FUTURE CRIMES

FUTURE CRIMES

Mysteries and Detection through Time and Space

edited by
MIKE ASHLEY

This collection first published in 2021 by
The British Library
96 Euston Road
London NW1 2DB

Cataloguing in Publication Data
A catalogue record for this publication is available from the British Library

ISBN 978 0 7123 5334 2
e-ISBN 978 0 7123 6738 7

Frontispiece illustration © The British Library Board.
Cover image © NRM/Pictorial Collection/Science & Society Picture Library.

EAST COAST INDUSTRIES
SERVED BY THE LNER

Cover design by Jason Anscomb
Text design and typesetting by Tetragon, London
Printed in England by TJ Books Limited, Padstow, Cornwall, UK

CONTENTS

INTRODUCTION 7

Elsewhen
Anthony Boucher 13

Puzzle for Spacemen
John Brunner 53

Legwork
Eric Frank Russell 85

Mirror Image
Isaac Asimov 147

The Flying Eye
Jacques Futrelle 169

Nonentity
E. C. Tubb 187

Death of a Telepath
George Chailey 213

Murder, 1986
P. D. James 221

Apple
Anne McCaffrey 249

The Absolutely Perfect Murder
Miriam Allen deFord 287

STORY SOURCES 301

INTRODUCTION

Crimes Beyond Time

Crime is, unfortunately, a part of daily life. If this were an anthology of utopias then there would be no crime, but we can be assured, just as there is crime today, there will be crime tomorrow, with mysteries and mayhem created by individuals, gangs—or even aliens—in new societies with new technologies, new powers and new laws.

This anthology brings together various examples of science fiction crime stories selected from the classic period with stories from as early as 1912 to as "recent" (in relative terms) as 1970. You may well ask whether these are genuine science fiction or genuine crime fiction and quite simply they are both, but the science-fiction element takes precedence. Here you will find how time travel helps, or maybe hinders, a crime; how a robot may or may not be a perfect witness; whether a telepath can commit a crime and be undetected; and how you track an alien that can make you believe anything!

There are several authors here who were known as much for their crime fiction as their science fiction—Anthony Boucher, Miriam Allen deFord and even Isaac Asimov—but there's also a crime-fiction writer not so well known for her science fiction, P. D. James.

Despite the science-fiction element the stories are true to crime-fiction protocols, and play fair with the reader, both as whodunnits and howdunnits.

In the early years of the twentieth century, before science fiction had a name, writers became fascinated with how science may help solve the crime. We are used today to the many TV series about forensic science, such as *CSI* or *Silent Witness*, and once upon a time their investigations were the stuff of science fiction. Not surprisingly it had been prompted by Sherlock Holmes, who had his own laboratory where he would experiment and occasionally produce monographs on such subjects as dating documents, identifying tobacco or tracking footsteps. This scientific analysis led to the proliferation of the scientific detective through such sleuths as R. Austin Freeman's Dr. Thorndyke, Arthur B. Reeve's Craig Kennedy and Edwin Balmer & William B. MacHarg's Luther Trant. These stories were sufficiently popular in their day for Hugo Gernsback to publish a specific magazine *Scientific Detective Stories* in 1930. Today most are dated, and I have not included any here, though their influence is evident in this collection's oldest story by Jacques Futrelle. For those interested in other scientific detective stories which have not dated I would recommend *The Measure of Malice*, one of the many excellent anthologies compiled by Martin Edwards for the British Library.

Scientific crime stories had in any case already moved beyond the forensic detective. They became investigations of major crimes, usually perpetrated by some mastermind. The most famous progenitor of these was Sax Rohmer's fiendish Dr. Fu Manchu who, in a long series of books starting with *The Mystery of Dr. Fu-Manchu* in 1913, developed increasingly extravagant schemes to try and take over the world, each time pursued and hindered, but rarely thwarted, by Assistant Commissioner Nayland Smith, once of Scotland Yard.

These megalomaniac scientists became a regular part of the sf crime scene. British thriller writer Edgar Wallace has his scientist create a micro-organism that can destroy all plant life in *The Green Rust* (1919) and American private-eye Stanford Beale has to save the world.

Murray Leinster produced a series of these starting with "The Darkness on Fifth Avenue" (1929) where Detective Inspector Hines investigates who had caused a total darkness to descend on New York. Over the next few months Leinster added three further stories with Hines tracking down the master criminal who has now found a way to create megastorms and, in the final story, block out the Sun and freeze the Earth.

Erle Stanley Gardner, in the years before he became famous for his Perry Mason cases, penned several megalomaniac crime stories such as "The Human Zero" (1931) where a super-scientist has found how to disintegrate matter and threatens millionaires with instant death, but does not reckon on private eye Sid Rodney.

These books and stories, though, are more thrillers than traditional crime and detection and the pulp magazines of the 1930s were full of their dastardly plots. They needed to be tamed and refocused with the more mature science fiction that began to appear in the 1940s.

Leading the way were writers like Eric Frank Russell, Anthony Boucher and Fredric Brown. Though British, Russell enjoyed reading the American crime pulps which found their way into Britain and he mastered their style which he was able to use in his first novel, *Sinister Barrier* (magazine, 1939), which involves a government agent trying to solve a series of mysterious deaths whilst the aliens among us who caused those deaths try to stop him. Anthony Boucher had already developed a reputation for his crime novels and he switched one of his private detectives, Fergus O'Breen, into his fantasy and sf. Stories by both of these writers are included here. Fredric Brown had been writing many

crime stories for the pulps before he switched to fantasy and sf
and he combined the two most cleverly in "Daymare" (1943), set
on another planet, where the detective has to unravel a puzzle of
how a man could be murdered at least five different ways, only for
the body to turn up a second time.

In 1948, John W. Campbell, the editor of *Astounding SF*, the
leading sf magazine of the 1940s, wrote that "in science fiction,
the ordinary detective story is impossible…", even though he had
written an excellent puzzle story in "Who Goes There?" (1938)
where scientists at an Antarctic base have to solve which amongst
them is actually a shape-shifting alien. Writers soon proved him
wrong.

A good example is *Needle* by Hal Clement, serialized in
Astounding SF in 1949. Here an alien policeman, who can take
over the mind and body of a human, is trying to find another of
its kind which had also taken a human host. Soon after Alfred
Bester penned *The Demolished Man* (serial, 1952) set in a world
where telepathy has been mastered and where you would think
crime had become impossible, and yet someone is murdered. Isaac
Asimov also equalled the task with *The Caves of Steel* (serial, 1953)
and *The Naked Sun* (serial, 1956). Here a human detective and his
robot companion try to solve crimes in societies where the moral
and ethical norms make it impossible for the crimes to have been
committed. Starting with "The Eyes Have It", and emulating
the works of John Dickson Carr, Randall Garrett produced an
ingenious series set in an alternate England and France where the
Plantagenet dynasty still held power and where magic works but
by strict rules. Lord Darcy, the Chief Forensic Investigator of the
Court of Normandy and his sorcerer advisor, Sean O'Lochlainn,
seek to solve crimes where even though sorcery may be employed,
it is all within a strict code of practice.

These works and others proved that the fields of crime fiction and science fiction could be seamlessly meshed together, and the theme continues to grow. Collected here are ten of the best examples from this intriguing field of fiction.

MIKE ASHLEY

ELSEWHEN

Anthony Boucher

Anthony Boucher was the best known pseudonym of William A. P. White (1911–68) who also wrote as H. H. Holmes and Herman W. Mudgett. He was as well respected in the fields of science fiction and fantasy as he was in crime fiction. The annual world mystery convention has been named Bouchercon since 1970. Boucher not only wrote fiction in all three fields, he was renowned as a book reviewer and critic, for which he won several Edgar Awards, and as an editor and anthologist. He was the co-founder of the Magazine of Fantasy and Science Fiction, *which he edited with J. Francis McComas from 1949 to 1954, and continued solo until 1958. His role as editor was enhanced by his knowledge of languages—he was fluent in French, Spanish and Portuguese.*

Boucher sold his first story to Weird Tales *in 1926 but spent most of the next few years developing a career in the theatre, acting, directing and as a playwright. He later transferred those skills to radio, scripting many Sherlock Holmes plays and writing his own series about detective Gregory Hood. His first novel was a mystery,* The Case of the Seven of Calvary *(1937) and amongst his crime novels is a classic locked-room mystery* Nine Times Nine *(1940, as H. H. Holmes).*

Boucher turned to fantasy and science fiction in 1941 starting with "Snulbug" where a magician summons a fairly useless demon. There was often an element of humour in Boucher's stories. Starting with The Case of the Crumpled Knave *(1939), Boucher wrote a series featuring the Irish-American private detective Fergus O'Breen, and he transferred him to crimes of the fantastic with "The Compleat Werewolf" (1942).*

O'Breen featured in six other short stories including the following. The full series along with all of Boucher's other sf and weird tales are collected in The Compleat Boucher *(1999). Another crossover is* Rocket to the Morgue *(1942) which includes several science-fiction personalities in thinly disguised roles.*

"**M**Y DEAR AGATHA," MR. PARTRIDGE ANNOUNCED AT THE breakfast table, "I have invented the world's first successful time machine."

His sister showed no signs of being impressed. "I suppose this will run the electric bill up even higher," she observed. "Have you ever stopped to consider, Harrison, what that workshop of yours costs us?"

Mr. Partridge listened meekly to the inevitable lecture. When it was over, he protested, "But, my dear, you have just listened to an announcement that no woman on earth has ever heard before. For ages man has dreamed of visiting the past and the future. Since the development of modern time-theory, he has even had some notion of how it might be accomplished. But never before in human history has anyone produced an actual working model of a time-travelling machine."

"Hm-m-m," said Agatha Partridge. "What good is it?"

"Its possibilities are untold." Mr. Partridge's pale little eyes lit up. "We can observe our pasts and perhaps even correct their errors. We can learn the secrets of the ancients. We can plot the uncharted course of the future—new conquistadors invading brave new continents of unmapped time. We can—"

"Will anyone pay money for that?"

"They will flock to me to pay it," said Mr. Partridge smugly.

His sister began to look impressed. "And how far can you travel with your time machine?"

Mr. Partridge buttered a piece of toast with absorbed concentration, but it was no use. His sister repeated the question: "How far can you go?"

"Not very far," Mr. Partridge admitted reluctantly. "In fact," he added hastily as he saw a more specific question forming, "hardly at all. And only one way. But remember," he went on, gathering courage, "the Wright brothers did not cross the Atlantic in their first model. Marconi did not launch radio with a world-wide broadcast. This is only the beginning and from this seed—"

Agatha's brief interest had completely subsided. "I thought so," she said. "You'd still better watch the electric bill."

It would be that way, Mr. Partridge thought, wherever he went, whomever he saw. "How far can you go?" "Hardly at all." "Good day, sir." People have no imagination. They cannot be made to see that to move along the time line with free volitional motion, unconditioned by the relentless force that pushes mankind along at the unchanging rate of—how shall one put it—one second per second—that to do this for even one little fraction of a second was as great a miracle as to zoom spectacularly ahead to 5900 A.D. He had, he could remember, felt disappointed at first himself—

The discovery had been made by accident. An experiment which he was working on—part of his long and fruitless attempt to recreate by modern scientific method the supposed results described in ancient alchemical works—had necessitated the setting up of a powerful magnetic field. And part of the apparatus within this field was a chronometer.

Mr. Partridge noted the time when he began his experiment. It was exactly fourteen seconds after nine thirty-one. And it was precisely at that moment that the tremor came. It was not a serious shock. To one who, like Mr. Partridge, had spent the past twenty years in southern California it was hardly noticeable, beyond the bother of a broken glass tube which had rolled off a table. But when he looked back at the chronometer, the dial read ten thirteen.

Time can pass quickly when you are absorbed in your work, but not so quickly as all that. Mr. Partridge looked at his pocket watch. It said nine thirty-two. Suddenly, in a space of seconds, the best chronometer available had gained forty-two minutes.

The more Mr. Partridge considered the matter, the more irresistibly one chain of logic forced itself upon him. The chronometer was accurate; therefore it had registered those forty-two minutes correctly. It had not registered them here and now; therefore the shock had jarred it to where it could register them. It had not moved in any of the three dimensions of space; therefore—

The chronometer had gone back in time forty-two minutes, and had registered those minutes in reaching the present again. Or was it only a matter of minutes? The chronometer was an eight-day one. Might it have been twelve hours and forty-two minutes? Forty-eight hours? Ninety-six? A hundred and ninety-two?

And why and how and—the dominant question in Mr. Partridge's mind—could the same device be made to work with a living being?

He had been musing for almost five minutes. It was now nine thirty-seven, and the dial read ten eighteen. Experimenting at random, he switched off the electromagnet, waited a moment, and turned it on again. The chronometer now read eleven o'clock.

Mr. Partridge remarked that he would be damned—a curiously prophetic remark in view of the fact that this great discovery was to turn him into a murderer.

It would be fruitless to relate in detail the many experiments which Mr. Partridge eagerly performed to verify and check his discovery. They were purely empirical in nature, for Mr. Partridge was that type of inventor which is short on theory but long on gadgetry. He did frame a very rough working hypothesis—that the sudden shock had caused the magnetic field to rotate into the temporal dimension, where it set up a certain—he groped for words—a certain negative potential of entropy, which drew things backward in time. But he would leave the doubtless highly debatable theory to the academicians. What he must do was perfect the machine, render it generally usable, and then burst forth upon an astonished world as Harrison Partridge, the first time traveller. His dry little ego glowed and expanded at the prospect.

There were the experiments in artificial shock which produced synthetically the earthquake effect. There were the experiments with the white mice which proved that the journey through time was harmless to life. There were the experiments with the chronometer which established that the time traversed varied directly as the square of the power expended on the electromagnet.

But these experiments also established that the time elapsed had not been twelve hours nor any multiple thereof, but simply forty-two minutes. And with the equipment at his disposal, it was impossible for Mr. Partridge to stretch that period any further than a trifle under two hours.

This, Mr. Partridge told himself, was ridiculous. Time travel at such short range, and only to the past, entailed no possible advantages. Oh, perhaps some piddling ones—once, after the mice had convinced him that he could safely venture himself, he had a lengthy piece of calculation which he wished to finish before dinner. An hour was simply not time enough for it; so at six o'clock he moved himself back to five again, and by working two hours in the space from five to six finished his task easily by dinner time. And one evening when, in his preoccupation, he had forgotten his favourite radio quiz programme until it was ending, it was simplicity itself to go back to the beginning and comfortably hear it through.

But though such trifling uses as this might be an important part of the work of the time machine once it was established—possibly the strongest commercial selling point for inexpensive home sets—they were not spectacular or startling enough to make the reputation of the machine and—more important—the reputation of Harrison Partridge.

The Great Harrison Partridge would have untold wealth. He could pension off his sister Agatha and never have to see her again. He would have untold prestige and glamour, despite his fat and his baldness, and the beautiful and aloof Faith Preston would fall into his arms like a ripe plum. He would—

It was while he was indulging in one of these dreams of power that Faith Preston herself entered his workshop. She was wearing a white sports dress and looking so fresh and immaculate that the whole room seemed to glow with her presence. She was all the youth and loveliness that had passed Mr. Partridge by, and his pulse galloped at her entrance.

"I came out here before I saw your sister," she said. Her voice was as cool and bright as her dress. "I wanted you to be the first to know. Simon and I are going to be married next month."

Mr. Partridge never remembered what was said after that. He imagined that she made her usual comments about the shocking disarray of his shop and her usual polite inquiries as to his current researches. He imagined that he offered the conventional good wishes and extended his congratulations, too, to that damned young whippersnapper Simon Ash. But all his thoughts were that he wanted her and needed her and that the great, the irresistible Harrison Partridge must come into being before next month.

Money. That was it. Money. With money he could build the tremendous machinery necessary to carry a load of power—and money was needed for that power, too—that would produce truly impressive results. To travel back even so much as a quarter of a century would be enough to dazzle the world. To appear at the Versailles peace conference, say, and expound to the delegates the inevitable results of their too lenient—or too strict?—terms. Or with unlimited money to course down the centuries, down the millennia, bringing back lost arts, forgotten secrets—

Money—

"Hm-m-m!" said Agatha. "Still mooning after that girl? Don't be an old fool."

He had not seen Agatha come in. He did not quite see her now. He saw a sort of vision of a cornucopia that would give him money that would give him the apparatus that would give him his time machine that would give him success that would give him Faith.

"If you must moon instead of working—if indeed you call this work—you might at least turn off a few switches," Agatha snapped. "Do you think we're made of money?"

Mechanically he obeyed.

"It makes you sick," Agatha droned on, "when you think how some people spend their money. Cousin Stanley! Hiring this Simon Ash as a secretary for nothing on earth but to look after his library and his collections. So much money he can't do anything but waste it! And all Great-uncle Max's money coming to him too, when we could use it so nicely. If only it weren't for Cousin Stanley, I'd be an heiress. And then—"

Mr. Partridge was about to observe that even as an heiress Agatha would doubtless have been the same intolerant old maid. But two thoughts checked his tongue. One was the sudden surprising revelation that even Agatha had her inner yearnings, too. And the other was an overwhelming feeling of gratitude to her.

"Yes," Mr. Partridge repeated slowly. "If it weren't for Cousin Stanley—"

*

By means as simple as this, murderers are made.

The chain of logic was so strong that moral questions hardly entered into the situation.

Great-uncle Max was infinitely old. That he should live another year was out of the question. And if his son Stanley were to predecease him, then Harrison and Agatha Partridge would be his only living relatives. And Maxwell Harrison was as infinitely rich as he was infinitely old.

Therefore Stanley must die. His life served no good end. Mr. Partridge understood that there are economic theories according to which conspicuous waste serves its purposes, but he did not care to understand them. Stanley alive was worth nothing. Stanley dead cleared the way for the enriching of the world by one of the greatest discoveries of mankind, which incidentally entailed great wealth and prestige for Mr. Partridge. And—a side issue, perhaps, but nonetheless as influential—the death of Stanley would leave his secretary Simon Ash without a job and certainly postpone his marriage to Faith, leaving her time to realize the full worth of Mr. Partridge.

Stanley must die, and his death must be accomplished with a maximum of personal safety. The means for that safety were at hand. For the one completely practical purpose of a short-range time machine, Mr. Partridge had suddenly realized, was to provide an alibi for murder.

The chief difficulty was in contriving a portable version of the machine which would operate over any considerable period of time. The first model had a travelling range of two minutes. But by the end of a week, Mr. Partridge had constructed a portable time machine which was good for forty-five minutes. He needed nothing more save a sharp knife. There was, Mr. Partridge thought, something crudely horrifying about guns.

*

That Friday afternoon he entered Cousin Stanley's library at five o'clock. This was an hour when the eccentric man of wealth always devoted himself to quiet and scholarly contemplation of his treasures. The butler, Bracket, had been reluctant to announce him, but "Tell my cousin," Mr. Partridge said, "that I have discovered a new entry for his bibliography."

The most recent of Cousin Stanley's collecting manias was fiction based upon factual murders. He had already built up the definitive library on the subject. Soon he intended to publish the definitive bibliography. And the promise of a new item was an assured open-sesame.

The ponderous gruff joviality of Stanley Harrison's greeting took no heed of the odd apparatus he carried. Everyone knew that Mr. Partridge was a crackpot inventor. That he should be carrying a strange framework of wires and magnets occasioned no more surprise than that an author should carry a sheaf of manuscript.

"Bracket tells me you've got something for me," Cousin Stanley boomed. "Glad to hear it. Have a drink? What is it?"

"No thank you." Something in Mr. Partridge rebelled at accepting the hospitality of his victim. "A Hungarian friend of mine was mentioning a novel about one Bela Kiss."

"Kiss?" Cousin Stanley's face lit up with a broad beam. "Splendid! Never could see why no one used him before. Woman killer. Landru type. Always fascinating. Kept 'em in empty gasoline tins. Never would have been caught if there hadn't been a gasoline shortage. Constable thought he was hoarding, checked the tins, found corpses. Beautiful! Now if you'll give me the details—"

Cousin Stanley, pencil poised over a P-slip, leaned over the desk. And Mr. Partridge struck.

He had checked the anatomy of the blow, just as he had checked the name of an obscure but interesting murderer. The knife went truly home, and there was a gurgle and the terrible spastic twitch of dying flesh.

Mr. Partridge was now an heir and a murderer, but he had time to be conscious of neither fact. He went through his carefully rehearsed motions, his mind numb and blank. He latched the windows of the library and locked each door. This was to be an impossible crime, one that could never conceivably be proved on him or on any innocent.

Mr. Partridge stood beside the corpse in the midst of the perfectly locked room. It was four minutes past five. He screamed twice, very loudly, in an unrecognizably harsh voice. Then he plugged his portable instrument into a floor outlet and turned a switch.

It was four nineteen. Mr. Partridge unplugged his machine. The room was empty and the door open. Mr. Partridge's gaze went to the desk. He felt, against all reason and knowledge, that there should be blood—some trace at least of what he had already done, of what was not to happen for three quarters of an hour yet.

Mr. Partridge knew his way reasonably well about his cousin's house. He got out without meeting anyone. He tucked the machine into the rumble seat of his car and drove off to Faith Preston's. Toward the end of his long journey across town he carefully drove through a traffic light and received a citation noting the time as four fifty. He reached Faith's at four fifty-four, ten minutes before the murder he had just committed.

Simon Ash had been up all Thursday night cataloguing Stanley Harrison's latest acquisitions. Still he had risen at his usual hour that

Friday to get through the morning's mail before his luncheon date with Faith. By four thirty that afternoon he was asleep on his feet.

He knew that his employer would be coming into the library in half an hour. And Stanley Harrison liked solitude for his daily five-o'clock gloating and meditation. But the secretary's work desk was hidden around a corner of the library's stacks, and no other physical hunger can be quite so dominantly compelling as the need for sleep.

Simon Ash's shaggy blond head sank onto the desk. His sleep-heavy hand shoved a pile of cards to the floor, and his mind only faintly registered the thought that they would all have to be alphabetized again. He was too sleepy to think of anything but pleasant things, like the sailboat at Balboa which brightened his week-ends, or the hiking trip in the Sierras planned for his next vacation, or above all Faith. Faith the fresh and lovely and perfect, who would be his next month—

There was a smile on Simon's rugged face as he slept. But he woke with a harsh scream ringing in his head. He sprang to his feet and looked out from the stacks into the library.

The dead hulk that slumped over the desk with the hilt protruding from its back was unbelievable, but even more incredible was the other spectacle. There was a man. His back was toward Simon, but he seemed faintly familiar. He stood close to a complicated piece of gadgetry. There was the click of a switch.

Then there was nothing.

Nothing in the room at all but Simon Ash and an infinity of books. And their dead owner.

Ash ran to the desk. He tried to lift Stanley Harrison, tried to draw out the knife, then realized how hopeless was any attempt to revive life in that body. He reached for the phone, then stopped as he heard the loud knocking on the door.

Over the raps came the butler's voice. "Mr. Harrison! Are you all right, sir?" A pause, more knocking, and then, "Mr. Harrison! Let me in, sir! Are you all right?"

Simon raced to the door. It was locked, and he wasted almost a minute groping for the key at his feet, while the butler's entreaties became more urgent. At last Simon opened the door.

Bracket stared at him—stared at his sleep-red eyes, his blood-red hands, and beyond him at what sat at the desk. "Mr. Ash, sir," the butler gasped. "What have you done?"

Faith Preston was home, of course. No such essential element of Mr. Partridge's plan could have been left to chance. She worked best in the late afternoons, she said, when she was getting hungry for dinner; and she was working hard this week on some entries for a national contest in soap carving.

The late-afternoon sun was bright in her room, which you might call her studio if you were politely disposed, her garret if you were not. It picked out the few perfect touches of colour in the scanty furnishings and converted them into bright aureoles surrounding the perfect form of Faith.

The radio was playing softly. She worked best to music, and that, too, was an integral portion of Mr. Partridge's plan.

Six minutes of unmemorable small talk—What are you working on? How lovely! And what have you been doing lately? Pottering around as usual. And the plans for the wedding?—and then Mr. Partridge held up a pleading hand for silence.

"When you hear the tone," the radio announced, "the time will be exactly five seconds before five o'clock."

"I forgot to wind my watch," Mr. Partridge observed casually. "I've been wondering all day exactly what time it was." He set his perfectly accurate watch.

He took a long breath. And now at last he knew that he was a new man. He was at last the Great Harrison Partridge. The last detail of his perfect plan had been checked off. His labours were over. In another four minutes Cousin Stanley would be dead. In another month or so Great-uncle Max would follow, more naturally. Then wealth and the new machine and power and glory and—

Mr. Partridge looked about the sun-bright garret as though he were a newborn infant with a miraculous power of vision and recognition. He was newborn. Not only had he made the greatest discovery of his generation; he had also committed its perfect crime. Nothing was impossible to this newborn Harrison Partridge.

"What's the matter?" Faith asked. "You look funny. Could I make you some tea?"

"No. Nothing. I'm all right." He walked around behind her and looked over her shoulder at the graceful nude emerging from her imprisonment in a cake of soap. "Exquisite, my dear," he observed. "Exquisite."

"I'm glad you like it. I'm never happy with female nudes; I don't think women sculptors ever are. But I wanted to try it."

Mr. Partridge ran a dry hot finger along the front of the soapen nymph. "A delightful texture," he remarked. "Almost as delightful as—" His tongue left the speech unfinished, but his hand rounded out the thought along Faith's cool neck and cheek.

"Why, Mr. Partridge!" She laughed.

The laugh was too much. One does not laugh at the Great Harrison Partridge, time traveller and perfect murderer. There was nothing in his plan that called for what followed. But something outside of any plans brought him to his knees, forced his arms around Faith's lithe body, pressed tumultuous words of incoherent ardour from his unwonted lips.

He saw fear growing in her eyes. He saw her hand dart out in instinctive defence and he wrested the knife from it. Then his own eyes glinted as he looked at the knife. It was little, ridiculously little. You could never plunge it through a man's back. But it was sharp—a throat, the artery of a wrist—

His muscles had relaxed for an instant. In that moment of nonvigilance, Faith had wrested herself free. She did not look backward. He heard the clatter of her steps down the stairs, and for a fraction of time the Great Harrison Partridge vanished and Mr. Partridge knew only fear. If he had aroused her hatred, if she should not swear to his alibi—

The fear was soon over. He knew that no motives of enmity could cause Faith to swear to anything but the truth. She was honest. And the enmity itself would vanish when she realized what manner of man had chosen her for his own.

It was not the butler who opened the door to Faith. It was a uniformed policeman, who said, "Whaddaya want here?"

"I've got to see Simon… Mr. Ash," she blurted out.

The officer's expression changed. "C'mon," and he beckoned her down the long hall.

Faith followed him, not perhaps so confused as she might ordinarily have been by such a reception. If the mild and repressed Mr. Partridge could suddenly change into a ravening wolf, anything was possible. The respectable Mr. Harrison might quite possibly be in some trouble with the police. But she had to see Simon. She needed reassuring, comforting—

The tall young man in plain clothes said, "My name is Jackson. Won't you sit down? Cigarette?" She waved the pack away nervously. "Hinkle says you wanted to speak to Mr. Ash?"

"Yes, I—"

"Are you Miss Preston? His fiancée?"

"Yes." Her eyes widened. "How did you—Oh, has something happened to Simon?"

The young officer looked unhappy. "I'm afraid something has. Though he's perfectly safe at the moment. You see, he—Damn it all, I never have been able to break such news gracefully."

The uniformed officer broke in. "They took him down to headquarters, miss. You see, it looks like he bumped off his boss."

Faith did not quite faint, but the world was uncertain for a few minutes. She hardly heard Lieutenant Jackson's explanations or the message of comfort that Simon had left for her. She simply held very tight to her chair until the ordinary outlines of things came back and she could swallow again.

"Simon is innocent," she said firmly.

"I hope he is." Jackson sounded sincere. "I've never enjoyed pinning a murder on as decent-seeming a fellow as your fiancé. But the case, I'm afraid, is too clear. If he is innocent, he'll have to tell us a more plausible story than his first one. Murderers that turn a switch and vanish into thin air are not highly regarded by most juries."

Faith rose. The world was firm again, and one fact was clear. "Simon is innocent," she repeated. "And I'm going to prove that. Will you please tell me where I can get a detective?"

The uniformed officer laughed. Jackson started to, but hesitated. The threatened guffaw turned into a not unsympathetic smile. "Of course, Miss Preston, the city's paying my salary under the impression that I'm one. But I see what you mean: You want a freer investigator, who won't be hampered by such considerations as the official viewpoint, or even the facts of the case. Well, it's your privilege."

"Thank you. And how do I go about finding one?"

"Acting as an employment agency's a little out of my line. But rather than see you tie up with some shyster shamus, I'll make a recommendation, a man I've worked with, or against, on a half dozen cases. And I think this set-up is just impossible enough to appeal to him. He likes lost causes."

"Lost?" It is a dismal word.

"And in fairness I should add they aren't always lost after he tackles them. The name's O'Breen—Fergus O'Breen."

Mr. Partridge dined out that night. He could not face the harshness of Agatha's tongue. Later he could dispose of her comfortably; in the meanwhile, he would avoid her as much as possible. After dinner he made a round of the bars on the Strip and played the pleasant game of "If only they knew who was sitting beside them." He felt like Harun-al-Rashid, and liked the glow of the feeling.

On his way home he bought the next morning's *Times* at an intersection and pulled over to the kerb to examine it. He had expected sensational headlines on the mysterious murder which had the police completely baffled. Instead he read:

SECRETARY SLAYS
EMPLOYER

After a moment of shock the Great Harrison Partridge was himself again. He had not intended this. He would not willingly cause unnecessary pain to anyone. But lesser individuals who obstruct the plans of the great must take their medicine. The weakling notion that had crossed his mind of confessing to save this innocent young man—that was dangerous nonsense that must be eradicated from his thoughts.

That another should pay for your murder makes the perfect crime even more perfect. And if the State chose to dispose of Simon Ash in the lethal-gas chamber—why, it was kind of the State to aid in the solution of the Faith problem.

Mr. Partridge drove home, contented. He could spend the night on the cot in his workshop and thus see that much the less of Agatha. He clicked on the workshop light and froze.

There was a man standing by the time machine. The original large machine. Mr. Partridge's feeling of superhuman self-confidence was enormous but easily undermined, like a vast balloon that needs only the smallest pin prick to shatter it. For a moment he envisioned a scientific master mind of the police who had deduced his method, tracked him here, and discovered his invention.

Then the figure turned.

Mr. Partridge's terror was only slightly lessened. For the figure was that of Mr. Partridge. There was a nightmare instant when he thought of Doppelganger, of Poe's William Wilson, of dissociated personalities, of Dr. Jekyll and Mr. Hyde. Then this other Mr. Partridge cried aloud and hurried from the room, and the entering one collapsed.

A trough must follow a crest. And now blackness was the inexorable aftermath of Mr. Partridge's elation. His successful murder, his ardour with Faith, his evening as Harun-al-Rashid, all vanished, to leave him an abject crawling thing faced with the double fear of madness and detection. He heard horrible noises in the room, and realized only after minutes that they were his own sobs.

Finally he pulled himself to his feet. He bathed his face in cold water from the sink, but still terror gnawed at him. Only one thing could reassure him. Only one thing could still convince him that he was the Great Harrison Partridge. And that was his noble machine. He touched it, caressed it as one might a fine and dearly loved horse.

Mr. Partridge was nervous, and he had been drinking more than his frugal customs allowed. His hand brushed the switch. He looked up and saw himself entering the door. He cried aloud and hurried from the room.

In the cool night air he slowly understood. He had accidentally sent himself back to the time he entered the room, so that upon entering he had seen himself. There was nothing more to it than that. But he made a careful mental note: Always take care, when using the machine, to avoid returning to a time-and-place where you already are. Never meet yourself. The dangers of psychological shock are too great.

Mr. Partridge felt better now. He had frightened himself, had he? Well, he would not be the last to tremble in fear of the Great Harrison Partridge.

Fergus O'Breen, the detective recommended—if you could call it that—by the police lieutenant, had his office in a ramshackle old building at Second and Spring. There were two, she imagined they were clients, in the waiting room ahead of Faith. One looked like the most sodden type of Skid Row loafer, and the elegant disarray of the other could mean nothing but the lower reaches of the upper layers of Hollywood.

The detective, when Faith finally saw him, inclined in costume toward the latter, but he wore sports clothes as though they were pleasantly comfortable, rather than as the badge of a caste. He was a thin young man, with sharpish features and very red hair. What you noticed most were his eyes—intensely green and alive with a restless curiosity. They made you feel that his work would never end until that curiosity had been satisfied.

He listened in silence to Faith's story, not moving save to make an occasional note. He was attentive and curious, but Faith's spirits sank as she saw the curiosity in the green eyes deaden to hopelessness. When she was through, he rose, lit a cigarette, and began pacing about the narrow inner office.

"I think better this way," he apologized. "I hope you don't mind. But what have I got to think about? Look: This is what you've told me. Your young man, this Simon Ash, was alone in the library with his employer. The butler heard a scream. Knocked on the door, tried to get in, no go. Ash unlocks the door from the inside. Police search later shows all other doors and windows likewise locked on the inside. And Ash's prints are on the murder knife. My dear Miss Preston, all that's better than a signed confession for any jury."

"But Simon is innocent," Faith insisted. "I know him, Mr. O'Breen. It isn't possible that he could have done a thing like that."

"I understand how you feel. But what have we got to go on besides your feelings? I'm not saying they're wrong; I'm trying to show you how the police and the court would look at it."

"But there wasn't any reason for Simon to kill Mr. Harrison. He had a good job. He liked it. We were going to get married. Now he hasn't any job or... or anything."

"I know." The detective continued to pace. "That's the one point you've got—absence of motive. But they've convicted without motive before this. And rightly enough. Murderers don't always think like the rational man. Anything can be a motive. The most outrageous and fascinating French murder since Landru was committed because the electric toaster didn't work right that morning. But let's look at motives. Mr. Harrison was a wealthy man; where does all that money go?"

"Simon helped draft his will. It all goes to libraries and foundations and things. A little to the servants, of course—"

"A little can turn the trick. But no near relatives?"

"His father's still alive. He's terribly old. But he's so rich himself that it'd be silly to leave him anything."

Fergus snapped his fingers. "Max Harrison! Of course. The superannuated robber-baron, to put it politely, who's been due to die any time these past ten years. And leave a mere handful of millions. There's a motive for you."

"How so?"

"The murderer could profit from Stanley Harrison's death, not directly if all his money goes to foundations, but indirectly from his father. Combination of two classic motives—profit and elimination. Who's next in line for old man Harrison's fortune?"

"I'm not sure. But I do know two people who are sort of second cousins or something. I think they're the only living relatives. Agatha and Harrison Partridge." Her eyes clouded a little as she mentioned Mr. Partridge and remembered his strange behaviour yesterday.

Fergus' eyes were brightening again. "At least it's a lead. Simon Ash had no motive and one Harrison Partridge had a honey. Which proves nothing, but gives you some place to start."

"Only—" Faith protested. "Only Mr. Partridge couldn't possibly have done it either."

Fergus stopped pacing. "Look, madam. I am willing to grant the unassailable innocence of one suspect on a client's word. Otherwise I'd never get clients. But if every individual who comes up is going to turn out to be someone in whose pureness of soul you have implicit faith and—"

"It isn't that. Not just that. Of course I can't imagine Mr. Partridge doing a thing like that—"

"You never can tell," said Fergus a little grimly. "Some of my best friends have been murderers."

"But the murder was just after five o'clock, the butler says. And Mr. Partridge was with me then, and I live way across town from Mr. Harrison's."

"You're sure of the time?"

"We heard the five-o'clock radio signal and he set his watch." Her voice was troubled and she tried not to remember the awful minutes afterward.

"Did he make a point of it?"

"Well... we were talking and he stopped and held up his hand and we listened to the bong."

"Hm-m-m." This statement seemed to strike the detective especially. "Well, there's still the sister. And anyway, the Partridges give me a point of departure, which is what I needed."

Faith looked at him hopefully. "Then you'll take the case?"

"I'll take it. God knows why. I don't want to raise your hopes, because if ever I saw an unpromising set-up it's this. But I'll take it. I think it's because I can't resist the pleasure of having a detective lieutenant shove a case into my lap."

"Bracket, was it usual for that door to be locked when Mr. Harrison was in the library?"

The butler's manner was imperfect; he could not decide whether a hired detective was a gentleman or a servant. "No," he said, politely enough but without a "sir." "No, it was most unusual."

"Did you notice if it was locked earlier?"

"It was not. I showed a visitor in shortly before the... before this dreadful thing happened."

"A visitor?" Fergus' eyes glinted. He began to have visions of all the elaborate possibilities of locking doors from the outside so that they seem locked on the inside. "And when was this?"

"Just on five o'clock, I thought. But the gentleman called here today to offer his sympathy, and he remarked, when I mentioned the subject, that he believed it to have been earlier."

"And who was this gentleman?"

"Mr. Harrison Partridge."

Hell, thought Fergus. There goes another possibility. It must have been much earlier if he was at Faith Preston's by five. And you can't tamper with radio time signals as you might with a clock. However—"Notice anything odd about Mr. Partridge? Anything in his manner?"

"Yesterday? No, I did not. He was carrying some curious contraption—I hardly noticed what. I imagine it was some recent invention of his which he wished to show to Mr. Harrison."

"He's an inventor, this Partridge? But you said yesterday. Anything odd about him today?"

"I don't know. It's difficult to describe. But there was something about him as though he had changed—grown, perhaps."

"Grown up?"

"No. Just grown."

"Now, Mr. Ash, this man you claim you saw—"

"Claim! Damn it, O'Breen, don't you believe me either?"

"Easy does it. The main thing for you is that Miss Preston believes you, and I'd say that's a lot. And I'm doing my damnedest to substantiate her belief. Now this man you saw, if that makes you any happier in this jail, did he remind you of anyone? Was there any suggestion—"

"I don't know. It's bothered me. I didn't get a good look, but there was something familiar—"

"You say he had some sort of machine beside him?"

Simon Ash was suddenly excited. "You've got it. That's it."

"That's what?"

"Who it was. Or who I thought it was. Mr. Partridge. He's some sort of a cousin of Mr. Harrison's. Screwball inventor."

"Miss Preston, I'll have to ask you more questions. Too many signposts keep pointing one way, and even if that way's a blind alley I've got to go up it. When Mr. Partridge called on you yesterday afternoon, what did he do to you?"

"Do to me?" Faith's voice wavered. "What on earth do you mean?"

"It was obvious from your manner earlier that there was something about that scene you wanted to forget. I'm afraid it'll have to be told. I want to know everything I can about Mr. Partridge, and particularly Mr. Partridge yesterday."

"He—Oh, no, I can't. Must I tell you, Mr. O'Breen?"

"Simon Ash says the jail is not bad after what he's heard of jails, but still—"

"All right. I'll tell you. But it was strange. I… I suppose I've known for a long time that Mr. Partridge was—well, you might say in love with me. But he's so much older than I am and he's very quiet and never said anything about it and—well, there it was, and I never gave it much thought one way or another. But yesterday— It was as though… as though he were possessed. All at once it seemed to burst out and there he was making love to me. Frightfully, horribly. I couldn't stand it. I ran away." Her slim body shuddered now with the memory. "That's all there was to it. But it was terrible."

"You pitched me a honey this time, Andy."

Lieutenant Jackson grinned. "Thought you'd appreciate it, Fergus."

"But look: What have you got against Ash but the physical

set-up of a locked room? The oldest cliché in murderous fiction, and not unheard of in fact. 'Locked rooms' can be unlocked. Remember the Carruthers case?"

"Show me how to unlock this one and your Mr. Ash is a free man."

"Set that aside for the moment. But look at my suspect, whom we will call, for the sake of novelty, X. X is a mild-mannered, inoffensive man who stands to gain several million by Harrison's death. He shows up at the library just before the murder. He's a crackpot inventor, and he has one of his gadgets with him. He shows an alibi-conscious awareness of time. He tries to get the butler to think he called earlier. He calls a witness' attention ostentatiously to a radio time signal. And most important of all, psychologically, he changes. He stops being mild-mannered and inoffensive. He goes on the make for a girl with physical violence. The butler describes him as a different man; he's grown."

Jackson nodded. "It's a good case. And the inventor's gadget, I suppose, explains the locked room?"

"Probably, when we learn what it was. You've got a good mechanical mind, Andy. That's right up your alley."

Jackson drew a note pad toward him. "Your X sounds worth questioning, to say the least. But this reticence isn't like you, Fergus. Why all this innuendo? Why aren't you telling me to get out of here and arrest him?"

Fergus was not quite his cocky self. "Because you see, that alibi I mentioned—well, it's good. I can't crack it. It's perfect."

Lieutenant Jackson shoved the pad away. "Run away and play," he said wearily.

"It couldn't be phony at the other end?" Fergus urged. "Some gadget planted to produce those screams at five o'clock to give a fake time for the murder?"

Jackson shook his head. "Harrison finished tea around four thirty. Stomach analysis shows the food had been digested just about a half-hour. No, he died at five o'clock, all right."

"X's alibi's perfect, then," Fergus repeated. "Unless… unless—" His green eyes blinked with amazed realization. "Oh, my dear God—" he said softly.

"Unless what?" Jackson demanded. There was no answer. It was the first time in history that the lieutenant had ever seen The O'Breen speechless.

Mr. Partridge was finding life pleasant to lead. Of course this was only a transitional stage. At present he was merely the—what was the transitional stage between cocoon and fully developed insect? Larva? Imago? Pupa? Outside of his own electro-inventive field, Mr. Partridge was not a well-informed man. That must be remedied. But let the metaphor go. Say simply that he was now in the transition between the meek worm that had been Mr. Partridge and the Great Harrison Partridge who would emerge triumphant when Great-uncle Max died and Faith forgot that poor foolish doomed young man.

Even Agatha he could tolerate more easily in this pleasant state, although he had nonetheless established permanent living quarters in his workroom. She had felt her own pleasure at the prospect of being an heiress, but had expressed it most properly by buying sumptuous mourning for Cousin Stanley—the most expensive clothes that she had bought in the past decade. And her hard edges were possibly softening a little—or was that the pleasing haze, almost like that of drunkenness, which now tended to soften all hard edges for Mr. Partridge's delighted eyes?

Life possessed pleasures that he had never dreamed of before. The pleasure, for instance, of his visit to the dead man's house to pay his respects, and to make sure that the butler's memory of time was not too accurately fixed. Risky, you say? Incurring the danger that one might thereby only fix it all the more accurately? For a lesser man, perhaps yes; but for the newly nascent Great Harrison Partridge a joyous exercise of pure skill.

It was in the midst of some such reverie as this that Mr. Partridge, lolling idly in his workshop with an unaccustomed tray of whiskey, ice and siphon beside him, casually overheard the radio announce the result of the fourth race at Hialeah and noted abstractedly that a horse named Karabali had paid forty-eight dollars and sixty cents on a two-dollar ticket. He had almost forgotten the only half-registered fact when the phone rang.

He answered, and a grudging voice said, "You can sure pick 'em. That's damned near five grand you made on Karabali."

Mr. Partridge fumbled with vocal noises.

The voice went on, "What shall I do with it? Want to pick it up tonight or—"

Mr. Partridge had been making incredibly rapid mental calculations. "Leave it in my account for the moment," he said firmly. "Oh, and—I'm afraid I've mislaid your telephone number."

"Trinity 2897. Got any more hunches now?"

"Not at the moment. I'll let you know."

Mr. Partridge replaced the receiver and poured himself a stiff drink. When he had downed it, he went to the machine and travelled two hours back. He returned to the telephone, dialled TR 2897, and said, "I wish to place a bet on the fourth race at Hialeah."

The same voice said, "And who're you?"

"Partridge. Harrison Partridge."

"Look, brother. I don't take bets by phone unless I see some cash first, see?"

Mr. Partridge hastily recalculated. As a result the next half hour was as packed with action as the final moments of his great plan. He learned about accounts, he ascertained the bookmaker's address, he hurried to his bank and drew out an impressive five hundred dollars which he could ill spare, and he opened his account and placed a two-hundred-dollar bet which excited nothing but a badly concealed derision.

Then he took a long walk and mused over the problem. He recalled happening on a story once in some magazine which proved that you could not use knowledge from the future of the outcome of races to make your fortune, because by interfering with your bet you would change the odds and alter the future. But he was not plucking from the future; he was going back into the past. The odds he had heard were already affected by what he had done. From his subjective point of view, he learned the result of his actions before he performed them. But in the objective physical temporospatial world, he performed those actions quite normally and correctly before their results.

It was perfect—for the time being. It could not, of course, be claimed as one of the general commercial advantages of the time machine. Once the Partridge principle became common knowledge, all gambling would inevitably collapse. But for this transitional stage it was ideal. Now, while he was waiting for Great-uncle Max to die and finance his great researches, Mr. Partridge could pass his time waiting for the telephone to inform him of the brilliant coup he had made. He could quietly amass an enormous amount of money and—

Mr. Partridge stopped dead on the sidewalk and a strolling couple ran headlong into him. He scarcely noticed the collision. He had had a dreadful thought. The sole acknowledged motive for his murder of Cousin Stanley had been to secure money for his researches. Now he learned that his machine, even in its present imperfect form, could provide him with untold money.

He had never needed to murder at all.

"My dearest Maureen," Fergus announced at the breakfast table, "I have discovered the world's first successful time machine."

His sister showed no signs of being impressed. "Have some more tomato juice," she suggested. "Want some tabasco in it? I didn't know that the delusions could survive into the hangover."

"But Macushla," Fergus protested, "you've just listened to an announcement that no woman on earth has ever heard before."

"Fergus O'Breen, Mad Scientist." Maureen shook her head. "It isn't a role I'd cast you for. Sorry."

"If you'd listen before you crack wise, I said 'discovered.' Not 'invented.' It's the damnedest thing that's ever happened to me in business. It hit me in a flash while I was talking to Andy. It's the perfect and only possible solution to a case. And who will ever believe me? Do you wonder that I went out and saturated myself last night?"

Maureen frowned. "You mean this? Honest and truly?"

"Black and bluely, my sweeting, and all the rest of the childish rigmarole. It's the McCoy. Listen." And he briefly outlined the case. "Now what sticks out like a sore thumb is this: Harrison Partridge establishing an alibi. The radio time signal, the talk with the butler—I'll even lay odds that the murderer himself gave those screams so there'd be no question as to time of death. Then you rub up against the fact that the alibi, like the horrendous dream of the young girl from Peru, is perfectly true.

"But what does an alibi mean? It's my own nomination for the most misused word in the language. It's come to mean a disproof, an excuse. But strictly it means nothing, but *elsewhere*. You know the classic gag: 'I wasn't there, this isn't the woman, and, anyway, she gave in.' Well, of those three redundant excuses, only the first is an alibi, an *elsewhere* statement. Now Partridge's claim of being elsewhere is true enough. He hasn't been playing with space, like the usual alibi builder. And even if we could remove him from elsewhere and put him literally on the spot, he could say: 'I couldn't have left the room after the murder; the doors were all locked on the inside.' Sure he couldn't—not *at that time*. And his excuse is not an *elsewhere*, but an *elsewhen*."

Maureen refilled his coffee cup and her own. "Hush up a minute and let me think it over." At last she nodded slowly. "And he's an eccentric inventor and when the butler saw him he was carrying one of his gadgets."

"Which he still had when Simon Ash saw him vanish. He committed the murder, locked the doors, went back in time, walked out through them in their unlocked past, and went off to hear the five-o'clock radio bong at Faith Preston's."

"But you can't try to sell the police on that. Not even Andy. He wouldn't listen to—"

"I know. Damn it, I know. And meanwhile that Ash, who seems a hell of a good guy—our kind of people, Maureen—sits there with the surest reserved booking for the lethal-gas chamber I've ever seen."

"What are you going to do?"

"I'm going to see Mr. Harrison Partridge. And I'm going to ask for an encore."

"Quite an establishment you've got here," Fergus observed to the plump bald little inventor.

Mr. Partridge smiled courteously. "I amuse myself with my small experiments," he admitted.

"I'm afraid I'm not much aware of the wonders of modern science. I'm looking forward to the more spectacular marvels, spaceships for instance, or time machines. But that wasn't what I came to talk about. Miss Preston tells me you're a friend of hers. I'm sure you're in sympathy with this attempt of hers to free young Ash."

"Oh, naturally. Most naturally. Anything that I can do to be of assistance—"

"It's just the most routine sort of question, but I'm groping for a lead. Anything that might point out a direction for me. Now, aside from Ash and the butler, you seem to have been the last person to see Harrison alive. Could you tell me anything about him? How was he?"

"Perfectly normal, so far as I could observe. We talked about a new item which I had unearthed for his bibliography, and he expressed some small dissatisfaction with Ash's cataloguing of late. I believe they had had words on the matter earlier."

"Nothing wrong with Harrison? No... no depression?"

"You're thinking of suicide? My dear young man, that hare won't start, I'm afraid. My cousin was the last man on earth to contemplate such an act."

"Bracket says you had one of your inventions with you?"

"Yes, a new, I thought, and highly improved frame for photostating rare books. My cousin, however, pointed out that the same improvements had recently been made by an Austrian *émigré* manufacturer. I abandoned the idea and reluctantly took apart my model."

"A shame. But I suppose that's part of the inventor's life, isn't it?"

"All too true. Was there anything else you wished to ask me?"

"No. Nothing really." There was an awkward pause. The smell of whiskey was in the air, but Mr. Partridge proffered no hospitality. "Funny the results a murder will have, isn't it? To think how this frightful fact will benefit cancer research."

"Cancer research?" Mr. Partridge wrinkled his brows. "I did not know that that was among Stanley's beneficiaries."

"Not your cousin's, no. But Miss Preston tells me that old Max Harrison has decided that since his only direct descendant is dead, his fortune might as well go to the world. He's planning to set up a medical foundation to rival Rockefeller's, and specializing in cancer. I know his lawyer slightly; he mentioned he's going out there tomorrow."

"Indeed," said Mr. Partridge evenly.

Fergus paced. "If you can think of anything, Mr. Partridge, let me know. I've got to clear Ash. I'm convinced he's innocent, but if he is, then this seems like the perfect crime at last. A magnificent piece of work, if you can look at it like that." He looked around the room. "Excellent small workshop you've got here. You can imagine almost anything coming out of it."

"Even," Mr. Partridge ventured, "your spaceships and time machines?"

"Hardly a spaceship," said Fergus.

Mr. Partridge smiled as the young detective departed. He had, he thought, carried off a difficult interview in a masterly fashion. How neatly he had slipped in that creative bit about Stanley's dissatisfaction with Ash! How brilliantly he had improvised a plausible excuse for the machine he was carrying!

Not that the young man could have suspected anything. It was patently the most routine visit. It was almost a pity that this was the case. How pleasant it would be to fence with a detective—master against master. To have a Javert, a Porfir, a Maigret on his trail and to admire the brilliance with which the Great Harrison Partridge should baffle him.

Perhaps the perfect criminal should be suspected, even known, and yet unattainable—

The pleasure of this parrying encounter confirmed him in the belief that had grown in him overnight. It is true that it was a pity that Stanley Harrison had died needlessly. Mr. Partridge's reasoning had slipped for once; murder for profit had not been an essential part of the plan.

And yet what great work had ever been accomplished without death? Does not the bell ring the truer for the blood of the hapless workman? Did not the ancients wisely believe that greatness must be founded upon a sacrifice? Not self-sacrifice, in the stupid Christian perversion of that belief, but a true sacrifice of another's flesh and blood.

So Stanley Harrison was the needful sacrifice from which should arise the Great Harrison Partridge. And were its effects not already visible? Would he be what he was today, would he so much as have emerged from the cocoon, purely by virtue of his discovery?

No, it was his great and irretrievable deed, the perfection of his crime, that had moulded him. In blood is greatness.

That ridiculous young man, prating of the perfection of the crime and never dreaming that—

Mr. Partridge paused and reviewed the conversation. There had twice been that curious insistence upon time machines. Then he had said—what was it?—"the crime was a magnificent piece of work," and then, "you can imagine almost anything coming out of this workshop." And the surprising news of Great-uncle Max's new will—

Mr. Partridge smiled happily. He had been unpardonably dense. Here was his Javert, his Porfir. The young detective did indeed suspect him. And the reference to Max had been a temptation, a trap. The detective could not know how unnecessary that fortune had now become. He had thought to lure him into giving away his hand by an attempt at another crime.

And yet, was any fortune ever unnecessary? And a challenge like that—so direct a challenge—could one resist it?

Mr. Partridge found himself considering all the difficulties. Great-uncle Max would have to be murdered today, if he planned on seeing his lawyer tomorrow. The sooner the better. Perhaps his habitual after-lunch siesta would be the best time. He was always alone then, dozing in his favourite corner of that large estate in the hills.

Bother! A snag. No electric plugs there. The portable model was out. And yet—Yes, of course. It could be done the other way. With Stanley, he had committed his crime, then gone back and prepared his alibi. But here he could just as well establish the alibi, then go back and commit the murder, sending himself back by the large machine here with wider range. No need for the locked-room effect. That was pleasing, but not essential.

An alibi for one o'clock in the afternoon. He did not care to use Faith again. He did not want to see her in his larval stage. He would let her suffer through her woes for that poor devil Ash, and then burst upon her in his glory as the Great Harrison Partridge. A perfectly reliable alibi. He might obtain another traffic ticket, though he had not yet been forced to produce his first one. Surely the police would be as good as—

The police. But how perfect. Ideal. To go to headquarters and ask to see the detective working on the Harrison case. Tell him, as a remembered afterthought, about Cousin Stanley's supposed quarrel with Ash. Be with him at the time Great-uncle Max is to be murdered.

At twelve thirty Mr. Partridge left his house for the central police station.

There was now no practical need for him to murder Maxwell Harrison. He had, in fact, not completely made up his mind to do so. But he was taking the first step in his plan.

*

Fergus could hear the old man's snores from his coign of vigilance. Getting into Maxwell Harrison's hermitlike retreat had been a simple job. The newspapers had for years so thoroughly covered the old boy's peculiarities that you knew in advance all you needed to know—his daily habits, his loathing for bodyguards, his favourite spot for napping.

His lack of precautions had up till now been justified. Servants guarded whatever was of value in the house; and who would be so wanton as to assault a man nearing his century who carried nothing of value on his person? But now—

Fergus had sighed with more than ordinary relief when he reached the spot and found the quarry safe. It would have been possible, he supposed, for Mr. Partridge to have gone back from his interview with Fergus for the crime. But the detective had banked on the criminal's disposition to repeat himself—commit the crime, in this instance, first, and then frame the *elsewhen*.

The sun was warm and the hills were peaceful. There was a purling stream at the deep bottom of the gully beside Fergus. Old Maxwell Harrison did well to sleep in such perfect solitude.

Fergus was on his third cigarette before he heard a sound. It was a very little sound, the turning of a pebble, perhaps; but here in this loneliness any sound that was not a snore or a stream seemed infinitely loud.

Fergus flipped his cigarette into the depths of the gully and moved, as noiselessly as was possible, toward the sound, screening himself behind scraggly bushes.

The sight, even though expected, was nonetheless startling in this quiet retreat: a plump bald man of middle age advancing on tiptoe with a long knife gleaming in his upraised hand.

Fergus flung himself forward. His left hand caught the

knife-brandishing wrist and his right pinioned Mr. Partridge's other arm behind him. The face of Mr. Partridge, that had been so bland a mask of serene exaltation as he advanced to his prey, twisted itself into something between rage and terror.

His body twisted itself, too. It was an instinctive, untrained movement, but timed so nicely by accident that it tore his knife hand free from Fergus' grip and allowed it to plunge downward.

The twist of Fergus' body was deft and conscious, but it was not quite enough to avoid a stinging flesh wound in the shoulder. He felt warm blood trickling down his back. Involuntarily he released his grip on Mr. Partridge's other arm.

Mr. Partridge hesitated for a moment, as though uncertain whether his knife should taste of Great-uncle Max or first dispose of Fergus. The hesitation was understandable, but fatal. Fergus sprang forward in a flying tackle aimed at Mr. Partridge's knees. Mr. Partridge lifted his foot to kick that advancing green-eyed face. He swung and felt his balance going. Then the detective's shoulder struck him. He was toppling, falling over backward, falling, falling—

The old man was still snoring when Fergus returned from his climb down the gully. There was no doubt that Harrison Partridge was dead. No living head could loll so limply on its neck.

And Fergus had killed him. Call it an accident, call it self-defence, call it what you will. Fergus had brought him to a trap, and in that trap he had died.

The brand of Cain may be worn in varying manners. To Mr. Partridge it had assumed the guise of an inspiring panache, a banner with a strange device. But Fergus wore his brand with a difference.

The shock of guilt did not bite too deeply into his conscience. He had brought about inadvertently and in person what he had hoped to bring the State to perform with all due ceremony. Human life, to be sure, is sacred; but believe too strongly in that precept, and what becomes of capital punishment or of the noble duties of war?

He could not blame himself morally, perhaps, for Mr. Partridge's death. But he could blame himself for professional failure in that death. He had no more proof than before to free Simon Ash, and he had burdened himself with a killing. A man killed at your hand in a trap of your devising—what more sure reason could deprive you of your licence as a detective? Even supposing, hopefully, that you escaped a murder rap.

For murder can spread in concentric circles, and Fergus O'Breen, who had set out to trap a murderer, now found himself being one.

Fergus hesitated in front of Mr. Partridge's workshop. It was his last chance. There might be evidence here—the machine itself or some document that could prove his theory even to the sceptical eye of Detective Lieutenant A. Jackson. House-breaking would be a small offence to add to his record now. The window on the left, he thought—

"Hi!" said Lieutenant Jackson cheerfully. "You on his trail, too?"

Fergus tried to seem his usual jaunty self. "Hi, Andy. So you've finally got around to suspecting Partridge?"

"Is he your mysterious X? I thought he might be."

"And that's what brings you out here?"

"No. He roused my professional suspicions all by himself. Came into the office an hour ago with the damnedest cock-and-bull story about some vital evidence he'd forgotten. Stanley Harrison's last words, it seems, were about a quarrel with Simon Ash. It didn't ring good—seemed like a deliberate effort to strengthen the case against Ash. As soon as I could get free, I decided to come out and have a further chat with the lad."

"I doubt if he's home," said Fergus.

"We can try." Jackson rapped on the door of the workshop. It was opened by Mr. Partridge.

Mr. Partridge held in one hand the remains of a large open-face ham sandwich. When he had opened the door, he picked up with the other hand the remains of a large whiskey and soda. He needed sustenance before this bright new adventure, this greater-than-perfect crime, because it arose from no needful compulsion and knew no normal motive.

Fresh light gleamed in his eyes as he saw the two men standing there. His Javert! Two Javerts! The unofficial detective who had so brilliantly challenged him, and the official one who was to provide his alibi. Chance was happy to offer him this further opportunity for vivid daring.

He hardly heeded the opening words of the official detective nor the look of dazed bewilderment on the face of the other. He opened his lips and the Great Harrison Partridge, shedding the last vestigial vestments of the cocoon, spoke:

"You may know the truth for what good it will do you. The life of the man Ash means nothing to me. I can triumph over him even though he live. I killed Stanley Harrison. Take that statement and do with it what you can. I know that an uncorroborated confession is useless to you. If you can prove it, you may have me. And I shall soon commit another sacrifice, and you are powerless to stop me. Because, you see, you are already too late." He laughed softly.

Mr. Partridge closed the door and locked it. He finished the sandwich and the whiskey, hardly noticing the poundings on the door. He picked up the knife and went to his machine. His face was a bland mask of serene exaltation.

Fergus for the second time was speechless. But Lieutenant Jackson had hurled himself against the door, a second too late. It was a matter of minutes before he and a finally aroused Fergus had broken it down.

"He's gone," Jackson stated puzzledly. "There must be a trick exit somewhere."

"'Locked room,'" Fergus murmured. His shoulder ached, and the charge against the door had set it bleeding again.

"What's that?"

"Nothing. Look, Andy. When do you go off duty?"

"Strictly speaking, I'm off now. I was making this check-up on my own time."

"Then let us, in the name of seventeen assorted demigods of drunkenness, go drown our confusions."

Fergus was still asleep when Lieutenant Jackson's phone call came the next morning. His sister woke him, and watched him come into acute and painful wakefulness as he listened, nodding and muttering, "Yes," or, "I'll be—"

Maureen waited till he had hung up, groped about, and found and lighted a cigarette. Then she said, "Well?"

"Remember that Harrison case I was telling you about yesterday?"

"The time-machine stuff? Yes."

"My murderer, Mr. Partridge—they found him in a gully out on his great-uncle's estate. Apparently slipped and killed himself while attempting his second murder—that's the way Andy sees it. Had a knife with him. So, in view of that and a sort of confession he made yesterday, Andy's turning Simon Ash loose. He still doesn't see how Partridge worked the first murder, but he doesn't have to bring it into court now."

"Well? What's the matter? Isn't that fine?"

"Matter? Look, Maureen macushla. I killed Partridge. I didn't mean to, and maybe you could call it justifiable; but I did. I killed him at one o'clock yesterday afternoon. Andy and I saw him at two; he was then eating a ham sandwich and drinking whiskey. The stomach analysis proves that he died half an hour after that meal, when I was with Andy starting out on a bender of bewilderment. So you see?"

"You mean he went back afterward to kill his uncle and then you... you saw him after you'd killed him only before he went back to be killed? Oh, how awful."

"Not just that, my sweeting. This is the humour of it: The time alibi, the elsewhen that gave the perfect cover up for Partridge's murder—it gives exactly the same ideal alibi to his own murderer."

Maureen started to speak and stopped. "Oh!" she gasped.

"What?"

"The time machine. It must still be there—somewhere— mustn't it? Shouldn't you—"

Fergus laughed, and not at comedy. "That's the payoff of perfection on this opus. I gather Partridge and his sister didn't love each other too dearly. You know what her first reaction was to the news of his death? After one official tear and one official sob, she went and smashed the hell out of his workshop."

PUZZLE FOR SPACEMEN

John Brunner

*John Brunner (1934–95) is not known for his crime fiction, though puzzles
and mysteries are evident in many of his stories, including the following.
He wrote a series of secret agent novels featuring a Jamaican operative
Max Curfew who appeared in* A Plague on Both Your Causes *(1969),*
Good Men Do Nothing *(1970) and* Honky in the Woodpile *(1971) but
they are not remembered. Better is* Black is the Colour *(1969), expanded
from his novella "This Rough Magic" (1956), about an investigation into
black magic set in London in the Swinging Sixties. In his later years
Brunner wrote a series featuring Mr. Secrett, a librarian who manages to
become involved in all manner of strange events. The stories were collected
posthumously as* The Man Who Was Secrett and Other Stories *(2013).*

Brunner is, of course, best known for the award-winning Stand on
Zanzibar *(1968), a bleak view of an overpopulated Earth, and other such
works of ominous portent,* The Jagged Orbit *(1969),* The Sheep Look
Up *(1972) and* The Shockwave Rider *(1975), but he wrote so much more.
The following story was included in Brunner's collection* No Future In
It *(1962) but its only other major outing was in* Special Wonder *(1970)
a tribute volume to Anthony Boucher compiled by J. Francis McComas.
Each contributor selected a story which they believed was one of Boucher's
favourites, and here it is.*

The ship was crammed absolutely as full as it could be with the very hardest kind of vacuum. The air circulators churned and sucked dutifully at nothing; the last of the normally luxuriant air-renewing plants in their transparent compartment on the sunward side of the ship had long ago turned brown and dead, because there was neither carbon dioxide nor oxygen; the chemical purifiers which would have been removing anthropotoxins if those had not already been removed much more effectively along with the other gas in the ship sat quietly and waited.

The only thing which visibly marred the almost sterile cleanness of the cabin was a long brown smear reaching out over the control panels as if it were a signpost pointing to the airlock. Its broader end splayed back towards the pilot's chair.

The man from whom it had issued floated in his restraining harness, the ragged ends of his G-suit swimming about him like fronds of seaweed in still water—the fabric had burst like an over-inflated balloon when the compressed gas inside had found it was pushing against nothing. His head—what was left of it—lolled on one side.

A man who has been subjected to fourteen pounds' explosive decompression is not a pretty sight.

Yannick Huyghens looked out at the cold stars and shivered. In the frame of the big port he could just see, if he craned his head close to the plastic, the dull red glow of the cooling jets on the ship which had just moved in to join the intricately interlinked combination of rotating parts which one day—one day—would be the completed Earth-Jupiter line-of-sight radio relay. At the moment it was a seemingly random collection of four ships—originally there had been only two—a myriad pieces of equipment, and ninety-three men, some of whose suit lights he could see out there as they went about their business of construction. But Yannick wasn't seeing all this to notice it; he could look beyond it and imagine the day when the chaos it now seemed was as perfect as the model which swung on its pivot on the corner of his desk—the culminating achievement of a life devoted to the business of building safe and useful additions to the sun's family of planets for the benefit of men.

"Watch it," said the public address speaker in the corner unemotionally, and the floor twisted under him. He yielded to the motion with automatic ease; it told him as eloquently as words that Louis Baron, his computerman, had completed his calculations and set up a stable relationship to include the ship which had recently arrived. Even as he watched, the dying glow of the tubes which he had just been able to see before, moved out of sight altogether, along with the distinctive irregular glinting of the holding chains.

There was a knock at the door, and without turning round, Yannick said, "Come in!"

It was Kurt Lochmann, his supply and time-and-movement superintendent, who entered. "Uh—I have the manifest of the cargo here, Yannick," he said.

"That's fine," said Yannick, still three years in the future and picturing the view from the supervisor's cabin in the completed station. "If you'll drop it on my desk, I'll be round to check it in a few minutes."

"I think I'd better do it," said Kurt. His Adam's apple bobbed up and down on his long, stringy neck and he swallowed hard.

Yannick turned away from the port and was about to demand why, when he saw that Kurt was not alone. In the doorway behind him stood a stranger. He wore an incongruous business suit of a smart blue shade, and carried a small attache case.

"Mr. Huyghens?" he said, coming forward and holding out his hand. "How do you do?"

Yannick ignored him. "All right, Kurt," he said. "Go check that cargo, after all. And make absolutely certain they've put in that batch of K69's they forgot last time. We could have been badly delayed by that."

Kurt nodded and went out, and Yannick turned his attention to the visitor, eyeing his Earthside clothing with astonishment. "What can we do for you?" he demanded.

"I've come out in connection with the matter of that ship you located recently. I'm Hal Jennings. I'm the assistant personnel manager of Creswell and Palmer, the owners."

Yannick scowled. "I see," he said. "Sit down."

He cleared a thick pile of circuit diagrams and progress reports, a keyboard computer and a half-finished sandwich to the side of his desk, and sat down himself. Jennings laid his case in front of him and rubbed his hands together briskly, a gesture Yannick loathed. "Now, Mr. Huyghens," he said. "About this dead man you found—"

"Don't say that," Yannick interrupted in a brittle voice, "We prefer to use the term 'casualty.' You know him?"

"Yes. That's to say, we believe we've established his identity. We have over three thousand pilots in our employ, you realize, but only one of our ships should have been anywhere near this area if he was running to schedule. If we're correct, he would have been running in under no-load from Pluto, though to date we haven't been able to obtain direct confirmation from our agency there. Our 'fax equipment isn't up to it. We'll have confirmation from them next week." He opened his case and took out a photograph. "Is this the man?"

Yannick ignored the picture. "How should I know?" he said in a tired voice.

Jennings blinked. "Well, I naturally assumed you would have been to look at the corpse—the casualty, rather."

"I have better things to do, Mr. Jennings. We all have. The man who did enter the ship—the one whom I sent to investigate when the pilot failed to acknowledge our calls—only came back on duty this morning. The shock upset him badly. We spent fifteen tons of valuable fuel on bringing the ship into our system and forty minutes' computer work on re-balancing the system afterwards; on top of which, if you count the man who went inside, we've lost sixty man-hours. We're out here to build a radio relay station—not to amuse ourselves with the results of a blowout. You can't expect us to do your people's work as well as our own."

"I'd have thought that the death of a human being was sufficient to warrant some departure from schedule," Jennings remarked, blankly.

"I'm not interested in the death of one human being, Mr. Jennings. I'm interested in the sanity of ninety-three of them."

"I don't quite follow you."

"Out here sanity is at a premium. It's too valuable to be risked. With the comparative solidity of a planet under one's feet, even if the planet isn't Earth, one can stand the strain of a long construction job. Similarly, working in space where one can see the familiar face of either the Earth or the moon. Here there's nothing for millions of miles in all directions. Nerves get ragged, living over a literally bottomless pit. To force men already in the constant shadow of death by blowout to occupy their minds with the consequences of a singularly unpleasant case of it would be criminal idiocy in its own right. The effect of such exposure on the progress of the work would be incalculably bad." He stared piercingly at his visitor. "I should have thought that you, as a personnel man, would have at least a faint idea of the probable result."

"I have more than a faint idea, Mr. Huyghens," answered Jennings rather stiffly. "I must confess, though, that I have specialized in the forms of space neurosis which are altogether more short-term—those which affect pilots and others on interplanetary trips. I don't know much about men forced to spend years at a time in isolated conditions."

"I do," said Yannick pointedly. "You'll understand me now, at any rate, when I say that I want you to get your business over as soon as possible. The mere presence of that casualty, looking over our shoulders the whole time, is enough to give my people the willies. When we 'faxed down the news, I expected your firm to just send up a pilot and get the ship out of the way. If it hadn't been for Oscar arguing about it, I'd have given the fellow a decent cremation and ourselves a chance to forget the whole thing."

"Oscar?"

"My foreman electronicist."

Jennings nodded. He seemed to notice for the first time that he still held the photo of the dead pilot, and put it back in his case. "Tell me, Mr. Huyghens," he said musingly, "have you any special reason for finding the—casualty—unnerving?"

"None, other than that I'm determined to get this station built without interruptions. And the fact that anyone who's blown his top sufficiently to try and breathe vacuum is a messy sight."

"You assume it was suicide?" Jennings suggested after a moment.

Yannick shrugged. "Why not? Enough rocket jockeys have gone space-happy for it to be a reasonable explanation. It wasn't an accident; a meteor big enough to tear clear through the skin would leave a hole you could see, and no one's noticed a rip in the hull since we hung it up here."

"I see." Jennings sat back and crossed his legs. "Excuse my asking silly questions, Mr. Huyghens, but this is in fact my first trip in space, aside from a few visits to the moon which were no more than glorified bus rides. I believe that the airlock of a ship can only be opened from inside. Isn't that so?"

"No," said Yannick. "You can open it from outside—obviously, or you couldn't get back in. What you're thinking of is the lunging-up switch, which opens both doors together. That's operated from the pilot's chair. It's normally only used on Earth."

"Thank you—that's what I meant." Jennings opened his case again and took out a sheet of graph paper with three lines—one red, one blue and one green—plotted across it. "You can read a psycho-profile?" he inquired, and Yannick nodded.

"Take a look at this one, then," said Jennings, passing it across the desk. "It's the last one we raised for Clore—I made it out myself, actually."

Yannick glanced cursorily at the paper; it was calibrated differently from those he was used to, but a check of the scale enabled him to follow it. He grunted.

"You'll see from that why I'm here," Jennings murmured.

"I see from this that there's something wrong with your methods of testing," contradicted Yannick. "According to this, Clore—you said Clore? Yes?—he was about as stable as Mother Earth."

"Exactly. That's why I was sent out, and not a pilot," said Jennings promptly. "As an engineer, Mr. Huyghens, you know just how costly interplanetary shipping space is. It cost my firm three thousand credits to get me here. If it hadn't been for that psycho-profile, we *would* just have breathed a silent sigh of relief and been glad enough to have got the ship back. Normally, if we lose a pilot we lose half a million credits' worth of space craft as well. It's a calculated risk, employing pilots who are nearing the limit of their margin of stability, and we seldom come out ahead on the deal. However, if we have here a pilot who was not within ten years of failing by any estimate we could make, by studying him—"

Yannick shuddered and turned his head.

"This is unique, Mr. Huyghens," pursued Jennings relentlessly. "Pluto to Earth under no-load is a long haul but a fast one, because of the additional reaction mass you carry instead of cargo. Clore should have taken it easily in his condition. If he did try to breathe space of his own accord, examination of the ship and in particular the log will point the way to further refinement of our testing methods."

Yannick fastened on an earlier remark of the other's. "Did you say you hadn't yet checked with Pluto whether it was Clore?" he asked.

"That's right. If he's too badly damaged for visual identification—"

"Oh, hell!" said Yannick fervently. "Mr. Jennings, this is nothing personal, but I am going to get you and your casualty out of our system at the first possible moment. I agree that your investigation is justified—I realize the risk of mental strain, and anything that can be done to eliminate it has my support. But by the same token, I'm responsible for ninety-three men here and now, not for an unknown number of another firm's pilots in the indefinite future. Is that understood?"

"Perfectly," said Jennings stiffly.

"All right, then." Yannick reached for the desk phone. "Charlie, where's Oscar at the moment?"

A rather pleasant light tenor voice answered him. "Out on Fourteen. Why, do you want him?"

Yannick's eyes ran over the master construction plot on the far wall as he spoke. "Yes, plug him in, will you?"

"Right away." A pause, and then a slow, rather gruff voice replaced the other.

"What is it, Yannick?"

"Oscar, we have to check with Pluto about that casualty we found. His firm have sent up someone to look into it. Could you jimmy-rig Fourteen to do the job?"

"Not jimmy-rig it," said Oscar, but before Yannick's face could reflect his annoyance, went on, "the whole damned thing tested out without a fault ten minutes ago. I was just about to put the welders on connecting it and Thirteen. Louis is figuring the re-balance now. Can't it wait?"

"For preference not."

"Well, to raise Pluto is asking a hell of a lot from a single unit. It can be done, of course. I'll have to swing the antenna and tie in a couple of power cables... Say an hour?"

"That's excellent. What can you send?"

"What do you want to send? Six groups is about all I can guarantee will get through."

"I'll have the message phoned down to you in a moment," said Yannick. There was the sound of a heavy sigh, and the circuit went dead. Yannick turned back to find Jennings already writing out his message in a neat, legible script.

He waited till he had finished, then took the paper from him and looked at it, shaking his head.

"What's wrong?" inquired Jennings anxiously. "I shall need to know all that."

"No 'fax, Mr. Jennings. What do you think this is—an Earth satellite? To raise Pluto with a single unit, we'll have to encode, compress the code into tenth-second blips, and repeat it fifty or a hundred times while we swing the beam across where we think Pluto is going to be when the message gets there. You Earth-bound desk pilots don't seem to have heard about relativity. Out here, we trip over it every time we fiddle with long-distance radio." He was leafing through the cypher manual as he spoke.

"Well, you're lucky. I can put your first eight words into one group—CJPUD means 'Request details and time of departure.' The name will have to go in clear, and so will the identity code of the ship, but I've a vague idea that there are some legal groups to cover the rest of it…" His voice tailed away as he swiftly turned pages.

"Put down WLMCY," said Jennings in a tight voice, and Yannick looked up in surprise.

"You know interplan code?"

"I've used it sometimes. That one stuck in my mind."

"What does it mean? I don't recognize it."

"It's probably never been used before, Mr. Huyghens. Largely because no one has ever been able to afford to use it. It happens to mean 'Information urgently required in course of investigation of unnatural death'." Dryly, he added, "Apparently the compilers of the manual thought there would be a police force in space to do the investigating."

Yannick frowned, but copied down the group. "With the pilot's name and the ship identification, plus our own tag, we get it into the six groups Oscar asked for." He reached for the phone again and dictated the message to Charlie for compression and recording preparatory to putting it on the beam.

"Now," said Jennings when he had finished, "I'd like to go out and look at the ship."

"Have you a strong stomach?" Yannick demanded.

"I don't know," Jennings answered seriously. "I've never seen a violent death."

Dear God! thought Yannick. And we—we walk and talk with it every day of our lives: waiting for the lifeline to fray through, the tank of propellant on a scooter to burst, the air-conditioning plants to blight or mutate into non-viable forms, the meteor to make a hole in a suit too big to slap a patch over—

He shut the thoughts deliberately out of his mind and got to his feet. "Very well, Mr. Jennings," he said heavily. "Come and see why we want to get rid of your property as soon as we can."

The airlock was cramped with two of them in it, and they waited stiffly while the air around them—too precious to be simply wasted on the void—was sucked to a minimum by powerful vacuum pumps. At length though, that was over, and they turned to step out into nowhere.

Someone was waiting outside for them to leave, staring patiently at the red eye of the cycling lamp which warned that reclamation was in progress; so long as there was any pressure in the interior of the lock, the cycling lamp was always lit. Behind the waiting man a two-seat scooter—little more than a gyro, a drive unit and the seats and controls themselves—swung idly at the end of a holding chain.

"Through with that scooter?" Jennings jumped as Yannick's voice echoed in his helmet, and then realized that the remark had not been addressed to him. The unknown who was entering the ship lifted his right arm in confirmation, and Yannick gestured to his companion to take the rear seat. After checking the fuel level, he settled himself in the harness and looked around him at the complex web of structural members, both floating free on tie-lines and already interlocked into completed units, which formed the system. Judging the strength of his movement precisely, he gave a tug on the holding chain, and the scooter changed attitude abruptly. Jennings gasped, and the sound reverberated in his ears as the stars spun about them. When Yannick again caught at the chain to cast it loose, they were aligned towards a gap in the ring, beyond which a shiny hull faintly threw back the light of the multiple floods under which the crewmen were working.

Then there was a short flare from the rear-placed jet, and they were on their way.

Once the acceleration had ended, it seemed to Jennings that it was the rest of the swinging system which was passing them, while they floated in timeless and moveless space. During the three minutes which their brief voyage took, he gained a pretty clear idea of the layout. He was able to see the enormous ingenuity which insured the cohesion of the drifting sections; he watched the tiny distant suit lights of the welders and electricians manhandling girders and banks of radio equipment into place. Once he glanced back to the airlock which they had left a minute before, and saw that the cycling lamp had gone out.

For a while he was badly puzzled by a little group of tiny moving objects apparently glowing with their own light against the black background of another gap in the ring. Then there was a minuscule change of orbit, and he caught the brilliance of an almost edge-on view of one of the searchlights. Instantly the dancing motes took on their true perspective, and he realized that they were particles of meteoric dust. Growing more accustomed to the level of brightness, he saw that such motes surrounded all the lamps.

"It's interesting," he said tentatively, "actually to *see* this interstellar dust which we're told is found in space."

"This is a bad patch," Yannick answered. "You know this station is in what they call a compromise orbit—an ellipse so designed that it's always in line-of-sight with both Earth and Jupiter when they're out of line with each other, transiting or eclipsed by the sun. It takes us across quite a lot of the solar system, but on the outer part of the swing we don't find so much of it. Here we're catching the backlog of the asteroid belt, which is full of the stuff. You've probably seen the belt which runs out around Earth itself—the one which produces the counterglow, you know."

"Yes, of course."

"Quiet a moment." Yannick spun the gyro, and the scooter's attitude changed again till its nose pointed slightly to one side of the airlock of the ship now looming up ahead of them; one nicely-judged burst from the jet, and the resultant of the two forces brought them with the gentlest of bumps up against the hull. Yannick clawed at the holding chain which hung on nothing beside him, and made fast.

"Some people," said Jennings with respect, "would have taken a dozen shots at that."

"I've had a little practice," answered Yannick dryly. He unclipped one of the powerful torches which served as headlights for the scooter, and used the holding chain to pull himself up to the lock.

Jennings followed him awkwardly, his arms and legs still tending to flail when they had nothing to give them purchase, and Yannick reached out to drag him in.

"Thanks," Jennings told him. "Hullo, what's happened here?" His gloved hand reached out and tapped on the hull surrounding the cycling lamp; the red-tinted glass covering the filament had been shattered.

"Probably bumped a pebble," said Yannick indifferently. "They aren't very strong, those lamps." He tugged at the handle of the door. "Steady yourself. Here's your pilot."

With a final glance at the broken lamp, Jennings crowded with him into the narrow lock, but since they were entering rather than leaving they passed almost straight through. Yannick stepped out across the floor of the cabin.

"Look," he said, and swung the torch. Jennings froze.

*

Preserved by the unchanging vacuum, Clore was not nice to look at. His face was smothered and discoloured with blood which had burst from his nose, ears and the corners of his eyes and had not been whipped away by the blast of air towards the place where they now stood. His mouth was frozen open in a tortured shape which might have produced a scream had there been air for the sound to ride.

After a while Yannick said with desperate sarcasm, "Seen enough?" The hand holding the torch trembled a little.

"I'm afraid not," said Jennings. The sound of heavy swallowing came clearly over the phones to Yannick. "May I have the torch?"

Yannick gave it to him and turned away. For what seemed like an eternity he could hear nothing but the sound of Jennings's breathing, and the slight click whenever he moved, caused by the magnets on his boots meeting and parting with the floor. He felt a cold resentment against the other, compounded of disgust that he should be forced into the presence of death, dislike at Jennings himself—an Earth-bound desk pilot—and visions of the time wasted by himself and his team. This Earth-Jupiter relay was to be the crowning achievement of his life; he had grown too anxious for its progress to suffer interruptions gladly.

"All right," said the other, twenty minutes later. "I've seen enough now."

"Did you find what you were looking for?" said Yannick, hope edging his voice.

"I've found one or two things. The log is missing, for a start, but if Clore went off his head he might have thrown it into the disposal chute, in which case his next change of course would have lost it somewhere in space. The most interesting thing is that there were two men in the ship when it left Pluto."

"What? How do you know?"

"Oh, the air purifiers are set to handle two men's respiration. There's nothing odd about that—it would have been one of our other employees cadging a lift. When it's cheaper in terms of fuel and time to make a slight detour in an available ship than to lay on a flight direct, we arrange for him to be trans-shipped when he crosses some other orbit."

"Well, what happened to him?"

"Oh, he would have transferred, of course. Pluto will tell us if Clore was to pass within hailing distance of one of our other vessels. As a matter of fact, you could probably tell me, couldn't you?"

Glad of something to distract his mind from the horror in the pilot's chair, Yannick closed his eyes and mentally reviewed the current ephemeris. At length he announced, "The best bet is probably the Mars-Jupiter freight orbit. With this rash of building on Io there's a lot of traffic on that lane, and just now it cuts clear across the Pluto to Earth line."

"Good. We haven't a regular Pluto to Mars service—you have to go via Earth. It would be worth trans-shipping him if he was making that journey. Could I contact our Mars office from here?"

"Easily. I suppose you want to have this man interrogated about Clore's state of mind during the first part of the flight?"

"Well, it's possible that the contrast between the company he enjoyed on the first leg and the isolation of the later part tipped the balance." Jennings handed back the torch. "Shall we go?"

As they climbed back into the seats of the scooter, a voice suddenly filled both their helmets.

"Chief? You there?"

"Here I am, Charlie," said Yannick, pausing as he was about to clip the torch back into place on the scooter. "What is it?"

"Oscar says to tell you that they sent that message to Pluto, and they're stripping down the boosters on Fourteen again."

"Thanks," said Yannick, and there was the click of the circuit being broken.

"Dismantling it?" inquired Jennings.

"Yes, why not?" Yannick jerked the scooter around again, looked for the main ship among the tangle of temporary planetoids, and jetted towards it. "Pluto's a working, ground-based installation. We don't have any trouble picking them up. Transmitting's different; we have to feed them a strong enough signal at the moment to be read in the eye of the sun."

There was a pause. Then Jennings said delicately, "Mr. Huyghens, how soon can I get in touch with Mars?"

"The sooner the better, frankly," said Yannick wearily, and Jennings subsided in silence. He was not welcome; to these men, anyone prying into violent death was ghoulish, because it was always a dreaded and imminent fact to them. Death in space was usually swift and accountable; if there was ever a mystery, the black maw of the void swallowed it beyond the reach of man. This case was not unique in itself, though it might be in the end; in any case he would be able to count on only grudging help from Yannick and his team. Yet paradoxically, that was all to the good.

Yannick killed their forward velocity by adding a sideways component which brought them bumping up against the hull of the main ship, and caught at the chain to make it fast. "Come along, Mr. Jennings," he said. "You can call Mars now."

"Oh, not now," said Jennings with a faint and deliberate sneer. "Until I get an answer from Pluto I won't know what to ask them about."

"Oh, *God!*" said Yannick from the bottom of his heart. "All right, Mr. Jennings. But oblige me by going and hiding in a corner. I mean don't get in anybody's way. You'll find an empty cabin on C deck you can use, and you can have lunch with us at one p.m. And so help me, if I catch you talking to *anybody* about the casualty, I'll shut you up on board that ship with it. Understood?"

"Of course," said Jennings acidly. For a moment Yannick had the impression that pure hatred was being transmitted over the helmet phones, and then he climbed into the airlock.

How, Yannick wondered sourly, could one man get to be so much of a nuisance in the space of a few short hours?

"Lord knows," said Kurt Lochmann from the other side of the desk, and Yannick realized with a start that he had spoken aloud. "I take it you're referring to that Earth-bound nosey-parker Jennings?"

"Who else? First the damned man loses me my lunch, because he insists on going out and poking around in that—ship. I had to go along because he'd never been in space before, and I wasn't going to risk letting a novice loose with a scooter in this system. When I got back I found a snarl in construction which took me three hours to clear. Then I had to put a communicator on to Pluto for him—more man-hours wasted. Now I've had to leave an operator I could use elsewhere on standby to pick up the answer. If he sticks around much longer I shall personally throw him off the ship." He crumpled a sheet of paper and threw it angrily into the disposal chute.

"I know," said Kurt sombrely. "The damned man doesn't *do* anything, but it's just his being here which is bad. I had a bad dream last night from it."

"Do this for me, will you, Kurt? As soon as you have a clerk available, make up a bill for services rendered and 'fax it back to Creswell and Palmer's head office on Earth. It'll make him unpopular at home and maybe they'll pull him out."

There was a knock at the door, and Yannick shouted for whoever it was to come in. The panel slid aside to reveal Louis Baron, the computerman, a thin man with inky fingers and a slide-rule in his pocket.

"What is it, Louis?" said Yannick.

"Thought you might care to see these figures," the newcomer told him. "I've been checking our orbit—the total orbit of the system, that is. Looks like we underestimated dust-drag a bit."

"Serious?"

"Lord, no!" said Louis, and Yannick relaxed. Anything which threatened the ultimate success of the station tended to make him terribly anxious. "Here are the figures."

Yannick took the papers and scrutinized them. "Seems reasonable," he nodded. "How—?"

The ring of the desk phone interrupted him, and he answered it with, "Huyghens."

"Charlie here, chief. I've had Pluto on the beam. Want the message?"

"Surely." Yannick seized the pencil nearest him and scribbled down the groups. One of them puzzled him, but he saw after a moment that it was a name—Klaus—in clear. "Okay," he said. "I got it. Thanks."

Shutting off the phone, he turned to Kurt. "Go and rout out Jennings, will you?" he requested. "Are they still within 'fax distance of Mars?"

"Don't move out of range till next week," said Kurt, rising. "I'll send him straight round."

Louis nodded to Yannick, and the two departed together. Yannick bent to the cypher manual, and when Jennings came in a little later, he looked up and nodded.

"Here's your reply from Pluto," he said. "And they took long enough about it. Seems you were right about there being two men on board. Clore left Pluto with another of your employees, an agent called Klaus, who was trying to make Mars. They arranged with Jupiter to have one of the ships from Io diverted to cross orbits with Clore and take off his passenger."

"Sounds reasonable," nodded Jennings. "Is there more?"

"I've got one last code group to work out. GVRMS," he muttered, turning pages.

"'Psychologically fit for spatial duties'," said Jennings promptly. "I've sent that one myself often enough."

"Sometimes wrongly," suggested Yannick unpleasantly.

"Oh, no," said Jennings quietly. "Always rightly."

The impudence of the man, thought Yannick wearily. With a tribute to his incompetence out there now, he can still make a ridiculous statement like that.

"All right," he said at length. "You can go around to the communications blister and get the operator to contact your Mars office. *Please* be as quick as you can; we need our channels for other things."

Jennings inclined his head and took the interpreted message, looking it over. "One thing, if you can spare a moment, Mr. Huyghens," he said. "How exactly does that red light alongside the airlock of a spaceship work?"

"A cycling lamp?" said Yannick. "Oh. If there's pressure in the lock—that is, between the two doors—it closes a circuit and switches on the light. It's just to warn anyone trying to enter from outside that the lock is occupied. It doesn't burn all the time—the closing of the inner door starts the pumps automatically, so that if someone comes in from outside he doesn't waste air."

"How far away could you see it?"

"Lord knows. A hundred miles if you were looking in the right direction, possibly." Yannick spoke as one explaining two plus two to a retarded child.

"It's kind of you to make it so clear," said Jennings. Yannick looked up sharply, wondering if he really had detected sarcasm in his voice. "How close would two ships approach when they had to trans-ship a passenger?"

"Their orbits would be pre-calculated by mutual agreement at the points of departure, and when they met, depending on the accuracy of the plotting, they would either sling across a line or—more likely—the bigger of the ships would send across a crewman with a scooter to pick the passenger up."

"Thank you," said Jennings again. He gathered up the message draft and went out.

After he had gone, Yannick turned sourly back to his work. What with waiting for Pluto's reply all through the past "night," he was falling behind. He set to determinedly and sorted out a progress report which should have gone off yesterday. He dictated a stinging account of the reasons for the delay—Jennings—and had just finished the stuff left over from yesterday when there was a hesitant knock at the door again, and Jennings returned.

"Well?" said Yannick. "All fixed? When are you moving out?"

Jennings sat down and adjusted the legs of his trousers delicately. "It looks as if you are going to be stuck with me for some time, Mr. Huyghens," he said. "In fact, not only me, but probably several other people, including the government's investigators. They won't take this lightly."

"Take what lightly?"

"Clore was murdered."

The silence remained for a long time, as solid and as heavy as if it were a physical thing. At last Yannick broke it, his voice sounding thin and far away.

"What are you talking about?" he said incredulously.

"I've been in touch with the duty shipmaster at our Sun Lake Port office on Mars. He confirmed that Klaus did leave Pluto with Clore, and was correctly trans-shipped—by scooter—to one of our heavy freighters from Io to Mars, the *Geertruida*. But because I happened to trust my psycho-profile of Clore, I asked for Klaus's confidential index. It turned out to be 18VY. Do you know what that is?"

Yannick shook his head dumbly.

"Potential homicidal instability. Triggered by a subconscious desire to kill without suffering the consequences. So long as they're surrounded by many people, they are quite safe. The classic cases are mostly from Earth during the pioneering stages; men without previous criminal records would go out into the wilderness with one companion and return and report him dead of a shooting accident or something similar. Since they *were* mostly unprovable, they frequently went unpunished. The classic case, which gives its name to the condition, is Packer's, back in 1874 in Utah. In that case it was combined with cannibalism."

Yannick's face twisted with nausea, but Jennings continued in the same level voice, "So you see, Mr. Huyghens, there will be an inquiry."

Visions of the entire job held up while strangers prowled and probed around the station filled Yannick's mind. He said, "Not while I'm in charge of this job, Jennings. If you want your pilot, take him out of here and don't come back. I don't care if Clore *was* murdered! I'm not going to stand for a bunch of ghouls breathing down our necks and flourishing that blowout in front of us for the next year or two."

"I'm sorry, Mr. Huyghens." Jennings was inexorable. "I know a little about the laws relating to criminal insanity. There has never before been a murder in space, except for those caused by maniacs who later committed suicide. Most deaths off the surface of a planet occur through accident or, more rarely, nervous breakdown. I think you'll find that the government will requisition accommodation here, for a start, rather than send up separate ships. Of course, my firm will be glad to give them space on the regular transports with which we service you—the good name of the company is at stake. I don't know who let this man Klaus slip out aboard an empty ship instead of riding a crewed freighter, but he will have considerable trouble to face—"

Yannick buried his head in his hands. He considered simply casting loose the ship and the dead man and sending it off into another orbit, and then dismissed it as hopeless. "Is there nothing we can do?" he said.

"Only one thing, Mr. Huyghens. Prove beyond doubt that this was in fact a murder."

Yannick stared. "You mean you aren't certain?" he demanded in a shaking voice.

"So far, we only have Klaus's known instability to guide us," said Jennings, leaning back in his chair. "Taken together with the fact that Clore was shown to be incapable of resorting to suicide at his last mental check-up, it's not proof—but it's grounds for investigation. As a psychologist, of course, I'm certain it was murder."

Yannick grunted and did not answer.

"Look, Huyghens," said Jennings abruptly, "I know how much this is going to affect you. The prejudice against coming into contact with violent death is an old one, especially when people are in daily dread of it happening to themselves. I'm from Earth, where we take it differently, and can't really appreciate it—"

"Putting a label on it doesn't make it any easier to live with," said Yannick.

"Exactly. Now there'll be another message in from our Mars office shortly—I've asked your operator to keep an eye out for it, and I hope you don't mind. So far I can see one possibility that may prove murder. I'm no detective, of course, but I think you'd rather settle the matter right away. It's the question of the cycling lamp. I asked our Mars office to find out whether the crewman who went across to collect Klaus from the *Geertruida* noticed if the cycling lamp was on when he passed through the airlock."

Yannick turned worried eyes on him. "I wondered why you were asking about that damned thing," he muttered. "But what does it prove? If the crewman noticed that it wasn't lit, Klaus need only say that it was broken, and so it is—you've seen it yourself."

"But it isn't broken," said Jennings gently.

"Damnation, man! I saw it myself—"

"And leapt to the wrong conclusion. I looked at it more closely, because, as I told you, this is my first time in space and I'm fascinated by the working of spaceships. At first I was as ready as you to accept it as out of order. But tell me, what purpose does the glass around the filament serve?"

Yannick sat up, sudden hope stirring in his mind. "To keep the vacuum!" he said.

"To keep the vacuum. The *filament* of the cycling bulb isn't broken, only the glass. It should have functioned as well in space without the glass as it did with. I take it that the only reason for having glass round it in space is the fragility of the wire. If we can obtain confirmation from the man who transferred Klaus to the *Geertruida* that the lamp did not light when he left the airlock, we have proof that the ship was already drained of air. In fact, that Klaus committed murder."

He rose to his feet. "Now all we have to do is to wait for the shipmaster on Mars to report. I hope for your sake, Mr. Huyghens, that the crewman kept his eyes open. I mean to find conclusive evidence of the crime if it's the last thing I do."

Looking at him, Yannick made a tentative admission to himself that perhaps Jennings was right, after all, perhaps the death of a man, on the strength of a couple of psychologists' reports, could be made into a justification for the holding up of his job, and the teetering of nearly a hundred men on the hair-line edge of sanity.

But he had never known Clore; his death meant nothing to a man who had worked space since the days when if you came back alive you were one of the lucky few. He knew this station, though, better than he knew himself. In a sense, it *was* himself—the product of his mind at least. It was always going to be more important to him.

He said nothing, and after hesitating a moment Jennings turned away and went out, carefully sliding the door to behind him.

God damn it! thought Yannick, angrily slapping the top of a pile of schematics. Would this Martian agency of Jennings's *never* find that crewman?

It was two days now since they reported that he had gone off on leave immediately on landing, and they would try to trace him. Even among the population of Mars—second now to Earth—it should not be so hard to find one man and ask him one simple question.

He hoped devoutly that the answer was going to be good.

The door opened without ceremony, and he tried to exchange the haggard look on his face for a smile to greet his visitor, but he failed. Instead he said, "Hullo, doc."

Dr. Meadows, who combined the functions of medical and mental officer, dietician and ecologist for the system, nodded his grey head and sat down. Without preamble, as if following up a previous train of thought, he remarked, "You don't look so good yourself, Yannick."

"Have I any reason to be? What's the visit for—about this man who went catatonic yesterday, I suppose?"

"Yes, of course." The doctor shrugged. "He'll have to go back to Earth at the first opportunity. And I fear there may be others later."

"It's that—casualty, I suppose."

"Definitely. Men in isolated conditions have always hated the presence of death—it's a basic prejudice which we shall probably never eliminate altogether. I've been reading up on it; it seems that even ocean-going sailors used to refuse to ship with a corpse. So long as it was just *there*, it could be tolerated; it could even be forgotten, for a while. If I'd been notified why Jennings was coming here, I would have advised you to keep his mission secret and give him a cover-up. As it is, everybody in the system knows who he is and why he's here, and the mere sight of him acts as a trigger."

"There are going to be a hell of a lot more triggers in a short time, unless we get proof of his crazy theory," said Yannick gloomily. "Doc, has he discussed it with you? Is he justified in suspecting murder?"

Meadows shook his head. "I don't know. But he's a good psychologist—he has to be, to hold down that post. I'd say that if his data are right, he's right."

Yannick jerked his thumb at the pile of papers on the desk. "I've got stuff here I should have dealt with three days ago," he said. "It's getting me down, too. You know what this job means to me, doc, don't you?"

Soberly, Meadows agreed that he did. "I can understand how holding it up affects you. Frankly—if you'll pardon what you might call doctor's privilege—I think it means entirely *too* much to you."

"Maybe it does," said Yannick tiredly. "Maybe it does. But I wouldn't change it if I could. Doc, suppose that we can't prove that the cycling lamp didn't light—that there was no pressure in the ship when Klaus left it? Is there another way to fix the time of the man's death?"

"State of the body? The vacuum will have preserved it. Consumption of food? People's appetites under no gravity vary from day to day—I know that from hard experience in trying to keep track of the eating habits right here. The log, Jennings tells me, is missing, which could equally well be due to Klaus covering his tracks or to a fit of madness by Clore, at least in the eyes of the law. Er—how about deviations from orbit—say failure to fire a correcting blast, or something?"

Yannick shook his head. "I've thought of that. When a long-run and a short-run ship cross orbits and want to match, the short-run ship, in this case the *Geertruida*, does the manoeuvring, because of the fuel expenditure. I already know that the plotting was good enough for them to avoid making any corrections—they matched to within twenty miles."

"Have you been giving a lot of thought to this?" asked Meadows. "It sounds like it."

Yannick gave a short, humourless laugh. "Yes, doc, I have. It's stupid, isn't it? I'm not interested in the blasted man himself, it's just that I'm so worried in case interference seriously hinders the job, I'm being compelled to look for every possible loophole. If I could just lay my hands on one item of proof that would get Jennings out of my hair, I'd be happy."

"Keep looking," said Meadows, rising. "I'll be getting along. See you at lunch."

For a long time Yannick remained looking at the spot where Meadows had been sitting. Just as he roused himself to get back to work, the phone interrupted him. He said, "Huyghens."

"Charlie, chief. We've had Mars on the beam for Jennings—he's coming round to see you now. I thought you might want to know before he hits you that they've found this crewman from the *Geertruida*, and he can't remember noticing whether the cycling lamp of Clore's ship was on or not. They say he just can't be sure."

Yannick's heart sank. "Thanks," he managed to say, and rang off. Looking up at Jennings as he came in through the door, he said, "I hope you're satisfied."

The bitterness in his tone seemed lost on Jennings, who shrugged. "It was just bad luck," he said. "Well, there isn't anything else we can do from this end, is there? I just came along to tell you I'm going to notify our head office on Earth and have the investigation proper commenced. I thought you'd want to know."

Can the man really be as thick-skinned as that? Yannick wondered in dumb incredulity as he watched the door close behind Jennings again.

He cursed, roundly and at length, the man who had put Klaus on board a no-load ship with one companion, instead of aboard a crewed ship where he would have been safe. He almost wished the man would repeat his murderous performance in a place where there were other people to tell the tale, but of course the very nature of his aberration made that impossible. Surely there must be *some* way to avoid the prospect of a bunch of grave-robbers coming out to trample over the horrid scene, to present its memory afresh to each of his already unnerved men every way they turned—

Try as he would, the problem which had defeated him a dozen times defeated him again; perhaps his very desperation was blinding him.

He looked at the model of the completed station on the corner of the desk. It would be much longer now before he saw the reality. Men would break down; replacements would have to be brought in and in their turn they would break down. He himself...

Picturing himself being taken away from the task which meant so much to him, he shuddered. *That* Jennings could do to him.

Sickly, he turned over the papers before him at random, finding things he had been given the day Jennings arrived and still hadn't attended to. What was this, now? Louis's figures on dust-drag. Never mind them, they could wait—

Dust!

He reached for the phone, his hand trembling with excitement. "Get me Louis," he said tensely. "Hurry!"

If only it were possible! But it must be.

The glass round an electric lamp served to preserve the vacuum; vacuum means "the empty thing"—and space is not empty. Weiszacker and Gamow had shown how planets could be formed from the inchoate dust of the Beginning, but they had not taken up all of it. Some of it remained to give Earth its counterglow; some of it was dancing out there in the light of the searchlights. A little of that would have entered Clore's ship, first when the discovery of his death was made, and then once more on the visit of Jennings and himself to the vessel—but only a trace, since at no time had both doors been opened. If the ship had been left open to space by Klaus long enough to have drained away all its air, it would have swept up a little of the dust of the place it was passing. A little. It would have to be *enough*.

His mind filled with a ghastly vision of Klaus, safe in his space-suit (he wondered what ingenious, devious excuse he had invented for putting it on), perhaps grinning in anticipation, slamming down the release of the airlock and blowing the air into space, while Clore, uttering that scream which was now frozen on his face, stretched out a frantic arm to stop him—and failed.

Suddenly he hated Klaus even more than he hated Jennings.

Then he would have stayed with the body—for hours? Days? The last shreds of air would have drifted out of the lock, and per-haps dust would have drifted in—it had to have drifted in. Until Klaus went outside when the proximity alarm light warned him of the nearness of the *Geertruida*, and closed the lock behind him from outside. He was safe; pilots had blown their air through insanity often enough before, and he had only to say that Clore was acting strangely when he left. After all, he had broken the cycling lamp on the lock, so no one could have told from the *Geertruida* that there was already no air in the hull. And with the log gone—easily done by the failing Clore later on—there was nothing to show when he died.

He realized that Louis had been shouting at him for ten sec-onds, demanding to know what he wanted, and he said, "Louis, do you have data on density and composition of the dust all along our orbit?"

"Of course," said Louis, faintly surprised.

"Could you tell the difference between a sample of this dust we're passing through now and that from somewhere between Pluto and the Mars-Jupiter orbit at the moment?"

"Heavens, yes! That one would be quite easy. You see, the orbit of Jupiter is pretty well swept clear by the mass of the planet and the Trojan asteroids. Inside the orbit the dust is mostly heavy stuff—what the inner planets are made of, and some of the asteroids. Outside Jupiter, the composition is very markedly different, it's similar to the giant planets themselves, fragments of ice, molecules of hydrogen, frozen ammonia and so on. The orbit of Jupiter almost forms an exact dividing line."

"Could you test the dust in that ship"—he didn't need to refer more directly to Clore's vessel—"and say whether the locks were opened to space inside or outside the orbit of Jupiter?"

Louis's voice reflected as much jubilation as Yannick himself felt. "I don't know, damn it," he said huskily. "But let's go and try."

"Mr. Huyghens, I'm afraid I have rather a serious admission to make," said Jennings, looking up with a smile from the report of Louis's spot analysis which he had in his lap. "You've been thinking of me as quite insensitive to your difficulties, and to the fact that you wanted to get this work ahead as fast as possible. Believe me, I wasn't. But I was trying to make things worse for you."

Yannick was temporarily speechless, and Jennings hurried on before he could master himself. "I've also lied to you regarding the imminence of an investigation. If I had gone to your communications room and sent a 'fax message to the police on Earth, they wouldn't have come out millions of miles. I had no concrete evidence to offer them; psychological tests have failed before, and aren't conclusive. If I'd notified my own firm, they would conveniently have overlooked it. The most that would have happened would have been the dismissal of the man on Pluto who was responsible for letting Klaus travel with Clore. That way, they stood to gain by the cost of one ship which could have been written off otherwise. As it is, Clore's dependants will sue my firm for negligence, and probably cost them a million.

"But I raised that profile of Clore myself. I *knew*—more certainly than I could put on paper—that he hadn't killed himself. I came out here fully expecting that I might have made a mistake; I was prepared to back down, in spite of that. The discovery that he had had a companion reassured me. For a while, with the discovery that the cycling lamp wasn't really broken, I hoped I could show proof. When that failed, I knew there was only one chance. As I told you, this is my first trip into space—I simply didn't look at things the way a man who had spent years in space could do. Obviously, you were the man to supply the answer—it was a puzzle for spacemen, not a 'desk pilot.'

"Since you were rigidly opposed either to wasting time from your project or probing into Clore's death, the only way I could elicit your aid was to point out that it was going to be worse for you if you didn't find that proof than if you did."

He looked squarely at Yannick. "I've broken one of the major rules by which I as a psychologist should live. I temporarily but knowingly endangered the sanity of members of your team. But I've adhered to a bigger and better precept. If I had consented to forget about Klaus, doubt would have been cast on the success of psychological testing—and I'm a psychologist. Space is too big and too menacing for the consequences of any mistake to go unremedied. If we can dispose of Klaus—and we can—we've added another piece of the jigsaw. The complete picture is perfectly safe space travel."

Yannick's sullen expression changed slowly, unwillingly—but irresistibly—into a smile. "You're a very clever man, Jennings," he said grudgingly. "You're probably too clever for your own good."

"I am," said Jennings levelly. "I've probably cost my firm a million credits in damages and incalculable goodwill. I've done myself out of my job, among other things. Yes, I'm too clever for my own good.

"But not, I like to think, for other people's good."

Eric Frank Russell

Eric Frank Russell (1905–1978) was one of Britain's leading sf writers in the 1950s, alongside Arthur C. Clarke and John Wyndham, but his reputation has faded since he more-or-less stopped writing in 1965. He honed his craft on reading American pulps in the 1930s and could muster a passable American idiom. He enjoyed pulp crime fiction. When he finalized his first novel, Sinister Barrier, which involves the investigation by a special government agent into a series of unusual and unexplained deaths, Russell modelled it on the American pulp G-Men. It clearly worked. John W. Campbell, Jr., bought it for the first issue of Unknown, and the novel, about aliens controlling humans, became instantly popular. Russell enjoyed creating strange mysteries investigated by the police in such early stories as "Shadow-Man" (1938) where the police try and find an invisible criminal, or "Seat of Oblivion" (1941) with the police trying to find a criminal who can possess other people. One of his last books, With a Strange Device (1964), issued in America as The Mindwarpers, was an expansion of a novella which first appeared in a detective pulp in 1956 and many critics argued it was not science fiction at all, but a Cold War thriller about the manipulation of scientists' minds. I have no doubt Russell would have made a good crime-fiction writer had he put his mind to it. The following story, written and set in 1955, pits human ingenuity against alien ability.

A S NEARLY AS AN ANDROMEDAN THOUGHT FORM CAN BE expressed in print, his name was Harasha Vanash. The formidable thing about him was his conceit. It was redoubtable because justified. His natural power had been tested on fifty hostile worlds and found invincible.

The greatest asset any living creature can possess is a brain capable of imagination. That is its strong point, its power centre. But to Vanash an opponent's mind was a weak spot, a chink in the armour, a thing to be exploited.

Even he had his limitations. He could not influence a mind of his own species armed with his own power. He could not do much with a brainless life form except kick it in the rumps. But if an alien could think and imagine, that alien was his meat.

Vanash was a twenty-four carat hypno, jewelled in every hole. Given a thinking mind to work upon at any range up to most of a mile, he could convince it in a split second that black was white, right was wrong, the sun had turned bright green, and the corner cop was King Farouk. Anything he imposed stayed stuck unless he saw fit to unstick it. Even if it outraged common sense, the victim would sign affidavits, swear to it upon the Bible, the Koran or whatever, and then be led away to have his head examined.

There was one terminal restriction that seemed to have the nature of a cosmos-wide law; he could not compel any life form to destroy itself by its own hand. At that point the universal instinct of self-survival became downright mulish and refused to budge.

However, he was well able to do the next best thing. He could do what a snake does to a rabbit, namely, obsess the victim with the idea that it was paralysed and completely unable to flee from certain death. He could not persuade a Bootean *appolan* to cut its own throat, but he could make it stand still while he performed that service.

Yes, Harasha Vanash had excellent basis for self-esteem. When one has walked into and out of fifty worlds one can afford to be confident about the fifty-first. Experience is a faithful and loving servant, always ready with a long, stimulating draught of ego when required.

So it was with nonchalance that he landed on Earth. The previous day he'd given the planet a look-over and his snooping had set off the usual rumours about flying saucers despite that his ship resembled no such object.

He arrived unseen in the hills, got out, sent the ship up to where its automechanisms would swing it into a distant orbit and make it a pinhead-sized moon. Among the rocks he hid the small, compact apparatus that could call it back when wanted.

The vessel was safe from interference up there, high in the sky. The chance of it being observed telescopically was very remote. If the creatures of Earth did succeed in detecting its presence, they could do nothing about it. They hadn't any rocketships. They could do no more than look and wonder and worry.

Yesterday's preliminary investigation had told him practically nothing about the shape and form of the dominant life. He hadn't got near enough for that. All he'd wanted to know was whether this planet was worthy of closer study and whether its highest life form had exploitable minds. It had not taken long to see that he'd discovered an especially juicy plum, a world deserving of eventual confiscation by the Andromedan horde.

The physical attributes of these future slaves did not matter much right now. Though not at all bizarre, he was sufficiently like them to walk around, sufficiently unlike to raise a yelp of alarm on sight. There would be no alarm. In spite of a dozen physical differences they'd be soothed, positively soothed. Because they'd never get a true view of him. Only an imaginary one. He could be a mental mock-up of anything, anybody.

Therefore, the first thing to do was to find a mediocrity who would pass unnoticed in a crowd, get his mental image firmly fixed and impress that on all other minds subsequently encountered until such time as it might be convenient to switch pictures.

Communication was no problem, either. He could read the questions, project the answers, and the other party's own mind could be compelled to supply accompanying camouflage. If they communicated by making noises with their mouths or by dexterous jiggling of their tails, it would work out the same. The other's mastered imagination would get his message while providing the noises and mouth movements or the appropriate tail-jigglings.

Leaving the landing place, he set forth through the hills, heading for a well-used road observed during his descent. A flight of primitive jetplanes arced across the eastward horizon. He paused long enough to watch them with approval. The trouble with prospective servants already discovered elsewhere was that they were a bit too stupid to be efficient. Not here, though.

He continued on his way, bearing no instrument other than a tiny compass needed for eventual return and take-off. No weapon. Not a knife, not a gun. There was no need to burden himself with lethal hardware. By self-evident logic, local weapons were the equals of themselves. Any time he wanted one he could make the nearest sucker hand over his own and feel happy to do it. It was that easy. He'd done it a dozen times before and could do it a dozen times again.

*

By the roadside stood a small filling station with four pumps. Vanash kept watch upon it from the shelter of thick bushes fifty yards away. Hm-m-m! bipeds, vaguely like himself but with semi-rigid limbs and a lot more hair. There was one operating a pump, another sitting in a car. He could not get a complete image of the latter because only the face and shoulders were visible. As for the former, the fellow wore a glossy-peaked cap bearing a metal badge, and uniformlike overalls with a crimson cipher on the pocket.

Neither example was suitable for mental duplication, he decided. One lacked sufficient detail, the other had far too much. Characters, who wore uniforms, usually took orders, had fixed duties, were liable to be noted and questioned if seen some place where they shouldn't be. It would be better to pick a subject able to move around at random.

The car pulled away. Peaked Cap wiped his hands on a piece of cotton waste and gazed along the road. Vanash maintained his watch. After a few minutes another car halted. This one had an aerial sticking from its roof and bore two individuals dressed alike; peaked caps, metal buttons and badges. They were heavy-featured, hard-eyed, had an official air about them. They wouldn't do either, thought Vanash. Too conspicuous.

Unconscious of this scrutiny, one of the cops said to the attendant, "Seen anything worth telling, Joe?"

"Not a thing. All quiet."

The police cruiser jerked forward and continued its patrol, Joe went into the station. Taking a flavour-seed from its small pack, Vanash chewed it and meditated while he bided his time. So they were mouth-talkers, nontelepathic, routine-minded and natural puppets for any hypno who cared to dangle them around.

Still, their cars, jetplanes and other gadgets proved that they enjoyed occasional flashes of inspiration. In Andromedan theory the rare touch of genius was all that menaced any hypno, since nothing else could sense his existence, follow his operations and pin him down.

It was a logical supposition—in terms of other-world logic. Everything the Andromedan culture possessed had been born one by one of numberless revealing shafts of revelation that through the centuries had sparked out of nothingness in the inexplicable way that such things do. But flashes of inspiration come spontaneously, of their own accord. They cannot be created to order no matter how great the need. Any species could go nuts for lack of one essential spark and, like everyone else, be compelled to wait its turn.

The trap in any foreign culture lies in the fact that no newcomer can know everything about it, imagine everything, guess everything. For instance, who could guess that the local life form were a bunch of chronic fidgets? Or that, because of it, they'd never had time to wait for genius? Vanash did not know, and could not suspect, that Earth had a tedious, conventional and most times unappreciated substitute for touches of genius. It was slow, grim, determined and unspectacular, but it was usable as and when required and it got results.

Variously it was called making the grade, slogging along, doing it the hard way, or just plain lousy legwork. Whoever heard of such a thing?

Not Vanash, nor any of his kind. So he waited behind the bushes until eventually a nondescript, mousy individual got out of a car, obligingly mooched around offering every detail of his features, mannerisms and attire. This specimen looked the unattached type that are a dime a dozen on any crowded city street. Vanash mentally photographed him from every angle, registered him to perfection and felt satisfied.

*

Five miles to the north along this road lay a small town, and forty miles beyond it a big city. He'd seen and noted them on the way down, deciding that the town would serve as training-ground before going to the city. Right now he could step boldly from cover and compel his model to drive him where he wanted to go.

The idea was tempting but unwise. Before he was through with this world its life form would become aware of inexplicable happenings in their midst and it would be safer not to locate the first of such events so near to the rendezvous with the ship. Peaked Cap might talk too loudly and too long about the amazing coincidence of a customer giving a lift to an exact twin. The victim himself might babble bemusedly about picking up somebody who made him feel as though looking into a mirror. Enough items like that, and a flash of revelation could assemble them into a picture of the horrid truth.

He let the customer go and waited for Joe to enter the building. Then he emerged from the bushes, walked half a mile northward, stopped and looked to the south.

The first car that came along was driven by a salesman who never, never, never picked up a hitcher. He'd heard of cases where free riders had bopped the driver and robbed him, and he wasn't going to be rolled if he could help it. So far as he was concerned, thumbers by the wayside could go on thumbing until next Thursday week.

He stopped and gave Vanash a lift and lacked the vaguest notion of why he'd done it. All he knew was that in a moment of mental aberration he'd broken the habit of a lifetime and picked up a thin-faced, sad and silent customer who resembled a middle-aged mortician.

"Going far?" asked the salesman, inwardly bothered by the weakness of his own resolution.

"Next town," said Vanash. Or the other one thought he said it, distinctly heard him saying it and would take a dying oath that it really had been said. Sneaking the town's name from the driver's mind and thrusting it back again, Vanash persuaded him to hear the addition of, "Northwood."

"Any particular part?"

"Doesn't matter. It's a small place. Drop me wherever you find convenient."

The driver grunted assent, offered no more conversation. His thoughts milled around, baffled by his own Samaritanism. Arriving in Northwood, he stopped the car.

"This do?"

"Thanks." Vanash got out. "I appreciate it."

"Think nothing of it," said the salesman, driving away bopless and unrolled.

Vanash watched him depart, then had a look around Northwood.

The place was nothing much. It had shops on one long main street and on two short side streets. A railroad depot with a marshalling yard. Four medium-sized industrial plants. Three banks, a post office, a fire station, a couple of municipal buildings. He estimated that Northwood held between four and five thousand Earthlings and that at least a third of them worked on outlying farms.

He ambled along the main street and was ignored by unsuspecting natives while practically rubbing shoulders with them. The experience gave him no great kick; he'd done it so often elsewhere that he now took it for granted and was almost bored by it. At one point a dog saw him, let go a howl of dismay and bolted with its tail between its legs. Nobody took any notice. Neither did he.

First lesson in pre-city education was gained inside a shop. Curious to see how the customers got what they wanted, he entered with a bunch of them. They used a medium of exchange in the form of printed paper and metal discs. That meant he'd save himself considerable trouble and inconvenience if he got hold of a supply of the stuff.

Moving to a crowded supermarket, he soon learned the relative values of money and a fair idea of its purchasing power. Then he helped himself to a small supply and was smart enough to do it by proxy. The technique was several times easier than falling off a log.

Standing unnoticed at one side, he concentrated attention on a plump, motherly shopper of obvious respectability. She responded by picking the purse of a preoccupied woman next to her. Sneaking the loot out of the market, she dropped it unopened on a vacant lot, went home, thought things over and held her head.

The take was forty-two dollars. Vanash counted it carefully, went to a cafeteria, splurged some of it on a square meal. By other methods he could have got the feed for free, but such tactics are self-advertising and can be linked up by a spark of inspiration. To his taste, some of the food was revolting, some passable, but it would do until he'd learned how to pick and choose.

One problem not yet satisfactorily resolved was that of what to do with the night. He needed sleep as much as any inferior life form and had to find some place for it. A snooze in the fields or a barn would be inappropriate; the master does not accept the hay while the servants snore on silk.

It took a little while to find out from observation, mind-pickings and a few questions to passers-by that he could bed down at an hotel or rooming house. The former did not appeal to him. Too public and, therefore, too demanding upon his resources for concealment. In an hotel he'd have less opportunity to let up for a while and be himself, which was a welcome form of relaxation.

But with a room of his own, free from constantly intruding servants armed with master-keys, he could revert to a normal, effortless state of mind, get his sleep, work out his plans in peace and privacy.

He found a suitable rooming house without much trouble. A blowzy female with four warts on her florid face showed him his hideout, demanded twelve dollars in advance because he had no luggage. Paying her, he informed her that he was William Jones, here for a week on business, and that he liked to be left alone.

In return, she intimated that her joint was a palace of peace for gentlemen, and that any bum who imported a hussy would be out on his neck. He assured her that he would not dream of such a thing, which was true enough because to him such a dream would have all the makings of a nightmare. Satisfied, she withdrew.

He sat on the edge of the bed and thought things over. It would have been an absurdly simple trick to have paid her in full without handing her a cent. He could have sent her away convinced that she had been paid. But she'd still be short twelve dollars and get riled about the mysterious loss. If he stayed on, he'd have to fool her again and again until at last the very fact that his payments coincided exactly with her losses would be too much even for an idiot.

A way out would be to nick someone for a week's rent, then move and take another boob. That tactic had its drawbacks. If the news got around and a hunt started after the bilker, he would have to change identities.

He wasn't averse to soaking a muttonhead or switching personalities, providing it was necessary. It irked him to have to do it frequently, for petty reasons hardly worth the effort. To let himself be the constant victim of trifling circumstances was to accept that these aliens were imposing conditions upon him. His ego resented such an idea.

All the same, he had to face a self-evident premise and its unavoidable conclusion. On this world one must have money to get around smoothly, without irritating complications. Therefore, he must acquire an adequate supply of the real thing or be continually called upon to create the delusion that he possessed it. No extraordinary intelligence was needed to divine which alternative gave the least trouble.

On other worlds the life forms had proved so sluggish and dull-witted, their civilizations so rudimentary, that it had not taken long to make a shrewd estimate of their worth as future foes and subsequent slaves. Here, the situation was a lot more complicated and required lengthier, more detailed survey. By the looks of it he'd be stalled quite a time. So he must get hold of money in quantities larger than that carried by the average individual. And when it ran out, he must get more.

Next day he devoted some time to tracing the flow of money back to a satisfactory source. Having found the source, he spent more time making careful study of it. In underworld jargon, he cased a bank.

The man lumbering along the corridor weighed two-fifty, had a couple of chins and a prominent paunch. At first sight, just a fat slob. First impressions can be very deceptive. At least half a dozen similarly built characters had been world heavyweight wrestling champs. Edward G. Rider was not quite in that category, but on rare occasion he could strew bodies around in a way that would make an onlooking chiseller offer his services as manager.

He stopped at a frosted glass door bearing the legend: UNITED STATES TREASURY—INVESTIGATION. Rattling the glass with a hammerlike knuckle, he entered without waiting for response, took a seat without being invited.

The sharp-faced individual behind the desk registered faint disapproval, said, "Eddie, I've got a smelly one for you."

"Have you ever given me one that wasn't?" Rider rested big hands on big kneecaps. "What's it this time? Another unregistered engraver on the rampage?"

"No. It's a bank robbery."

Rider frowned, twitched heavy eyebrows. "I thought we were interested only in counterfeit currency and illegal transfers of capital. What has a heist to do with us? That's for the police, isn't it?"

"The police are stuck with it."

"Well, if the place was government insured they can call in the Feds."

"It's not insured. We offered to lend a hand. You are the boy who will lend it."

"Why?"

The other drew a deep breath, explained rapidly, "Some smartie took the First Bank of Northwood for approximately twelve thousand—and nobody knows how. Captain Harrison, of the Northwood police, says the puzzle is a stinker. According to him, it looks very much as though at long last somebody has found a technique for committing the perfect crime."

"He would say that if he feels thwarted. How come we're dragged into it?"

"On checking up with the bank Harrison found that the loot included forty one-hundred dollar bills consecutively numbered. Those numbers are known. The others are not. He phoned us to give the data, hoping the bills might turn up and we could backtrack on them. Embleton handled the call, chatted a while, got interested in this perfect crime thesis."

"So?"

"He consulted with me. We both agreed that if somebody has learned how to truck lettuce the way he likes, he's as much a menace to the economy as any large-scale counterfeiter."

"I see," said Rider, doubtfully.

"Then I took the matter up at high level. Ballantyne himself decided that we're entitled to chip in, just in case something's started that can go too far. I chose you. The whole office block will sit steadier without your size fourteen boots banging around." He moved some papers to his front, picked up a pen. "Get out to Northwood and give Chief Harrison a boost."

"Now?"

"Any reason why it should be tomorrow or next week?"

"I'm baby-sitting tonight."

"Don't be silly."

"It's not silly," said Rider. "Not with this baby."

"You ought to be ashamed. You're not long married. You've got a sweet and trusting wife."

"She's the baby," Rider informed. "I promised her faithfully and fervently that I'd—"

"And I promised Harrison and Ballantyne that you'd handle this with your usual elephantine efficiency," the other interrupted, scowling. "Do you want to hold down your job or do you want out? Phone your wife and tell her duty comes first."

"Oh, all right." He went out, slammed the door, tramped surlily along the corridor, entered a booth and took twenty-two minutes to do the telling.

Chief Harrison was tall, lean and fed up. He said, "Why should I bother to tell you what happened? Direct evidence is better than secondhand information. We've got the actual witness here. I sent for him when I learned you were coming." He flipped a switch on the desk-box. "Send Ashcroft in."

"Who's he?" Rider asked.

"Head teller of the First Bank, and a worried man." He waited for the witness to enter, made an introduction. "This is Mr. Rider, a special investigator. He wants to hear your story."

Ashcroft sat down, wearily rubbed his forehead. He was a white-haired, dapper man in the early sixties. Rider weighed him up as the precise, somewhat finicky but solid type often described as a pillar of the community.

"So far I've told it about twenty times," Ashcroft complained, "and each time it sounds a little madder. My mind is spinning with the thoughts of it. I just can't find any plausible—"

"Don't worry yourself," advised Rider in soothing tones. "Just give me the facts as far as they go."

"Each week we make up the pay-roll for the Dakin Glass Company. It varies between ten and fifteen thousand dollars. The day before the company sends around a messenger with a debit-note calling for the required sum and stating how they want it. We then get it ready in good time for the following morning."

"And then?"

"The company collects. They send around a cashier accompanied by a couple of guards. He always arrives at about eleven o'clock. Never earlier than ten to eleven or later than ten past."

"You know the cashier by sight?"

"There are two of them, Mr. Swain and Mr. Letheren. Either of them might come for the money. One relieves the other from time to time. Or one comes when the other is too busy, or ill, or on vacation. Both have been well-known to me for several years."

"All right, carry on."

"When the cashier arrives he brings a locked leather bag and has the key in a pocket. He unlocks the bag, hands it to me. I fill it in such manner that he can check the quantities, pass it back together with a receipt slip. He locks the bag, puts the key in his pocket, signs the slip and walks out. I file the receipt and that's all there is to it."

"Seems a bit careless to let the same fellow carry both the bag and the key," Rider commented.

Chief Harrison chipped in with, "We've checked on that. A guard carries the key. He gives it to the cashier when they arrive at the bank, takes it back when they leave."

Nervously licking his lips, Ashcroft went on, "Last Friday morning we had twelve thousand one hundred eighty-two dollars ready for the Dakin plant. Mr. Letheren came in with the bag. It was exactly ten-thirty."

"How do you know that?" inquired Rider, sharply. "Did you look at the clock? What impelled you to look at it?"

"I consulted the clock because I was a little surprised. He was ahead of his usual time. I had not expected him for another twenty minutes or so."

"And it was ten-thirty? You're positive of that?"

"I am absolutely certain," said Ashcroft, as though it was the only certainty in the whole affair. "Mr. Letheren came up to the counter and gave me the bag. I greeted him, made a casual remark about him being early."

"What was his reply?"

"I don't recall the precise wording. I'd no reason to take especial note of what he said and I was busy tending the bag." He frowned with effort of thought. "He made some commonplace remark about it being better to be too early than too late."

"What occurred next?"

"I gave him the bag and the slip. He locked the bag, signed the slip and departed."

"Is that all?" Rider asked.

"Not by a long chalk," put in Chief Harrison. He nodded encouragingly at Ashcroft. "Go on, give him the rest of it."

"At five to eleven," continued the witness, his expression slightly befuddled, "Mr. Letheren came back, placed the bag on the counter and looked at me sort of expectantly. So I said, 'Anything wrong, Mr. Letheren?' He answered, 'Nothing so far as I know. Ought there to be?'"

He paused, rubbed his forehead again. Rider advised, "Take your time with it. I want it as accurately as you can give it."

Ashcroft pulled himself together. "I told him there was no reason for anything to be wrong because the money had been checked and rechecked three times. He then displayed some impatience and said he didn't care if it had been checked fifty times so long as I got busy handing it over and let him get back to the plant."

"That knocked you onto your heels, eh?" Rider suggested, with a grim smile.

"I was flabbergasted. At first I thought it was some kind of joke, though he isn't the type to play such tricks. I told him I'd already given him the money, about half an hour before. He asked me if I was cracked. So I called Jackson, a junior teller, and he confirmed my statement. He had seen me loading the bag."

"Did he also see Letheren taking it away?"

"Yes, sir. And he said as much."

"What was Letheren's answer to that?"

"He demanded to see the manager. I showed him into Mr. Olsen's office. A minute later Mr. Olsen called for the receipt slip. I took it out of the file and discovered there was no signature upon it."

"It was blank?"

"Yes. I can't understand it. I watched him sign that receipt myself. Nevertheless there was nothing on it, not a mark of any sort." He sat silent and shaken, then finished, "Mr. Letheren insisted that Mr. Olsen cease questioning me and call the police. I was detained in the manager's office until Mr. Harrison arrived."

Rider stewed it over, then asked, "Did the same pair of guards accompany Letheren both times?"

"I don't know. I did not see his escort on either occasion."

"You mean he came unguarded?"

"They are not always visible to the bank's staff," Harrison put in. "I've chased that lead to a dead end."

"How much did you learn on the way?"

"The guards deliberately vary their routine so as to make their behaviour unpredictable to anyone planning a grab. Sometimes both accompany the cashier to the counter and back. Sometimes they wait outside the main door, watching the street. Other times one remains in the car while the other mooches up and down near the bank."

"They are armed, I take it?"

"Of course." He eyed Rider quizzically. "Both guards swear that last Friday morning they escorted Letheren to the bank once and only once. That was at five to eleven."

"But he was there at ten-thirty," Ashcroft protested.

"He denies it," said Harrison. "So do the guards."

"Did the guards say they'd actually entered the bank?" inquired Rider, sniffing around for more contradictory evidence.

"They did not enter on arrival. They hung around outside the front door until Letheren's delay made them take alarm. At that point they went inside with guns half-drawn. Ashcroft couldn't see them because by then he was on the carpet in Olsen's office."

"Well, you can see how it is," commented Rider, staring hard at the unhappy Ashcroft. "You say Letheren got the money at ten-thirty. He says he did not. The statements are mutually opposed. Got any ideas on that?"

"You don't believe me, do you?" said Ashcroft, miserably.

"I don't disbelieve you, either. I'm keeping judgment suspended. We're faced with a flat contradiction of evidence. It doesn't follow that one of the witnesses is a liar and thus a major suspect. Somebody may be talking in good faith but genuinely mistaken."

"Meaning me?"

"Could be. You're not infallible. Nobody is." Rider leaned forward, gave emphasis to his tones. "Let's accept the main points at face value. If you've told the truth, the cash was collected at ten-thirty. If Letheren has told the truth, he was not the collector. Add those up and what do you get? Answer: the money was toted away by somebody who was not Letheren. And if that answer happens to be correct, it means that you're badly mistaken."

"I've made no mistake," Ashcroft denied. "I know what I saw. I saw Letheren and nobody else. To say otherwise is to concede that I can't trust the evidence of my own eyes."

"You've conceded it already," Rider pointed out.

"Oh, no I haven't."

"You told us that you watched him sign the receipt slip. With your own two eyes you saw him append his signature." He waited for comment that did not come, ended, "There was nothing on the slip."

Ashcroft brooded in glum silence.

"If you were deluded about the writing, you could be equally deluded about the writer."

"I don't suffer from delusions."

"So it seems," said Rider, dry voiced. "How do you explain that receipt?"

"I don't have to," declared Ashcroft with sudden spirit. "I've given the facts. It's for you fellows to find the explanation."

"That's right enough," Rider agreed. "We don't resent being reminded. I hope you don't resent being questioned again and again. Thanks for coming along."

"Glad to be of help." He went out, obviously relieved by the end of the inquisition.

Harrison found a toothpick, chewed it, said, "It's a heller. Another day or two of this and you'll be sorry they sent you to show me how."

Meditatively studying the police chief, Rider informed, "I didn't come to show you how. I came to help because you said you needed help. Two minds are better than one. A hundred minds are better than ten. But if you'd rather I beat it back home—"

"Nuts," said Harrison. "At times like this I sour up on everyone. My position is different from yours. When someone takes a bank, right under my nose, he's made a chump of me. How'd you like to be both a police chief and a chump?"

"I think I'd accept the latter definition when and only when I'd been compelled to admit defeat. Are you admitting it?"

"Not on your life."

"Quit griping then. Let's concentrate on the job in hand. There's something mighty fishy about this business of the receipt. It looks cockeyed."

"It's plain as pie to me," said Harrison. "Ashcroft was deluded or tricked."

"That isn't the point," Rider told him. "The real puzzle is that of *why* he was outsmarted. Assuming that he and Letheren are both innocent, the loot was grabbed by someone else, by somebody unknown. I don't see any valid reason why the culprit should risk bollixing the entire set-up by handing in a blank receipt that might be challenged on the spot. All he had to do to avoid it was to scrawl Letheren's name. Why didn't he?"

Harrison thought it over. "Maybe he feared Ashcroft would recognize the signature as a forgery, take a closer look at him and yell bloody murder."

"If he could masquerade as Letheren well enough to get by, he should have been able to imitate a signature well enough to pass scrutiny."

"Well, maybe he didn't sign because he couldn't," Harrison ventured, "not being able to write. I know of several hoodlums who can write only because they got taught in the jug."

"You may have something there," Rider conceded. "Anyway, for the moment Ashcroft and Letheren appear to be the chief suspects. They'll have to be eliminated before we start looking elsewhere. I presume you've already checked on both of them?"

"And how!" Harrison used the desk-box. "Send in the First Bank file." When it came, he thumbed through its pages. "Take Ashcroft first. Financially well-fixed, no criminal record, excellent character, no motive for turning bank robber. Jackson, the junior teller, confirms his evidence to a limited extent. Ashcroft could not have hidden the Dakin consignment any place. We searched the bank from top to bottom, during which time Ashcroft did not leave the place for one minute. We found nothing. Subsequent investigation brought out other items in his favour... I'll give you the details later on."

"You're satisfied that he is innocent?"

"Almost, but not quite," said Harrison. "He could have handed the money to an accomplice who bears superficial resemblance to

Letheren. That tactic would have finagled the stuff clean out of the bank. I wish I could shake down his home in search of his split. One bill with a known number would tie him down but good." His features became disgruntled, "Judge Maxon refused to sign a search warrant on grounds of insufficient justification. Said he's got to be shown better cause for reasonable suspicion. I'm compelled to admit that he's right."

"How about the company's cashier, Letheren?"

"He's a confirmed bachelor in the late fifties. I won't weary you with his full background. There's nothing we can pin on him."

"You're sure of that?"

"Judge for yourself. The company's car remained parked outside the office all morning until ten thirty-five. It was then used to take Letheren and his guards to the bank. It couldn't reach the bank in less than twenty minutes. There just wasn't enough time for Letheren to make the first call in some other car, return to the plant, pick up the guards and make the second call."

"Not to mention hiding the loot in the interim," Rider suggested.

"No, he could not have done it. Furthermore, there are forty people in the Dakin office and between them they were able to account for every minute of Letheren's time from when he started work at nine o'clock up to when he left for the bank at ten thirty-five. No prosecutor could bust an alibi like that!"

"That seems to put him right out of the running."

Harrison scowled and said, "It certainly does—but we've since found five witnesses who place him near the bank at ten-thirty."

"Meaning they support the statements of Ashcroft and Jackson?"

"Yes, they do. Immediately after the case broke I put every available man onto the job of asking questions the whole length of the street and down the nearest side-streets. The usual lousy legwork. They found three people prepared to swear they'd seen Letheren entering the bank at ten-thirty. They didn't know him by sight, but they were shown Letheren's photograph and identified him."

"Did they notice his car and give its description?"

"They didn't see him using a car. He was on foot at the time and carrying the bag. They noticed and remembered him only because a mutt yelped and went hell-for-leather down the street. They wondered whether he'd kicked it and why."

"Do they say he *did* kick it?"

"No."

Rider thoughtfully rubbed two chins. "Then I wonder why it behaved like that. Dogs don't yelp and bolt for nothing. Something must have hurt or scared it."

"Who cares?" said Harrison, having worries enough. "The boys also found a fellow who says he saw Letheren a few minutes later, coming out of the bank and still with the bag. He didn't notice any guards hanging around. He says Letheren started walking along the street as though he hadn't a care in the world, but after fifty yards he picked up a prowling taxi and rolled away."

"You traced the driver?"

"We did. He also recognized the photo we showed him. Said he'd taken Letheren to the Cameo Theater on Fourth Street, but did not see him actually enter the place. Just dropped him, got paid and drove off. We questioned the Cameo's staff, searched the house. It got us nowhere. There's a bus terminal nearby. We gave everyone there a rough time and learned nothing."

"And that's as far as you've been able to take it?"

"Not entirely. I've phoned the Treasury, given them the numbers of forty bills. I've put out an eight-state alarm for a suspect

answering to Letheren's description. Right now the boys are armed
with copies of his pic and are going the rounds of hotels and
rooming houses. He must have holed up somewhere and it could
have been right in this town. Now I'm stuck. I don't know where
to look next."

Rider lay back in his chair which creaked in protest. He mused
quite a time while Harrison slowly masticated the toothpick.

Then he said, "Excellent character, financial security and no
apparent motive are things less convincing than the support of
other witnesses. A man can have a secret motive strong enough
to send him right off the rails. He could be in desperate need of
ten or twelve thousand in ready cash merely because he's got to
produce it a darned sight quicker than he can raise it by legitimate
realization of insurance, stocks and bonds. For example, what if
he's got twenty-four hours in which to find ransom money?"

Harrison popped his eyes. "You think we should check on
Ashcroft's and Letheren's kin and see if any one of them is missing
or has been missing of late?"

"Please yourself. Personally, I doubt that it's worth the bother.
A kidnapper risks the death penalty. Why should he take a chance
like that for a measly twelve thousand when he endangers himself
no more by sticking a fatter victim for a far bigger sum? Besides,
even if a check did produce a motive it wouldn't tell us how the
robbery was pulled or enable us to prove it to the satisfaction of
a judge and jury."

"That's right enough," Harrison agreed. "All the same, the
check is worth making. It'll cost me nothing. Except for Ashcroft's
wife, the relatives of both men live elsewhere. It's just a matter of
getting the co-operation of police chiefs."

"Do it if you wish. And while we're making blind passes in
the dark, get someone to find out whether Letheren happens

to be afflicted with a no-good brother who could exploit a close family likeness. Maybe Letheren is the suffering half of a pair of identical twins."

"If he is," growled Harrison, "he's also an accessory after the fact because he can guess how the job was done and who did it, but he's kept his lips buttoned."

"That's the legal viewpoint. There's a human one as well. If one feels disgrace, one doesn't invite it. If you had a brother with a record as long as your arm, would you advertise it all over town?"

"For the fun of it, no. In the interests of justice, yes."

"All men aren't alike and thank God they're not." Rider made an impatient gesture. "We've gone as far as we can with the two obvious suspects. Let's work out what we can do with a third and unknown one."

Harrison said, "I told you I've sent out an alarm for a fellow answering to Letheren's description."

"Yes, I know. Think it will do any good?"

"It's hard to say. The guy may be a master of make-up. If so, he'll now look a lot different from the way he did when he pulled the job. If the resemblance happens to be real, close and unalterable, the alarm may help nail him."

"That's true. However, unless there's an actual blood relationship—which possibility you're following up anyway—the likeness can hardly be genuine. It would be too much of a coincidence. Let's say it's artificial. What does that tell us?"

"It was good," Harrison responded. "Good enough to fool several witnesses. Far too good for comfort."

"You said it," endorsed Rider. "What's more, an artist so exceptionally accomplished could do it again and again and again, working his way through a series of personalities more or less of his physical build. Therefore he may really look as much like Letheren as I look like a performing seal. We haven't his true description and the lack is a severe handicap. Offhand, I can think of no way of discovering what he looks like right now."

"Me neither," said Harrison, becoming morbid.

"There's one chance we've got, though. Ten to one his present appearance is the same as it was before he worked his trick. He'd no reason to disguise himself while casing the job and making his plans. The robbery was so smooth and well-timed that it must have been schemed to perfection. That kind of planning requires plenty of preliminary observation. He could not cotton onto Dakin's collecting habits and Letheren's appearance at one solitary go. Not unless he was a mind reader."

"I don't believe in mind readers," Harrison declared. "Nor astrologers, swamis or any of their ilk."

Ignoring it, Rider ploughed stubbornly on, "So for some time prior to the robbery he had a hideout in this town or fairly close to it. Fifty or more people may have seen him repeatedly and be able to describe him. Your boys won't find him by circling the dives and dumps and showing a photo, because he didn't look like the photo. The problem now is to discover the hideout, learn what he looked like."

"Easier said than done."

"It's hard sledding, chief, but let's keep at it. Eventually we'll get ourselves somewhere even if only into a padded cell."

He lapsed into silence, thinking deeply. Harrison concentrated attention on the ceiling. They did not know it, but they were employing Earth's on-the-spot substitute for a rare flash of genius. A couple of times Rider opened his mouth as if about to say something, changed his mind, resumed his meditating.

In the end, Rider said, "To put over so convincingly the gag that he was Letheren he must not only have looked like him but also dressed like him, walked like him, behaved like him, smelled like him."

"He was Letheren to the spit," answered Harrison. "I've questioned Ashcroft until we're both sick of it. Every single detail was Letheren right down to his shoes."

Rider asked, "How about the bag?"

"The bag?" Harrison's lean face assumed startlement followed by self-reproach. "You've got me there. I didn't ask about it. I slipped up."

"Not necessarily. There may be nothing worth learning. We'd better be sure on that point."

"I can find out right now." He picked up the phone, called a number, said, "Mr. Ashcroft, I've another question for you. About that bag you put the money into—was it the actual one always used by the Dakin people?"

The voice came back distinctly, "No, Mr. Harrison, it was a new one."

"*What?*" Harrison's face purpled as he bellowed, "Why didn't you say so at the start?"

"You didn't ask me and, therefore, I didn't think of it. Even if I had thought of it of my own accord I wouldn't have considered it of any importance."

"Listen, it's for me and not for you to decide what evidence is, or is not, important." He fumed a bit, threw the listening Rider a look of martyrdom, went on in tones edged with irritation. "Now let's get this straight, once and for all. Apart from being new, was the bag identically the same as the one Dakin uses?"

"No, sir. But it was very similar. Same type, same brass lock, same general appearance. It was slightly longer and about an inch deeper. I remember that when I was putting the money into it I wondered why they'd bought another bag and concluded that the purpose was to let Mr. Letheren and Mr. Swain have one each."

"Did you notice any distinguishing mark upon it, a price tag, a maker's sticker, initials, code letters, serial number, or anything like that?"

"Nothing at all. It didn't occur to me to look. Not knowing what was to come, I—"

The voice cut off in mid-sentence as Harrison irefully slammed down the phone. He stared hard at Rider who said nothing.

"For your information," Harrison told him, "I can say that there are distinct advantages in taking up the profession of latrine attendant. Sometimes I am sorely tempted." He breathed heavily, switched the desk-box. "Who's loafing around out there?"

Somebody replied, "It's Kastner, chief."

"Send him in."

Detective Kastner entered. He was a neatly attired individual who had the air of knowing how to get around in a sink of iniquity.

"Jim," ordered Harrison, "beat it out to the Dakin plant and borrow their cash-bag. Make certain it's the one they use for weekly collections. Take it to every store selling leather goods and follow up every sale of a similar bag within the last month. If you trace a purchaser, make him prove that he still possesses his bag, get him to say where he was and what he was doing at ten-thirty last Friday morning."

"Right, chief."

"Phone me the details if you latch onto anything significant."

After Kastner had gone, Harrison said, "That bag was bought specifically for the job. Therefore, the purchase is likely to be a recent one and probably made in this town. If we can't trace a sale through local stores, we'll inquire farther afield."

"You do that," Rider agreed. "Meanwhile, I'll take a couple of steps that may help."

"Such as what?"

"We're a scientific species, living in a technological age. We've got extensive, well-integrated communications networks and huge, informative filing systems. Let's use what we've got, eh?"

"What's on your mind?" Harrison asked.

Rider said, "A robbery so smooth, neat and easy is something that begs to be repeated *ad lib*. Maybe he's done it before. There's every likelihood that he'll do it again."

"So—?"

"We have his description, but it isn't worth much." He leaned forward. "We also have full details of his method and those *are* reliable."

"Yes, that's true."

"So let's boil down his description to the unalterable basics of height, weight, build, colour of eyes. The rest can be ignored. Let's also condense his technique, reduce it to the bare facts. We can summarize the lot in five hundred words."

"And then?"

"There are six thousand two hundred eighty banks in this country, of which slightly more than six thousand belong to the Bank Association. I'll get Washington to run off enough handbills for the Association to send its entire membership. They'll be put on guard against a similar snatch, asked to rush us full details if any get taken despite the warning or already had been taken before they got it."

"That's a good idea," Harrison approved. "Some other police chief may nurse a couple of items that we lack, while we're holding a couple that he wants. A get-together may find us holding enough to solve both cases."

"There's a slight chance that we can take it farther still," said Rider. "The culprit may have a record. If he has not, we're out of luck. But if he's done it before, and been pinched, we can find his card in no time at all." He pondered reminiscently, added, "That filing system in Washington is really something."

"I know of it, of course, but haven't seen it," Harrison commented.

"Friend of mine down there, a postal inspector, found it handy not long ago. He was hunting a fellow selling fake oil stock through the mails. This character had taken at least fifty suckers by means of some classy print-work including official looking reserve reports, certificates and other worthless documents. There was no description of him. Not a victim had seen him in the flesh."

"That's not much to go on."

"No, but it was enough. Attempts by postal authorities to trap him had failed. He was a wily bird and that in itself was a clue. Obviously he was a swindler sufficiently experienced to have a record. So this friend took what little he'd got to the F.B.I."

"What happened?"

"A *modus operandi* expert coded the data and fed it into the high-speed extractor, like giving the scent to a hound. Electronic fingers raced over slots and punch-holes in a million cards a darned sight faster than you could blow your nose. Rejecting muggers, heistmen and various toughies, the fingers dug out maybe four thousand confidence tricksters. From those they then extracted perhaps six hundred bond-pushers. And from those they picked a hundred who specialized in phony oil stocks. And from those they took twelve who kept out of sight by operating through the mails."

"That narrowed it down," Harrison conceded.

"The machine ejected twelve cards," Rider continued. "An extra datum might have enabled it to throw out one and only one. But that was as far as it could go; it couldn't use what it hadn't been given. Not that it mattered. A quick check of other records showed that four of the twelve were dead and six more were languishing in the clink. Of the remaining two, one was picked up, proved himself in the clear. That left the last fellow. The postal authorities now had his name, mug-shot, prints, habits, associates and everything but his mother's wedding certificate. They grabbed him within three weeks."

"Nice work. Only thing I don't understand is why they keep dead men's cards on file."

"That's because evidence comes up—sometimes years later—proving them responsible for old, unsolved crimes. The evil that men do lives after them; the good, if any, is interred with their bones." He eyed the other, ended, "The slaves of the filing system don't like cases left open and unfinished. They like to mark them closed even if it takes half a lifetime. They're tidy-minded, see?"

"Yes, I see." Harrison thought a while, remarked, "You'd think a criminal would go honest once on the files, or at least have the sense not to repeat."

"They always repeat. They get in a rut and can't jack themselves out of it. I never heard of a counterfeiter who turned gunman or bicycle thief. This fellow we're after will pull the same stunt again by substantially the same method. You wait and see." He signed to the phone. "Mind if I make a couple of long-distance calls?"

"Help yourself. I don't pay for them."

"In that case I'll have three. The little woman is entitled to some vocal fondling."

"Go right ahead." Registering disgust, Harrison heaved himself erect, went to the door. "I'll get busy someplace else. If one thing turns my stomach, it's the spectacle of a big man cooing a lot of slop."

Grinning to himself, Rider picked up the phone. "Get me the United States Treasury, Washington, Extension 417, Mr. O'Keefe."

Over the next twenty-four hours the steady, tiresome but determined pressure of Earth technique was maintained. Patrolmen asked questions of store owners, local gossips, tavern keepers, parolees, stool pigeons, any and every character who by remote chance might give with a crumb of worthwhile information. Plainclothes detectives knocked on doors, cross-examined all who responded, checked back later on any who'd failed to answer. State troopers shook down outlying motels and trailer parks, quizzed owners, managers, assistants. Sheriffs and deputies visited farms known to take occasional roomers.

In Washington, six thousand leaflets poured from a press while not far away another machine addressed six thousand envelopes. Also nearby, electronic fingers sought a specific array of holes and slots among a million variously punched cards. Police of half a dozen towns and cities loped around, checked on certain people, phoned their findings to Northwood, then carried on with their own work.

As usual, first results were represented by a stack of negative information. None of Ashcroft's relatives were missing or had been of late. There was no black sheep in Letheren's family, he had no twin, his only brother was ten years younger, was highly respected, bore no striking likeness and, in any case, had an unbreakable alibi.

No other bank had yet reported being soaked by an expert masquerader. Rooming houses, hotels and other possible hideouts failed to produce a clue to anyone resembling Letheren's photograph.

The silent searcher through the filing system found forty-one bank swindlers, living and dead. But not one with the same *modus operandi* or anything closely similar. Regretfully it flashed a light meaning, "No record."

However, from the deductive viewpoint enough negatives can make a few positives. Harrison and Rider stewed the latest news, came to the same conclusions. Ashcroft and Letheren were well-nigh in the clear. The unknown culprit was a newcomer to crime and his first success would induce him to do it again. Such a master of make-up had previously concealed himself under some identity other than that now being sought.

First break came in the late afternoon. Kastner walked in, tipped his hat onto the back of his head and said, "I may have something."

"Such as what?" asked Harrison, his features alert.

"There's no great demand for that particular kind of bag and only one store sells them in this town. Within the last month they've got rid of three."

"Paid for by cheque?"

"Cash on the nail." Kastner responded with a grim smile to the other's look of disappointment, went on, "But two of the buyers were local folk, recognized and known. Both made their purchases about three weeks ago. I chased them up. They've still got their bags and can account for their time last Friday morning. I've checked their stories and they hold good and tight."

"How about the third buyer?"

"That's what I'm coming to, chief. He looks good to me. He bought his bag the afternoon before the robbery. Nobody knows him."

"A stranger?"

"Not quite. I got a detailed description of him from Hilda Cassidy, the dame who waited on him. She says he was a middle-aged, thin-faced, meek sort of character with a miserable expression. Looked like an unhappy embalmer."

"Then what makes you say he's not quite a stranger?"

"Because, chief, there are eleven stores selling leather goods of one kind or another. I've lived here quite a piece, but I had to hunt around to find the one handling this kind of bag. So I figured that this miserable guy would have had to do some going the rounds, too. I tried all the stores a second time, giving them this new description."

"And—?"

"Three of them remembered this fellow looking for what they don't stock. All confirmed the description." He paused, added, "Sol Bergman, of the Travel Mart, says the guy's face was slightly familiar. Doesn't know who he is and can't make a useful guess. But he's sure he's seen him two or three times before."

"Maybe an occasional visitor from somewhere a good way out."

"That's how it looks to me, chief."

"A good way out means anywhere within a hundred-mile radius," growled Harrison. "Perhaps even farther." He eyed Kastner sourly. "Who got the longest and closest look at him?"

"The Cassidy girl."

"You'd better bring her in, and fast."

"I did bring her. She's waiting outside."

"Good work, Jim," approved Harrison, brightening. "Let's see her."

Kastner went out and brought her in. She was a tall, slender, intelligent person in the early twenties. Cool and composed, she sat with hands folded in her lap, answered Harrison's questions while he got the suspect's description in as complete detail as she was able to supply.

"More darned legwork," Harrison complained as she finished. "Now the boys will have to make all the rounds again looking for a lead on *this* guy."

Rider chipped in, "If he's an out-of-towner, you'll need the co-operation of all surrounding authorities."

"Yes, of course."

"Maybe we can make it lots easier for them." He glanced inquiringly across the desk toward the girl. "That is, if Miss Cassidy will help."

"I'll do anything I can," she assured.

"What's on your mind?" Harrison asked.

"We'll get Roger King to lend a hand."

"Who's he?"

"A staff artist. Does cartoon work on the side. He's good, very good." He switched attention to the girl. "Can you come round early and spend the morning here?"

"If the boss will let me."

"He will," put in Harrison. "I'll see to that."

"All right," said Rider to the girl. "You come round. Mr. King will show you a number of photographs. Look through them carefully and pick out distinguishing features that correspond with those of the man who bought that bag. A chin here, a mouth there, a nose somewhere else. Mr. King will make a composite drawing from them and will keep altering it in accordance with your instructions until he's got it right. Think you can do that?"

"Oh, sure," she said.

"We can do better," Kastner announced. "Sol Bergman is the eager-beaver type. He'll be tickled to death to assist."

"Then get him to come along, too."

Kastner and the girl departed as Rider said to Harrison, "Know a local printer who can run off a batch of copies within a few hours?"

"You bet I do."

"Good!" He gestured to the phone. "Can I hoist the bill another notch?"

"For all I care you can make the mayor faint at the sight of it," said Harrison. "But if you intend to pour primitive passion through the line, say so and let me get out."

"Not this time. She may be pining somewhat, but duty comes first." He took up the instrument. "Treasury Headquarters, Washington, Extension 338. I want Roger King."

Copies of the King sketch were mailed out along with a description and pick-up request. They had not been delivered more than a few minutes when the phone whirred and Harrison grabbed it: "Northwood police."

"This is the State Police Barracks, Sergeant Wilkins speaking. We just got that 'Wanted' notice of yours. I know that fellow. He lives right on my beat."

"Who is he?"

"Name of William Jones. Runs a twenty-acre nursery on Route Four, a couple of hours' away from your town. He's a slightly surly type, but there's nothing known against him. My impression is that he's pessimistic but dead straight. You want us to pick him up?"

"Look, are you sure he's the fellow?"

"It's his face on that drawing of yours and that's as far as I go. I've been in the business as long as you, and I don't make mistakes about faces."

"Of course not, sergeant. We'd appreciate it if you'd bring him in for questioning."

"I'll do that."

He cut off. Harrison lay back, absently studied his desk while his mind juggled around with this latest news.

After a while, he said, "I could understand it better if this Jones was described as a one-time vaudeville actor such as a quick-change impressionist. A fellow operating a nursery out in the wilds sounds a bit of a hick to me. Somehow I can't imagine him doing a bank job as slick as this one."

"He might be just an accomplice. He got the bag beforehand, hid the cash afterward, perhaps acted as lookout man while the robbery was taking place."

Harrison nodded. "We'll find out once he's here. He'll be in trouble if he can't prove he made an innocent purchase."

"What if he does prove it?"

"Then we'll be right back where we started." Harrison gloomed at the thought of it. The phone called for attention and he snatched it up. "Northwood police."

"Patrolman Clinton here, chief. I just showed that drawing to Mrs. Bastico. She has a rooming house at 157 Stevens. She swears that guy is William Jones who roomed with her ten days. He came without luggage but later got a new bag like the Dakin one. Saturday morning he cleared out, taking the bag. He'd overpaid by four days' rent, but he beat it without a word and hasn't come back."

"You stay there, Clinton. We'll be right out." He licked anticipatory lips, said to Rider, "Come on, let's get going."

Piling into a cruiser, they raced to 157 Stevens. It was a dilapidated brownstone with well-worn steps.

Mrs. Bastico, a heavy-featured female with several warts, declaimed in self-righteous tones, "I've never had the cops in this house. Not once in twenty years."

"You've got 'em now," informed Harrison. "And it gives the place a touch of respectability. Now, what d'you know about this Jones fellow?"

"Nothing much," she answered, still miffed. "He kept to himself. I don't bother roomers who behave."

"Did he say anything about where he'd come from, or where he was going to, or anything like that?"

"No. He paid in advance, told me his name, said he was on local business, and that was that. He went out each morning, came back at a decent hour each night, kept sober and interfered with nobody."

"Did he have any visitors?" He extracted Letheren's photograph. "Someone like this, for example?"

"Officer Clinton showed me that picture yesterday. I don't know him. I never saw Mr. Jones talking to another person."

"Hm-m-m!" Harrison registered disappointment. "We'd like a look at his room. Mind if we see it?"

Begrudgingly she led them upstairs, unlocked the door, departed and left them to rake through it at will. Her air was that of one allergic to police.

They searched the room thoroughly, stripping bedclothes, shifting furniture, lifting carpets, even unbolting and emptying the washbasin waste-trap. It was Patrolman Clinton who dug out of a narrow gap between floorboards a small, pink transparent wrapper, also two peculiar seeds resembling elongated almonds and exuding a strong, aromatic scent.

Satisfied that there was nothing else to be found, they carted these petty clues back to the station, mailed them to the State Criminological Laboratory for analysis and report.

Three hours afterward William Jones walked in. He ignored Rider, glowered at the uniformed Harrison, demanded, "What's the idea of having me dragged here? I've done nothing."

"Then what have you got to worry about?" Harrison assumed his best tough expression. "Where were you last Friday morning?"

"That's an easy one," said Jones, with a touch of spite. "I was in Smoky Fall's getting spares for a cultivator."

"That's eighty miles from here."

"So what? It's a lot less from where I live. And I can't get those spares any place nearer. If there's an agent in Northwood, you find him for me."

"Never mind about that. How long were you there?"

"I arrived about ten in the morning, left in the mid-afternoon."

"So it took you about five hours to buy a few spares?"

"I ambled around a piece. Bought groceries as well. Had a meal there, and a few drinks."

"Then there ought to be plenty of folk willing to vouch for your presence there?"

"Sure are," agreed Jones with disconcerting positiveness.

Harrison switched his desk-box, said to someone, "Bring in Mrs. Bastico, the Cassidy girl and Sol Bergman." He returned attention to Jones. "Tell me exactly where you went from time of arrival to departure, and who saw you in each place." He scribbled rapidly as the other recited the tale of his Friday morning shopping trip. When the story ended, he called the Smoky Falls police, briefed them swiftly, gave them the data, asked for a complete check-up.

Listening to this last, Jones showed no visible alarm or apprehension. "Can I go now? I got work to do."

"So have I," Harrison retorted. "Where have you stashed that leather cash-bag?"

"What bag?"

"The new one you bought Thursday afternoon."

Eyeing him incredulously, Jones said, "Hey, what are you trying to pin on me? I bought no bag. Why should I? I don't need a new bag."

"You'll be telling me next that you didn't hole-up in a rooming house on Stevens."

"I didn't. I don't know of any place on Stevens. And if I did, I wouldn't be seen dead there."

*

They argued about it for twenty minutes. Jones maintained with mulish stubbornness that he'd been working on his nursery the whole of Thursday and had been there most of the time he was alleged to be at the rooming house. He'd never heard of Mrs. Bastico and didn't want to. He'd never bought a Dakin-type bag. They could search his place and welcome—if they found such a bag it'd be because they'd planted it on him.

A patrolman stuck his head through the doorway and announced, "They're here, chief."

"All right. Get a line-up ready."

After another ten minutes Harrison led William Jones into a back room, stood him in a row consisting of four detectives and half a dozen nondescripts enlisted from the street. Sol Bergman, Hilda Cassidy and Mrs. Bastico appeared, looked at the parade, pointed simultaneously and in the same direction.

"That's him," said Mrs. Bastico.

"He's the man," endorsed the Cassidy girl.

"Nobody else but," Sol Bergman confirmed.

"They're nuts," declared Jones, showing no idea of what it was all about.

Taking the three witnesses back to his office, Harrison queried them for a possible mistake in identity. They insisted they were not mistaken, that they could not be more positive. William Jones was the man, definitely and absolutely.

He let them go, held Jones on suspicion pending a report from Smoky Falls. Near the end of the twenty-four hours legal holding limit the result of the check came through. No less than thirty-two people accounted fully for the suspect's time all the way from ten to three-thirty. Road-checks had also traced him all the way to that town and all the way back. Other witnesses had placed him at the nursery at several times when he was said to have been at Mrs. Bastico's. State troopers had searched the Jones property. No bag. No money identifiable as loot.

"That's torn it," growled Harrison. "I've no choice but to release him with abject apologies. What sort of a lousy, stinking case is this, when everybody mistakes everybody for everybody else?"

Rider massaged two chins, suggested, "Maybe we ought to try checking on that as well. Let's have another word with Jones before you let him loose."

Slouching in, Jones looked considerably subdued and only too willing to help with anything likely to get him home.

"Sorry to inconvenience you so much, Mr. Jones," Rider soothed. "It couldn't be avoided in the circumstances. We're up against a mighty tough problem." Bending forward, he fixed the other with an imperative gaze. "It might do us a lot of good if you'd think back carefully and tell us if there's any time you've been mistaken for somebody else."

Jones opened his mouth, shut it, opened it again. "Jeepers, that very thing happened about a fortnight ago."

"Give us the story," invited Rider, a glint in his eyes.

"I drove through here nonstop and went straight on to the city. Been there about an hour when a fellow yelled at me from across the street. I didn't know him, thought at first he was calling someone else. He meant me all right."

"Go on," urged Harrison, impatient as the other paused.

"He asked me in a sort of dumbfounded way how I'd got there. I said I'd come in my car. He didn't want to believe it."

"Why not?"

"He said I'd been on foot and thumbing a hitch. He knew it because he'd picked me up and run me to Northwood. What's more, he said, after dropping me in Northwood he'd driven straight to the city, going so fast that nothing had overtaken him on the way. Then he'd parked his car, started down the street, and the first thing he'd seen was me strolling on the other side."

"What did you tell him?"

"I said it couldn't possibly have been me and that his own story proved it."

"That fazed him somewhat, eh?"

"He got sort of completely baffled. He led me right up to his parked car, said, 'Mean to say you didn't take a ride in that?' and, of course, I denied it. I walked away. First I thought it might be some kind of gag. Next, I wondered if he was touched in the head."

"Now," put in Rider carefully, "we must trace this fellow. Give us all you've got on him."

Thinking deeply, Jones said, "He was in his late thirties, well-dressed, smooth talker, the salesman type. Had a lot of pamphlets, colour charts and paint cans in the back of his car."

"You mean in the trunk compartment? You got a look inside there?"

"No. They were lying on the rear seat, as though he was in the habit of grabbing them out in a hurry and slinging them in again."

"How about the car itself?"

"It was the latest model *Flash*, duotone green, white sidewalls, a radio. Didn't notice the tag number."

They spent another ten minutes digging more details regarding appearance, mannerisms and attire. Then Harrison called the city police, asked for a trace.

"The paint stores are your best bet. He's got all the looks of a drummer making his rounds. They should be able to tell you who called on them that day."

City police promised immediate action. Jones went home, disgruntled, but also vastly relieved. Within two hours this latest lead had been extended. A call came from the city.

"Took only four visits to learn what you want. That character is well known to the paint trade. He's Burge Kimmelman, area representative of Acme Paint & Varnish Company of Marion, Illinois. Present whereabouts unknown. His employers should be able to find him for you."

"Thanks a million!" Harrison disconnected, put through a call to Acme Paint. He yapped a while, dumped the phone, said to Rider, "He's somewhere along a route a couple of hundred miles south. They'll reach him at his hotel this evening. He'll get here tomorrow."

"Good."

"Or is it?" asked Harrison, showing a trace of bitterness. "We're sweating ourselves to death tracing people and being led from one personality to another. That sort of thing can continue to the crack of doom."

"And it can continue until something else cracks," Rider riposted. "The mills of *man* grind slowly, but they grind exceeding small."

Elsewhere, seven hundred miles westward, was another legworker. Organized effort can be very formidable but becomes doubly so when it takes to itself the results of individual effort.

This character was thin-faced, sharp-nosed, lived in an attic, ate in an automat, had fingers dyed with nicotine and for twenty years had nursed the notion of writing the Great American Novel but somehow had never gotten around to it.

Name of Arthur Pilchard and, therefore, referred to as Fish—a press reporter. What is worse, a reporter on a harum-scarum tabloid. He was wandering past a desk when somebody with ulcers and a sour face shoved a slip of paper at him.

"Here, Fish. Another saucer nut. Get moving!"

Hustling out with poor grace, he reached the address given on the slip, knocked on the door. It was answered by an intelligent young fellow in his late teens or early twenties.

"You George Lamothe?"

"That's me," agreed the other.

"I'm from the *Call*. You told them you'd got some dope on a saucer. That right?"

Lamothe looked pained. "It's not a saucer and I didn't describe it as such. It's a spherical object and it's not a natural phenomenon."

"I'll take your word for it. When and where did you see it?"

"Last night and the night before. Up in the sky."

"Right over this town?"

"No, but it is visible from here."

"I've not seen it. So far as I know, you're the only one who has. How d'you explain that?"

"It's extremely difficult to see with the naked eye. I own an eight-inch telescope."

"Built it yourself?"

"Yes."

"That takes some doing," commented Art Pilchard admiringly. "How about showing it to me?"

Lamothe hesitated, said, "All right," led him upstairs. Sure enough a real, genuine telescope was there, its inquisitive snout tilted toward a movable roof-trap.

"You've actually seen the object through that?"

"Two successive nights," Lamothe confirmed. "I hope to observe it tonight as well."

"Any idea what it is?"

"That's a matter of guesswork," evaded the other, becoming wary. "All I'm willing to say is that it's located in a satellite orbit, it's perfectly spherical and appears to be an artificial construction of metal."

"Got a picture of it?"

"Sorry, I lack the equipment."

"Maybe one of our cameramen could help you there."

"If he has suitable apparatus," Lamothe agreed.

Pilchard asked twenty more questions, finished doubtfully, "What you can see anyone else with a telescope could see. The world's full of telescopes, some of them big enough to drive a locomotive through. How come nobody yet has shouted the news? Got any ideas on that?"

With a faint smile, Lamothe said, "Everyone with a telescope isn't staring through it twenty-four hours per day. And even when he is using it he's likely to be studying a specific area within the starfield. Moreover, if news gets out it's got to start somewhere. That's why I phoned the *Call*."

"Dead right!" agreed Pilchard, enjoying the savoury odour of a minor scoop.

"Besides," Lamothe went on, "others *have* seen it. I phoned three astronomical friends last night. They looked and saw it. A couple of them said they were going to ring up nearby observatories and draw attention to it. I mailed a full report to an observatory today, and another to a scientific magazine."

"Hells bells!" said Pilchard, getting itchy feet. "I'd better rush this before it breaks in some other rag." A fragment of suspicion came into his face. "Not having seen this spherical contraption myself, I'll have to check on it with another source. By that, I don't mean I think you're a liar. I have to check stories or find another job. Can you give me the name and address of one of these astronomical friends of yours?"

Lamothe obliged, showed him to the door. As Pilchard hastened down the street toward a telephone booth, a police cruiser raced up on the other side. It braked outside Lamothe's house. Pilchard recognized the uniformed cop who was driving but not the pair of burly men in plainclothes riding with him. That was strange because as a reporter of long standing he knew all the local detectives and called them by their first names. While he watched from a distance, the two unknowns got out of the cruiser, went to Lamothe's door, rang the bell.

Bolting round the corner, Pilchard entered the booth, called long distance, rammed coins into the box.

"Alan Reed? My name's Pilchard. I write up astronomical stuff. I believe you've seen a strange metal object in the sky. Hey?" He frowned. "Don't give me that! Your friend George Lamothe has seen it, too. He told me himself that he phoned you about it last night." He paused, glowered at the earpiece. "Where's the sense of repeating, 'No comment,' like a parrot? Look, either you've seen it or you haven't—and so far you've not denied seeing it." Another pause, then in leery tones, "Mr. Reed, has someone ordered you to keep shut?"

He racked the phone, shot a wary glance toward the corner, inserted more coins, said to somebody, "Art here. If you want to feature this, you'll have to move damn fast. You'll run it only if you're too quick to be stopped." He listened for the click of the tape being linked in, recited rapidly for five minutes. Finishing, he returned to the corner, looked along the street. The cruiser was still there.

In a short time a flood of *Calls* hit the streets. Simultaneously a long chain of small-town papers took the same news off their wire-service, broke into a rash of two-inch headlines.

SPACE PLATFORM IN SKY.
OURS OR THEIRS?

Late in the following morning Harrison ploughed doggedly through routine work. At one side of his office Rider sat with columnar legs stretched straight out and read slowly and carefully through a wad of typed sheets.

The wad was the fruit of legwork done by many men. It traced, with a few gaps, the hour by hour movements of one William Jones known to be not the real William Jones. He'd been seen wandering around Northwood like a rubbernecking tourist. He'd been seen repeatedly on the main street and examining its shops. He'd been seen in a supermarket around the time a customer's purse had been stolen. He'd eaten meals in cafes and restaurants, drunk beer in bars and taverns.

Ashcroft, Jackson and another teller remembered a Joneslike stranger making idle inquiries in the bank during the week preceding the robbery. Letheren and his guards recalled the mirror-image of William Jones hanging around when they made the previous collection. Altogether, the tediously gathered report covered most of the suspect's time in Northwood, a period amounting to ten days.

Finishing his perusal, Rider closed his eyes, mulled the details over and over while his mind sought a new lead. While he was doing this, a muted radio sat on a ledge and yammered steadily, squirting across the office the reduced voice of an indignant commentator.

"The whole world now knows that someone has succeeded in establishing an artificial satellite up there in the sky. Anyone with a telescope or good binoculars can see it for himself at night. Why, then, does authority insist on pretending that the thing doesn't exist? If potential enemies are responsible, let us be told as much—the enemies already know it, anyway. If we are responsible, if this is our doing, let us be told as much—the enemies already are grimly aware of it. Why must we be denied information possessed by possible foes? Does somebody think we're a bunch of irresponsible children? Who are these brasshats who assign to themselves the right to decide what we may be told or not told? Away with them! Let the government speak!"

"Yeah," commented Harrison, glancing up from his work, "I'm with him there. Why don't they say outright whether it's ours or theirs? Some of those guys down your way have a grossly exaggerated idea of their own importance. A hearty kick in the pants would do them a lot—" He shut up, grabbed the phone. "Northwood police." A weird series of expressions crossed his lean features as he listened. Then he racked the phone, said, "It gets nuttier every minute."

"What's it this time?"

"Those seeds. The laboratory can't identify them."

"Doesn't surprise me. They can't be expected to know absolutely everything."

"They know enough to know when they're stuck," Harrison gave back. "So they sent them to some firm in New York where they know everything knowable about seeds. They've just got a reply."

"Saying what?"

"Same thing—not identifiable. New York went so far as to squeeze out the essential oils and subject remaining solids to destructive distillation. Result: the seeds just aren't known." He emitted a loud sniff, added, "They want us to send them another dozen so they can make them germinate. They want to see what comes up."

"Forget it," advised Rider. "We don't have any more seeds and we don't know where to find 'em."

"But we do have something darned peculiar," Harrison persisted. "With those seeds we sent a pink, transparent wrapper, remember? At the time I thought it was just a piece of coloured cellophane. The lab says it isn't. They say it's organic, cellular and veined, and appears a subsection of the skin of an unknown fruit."

"… A tactic long theorized and believed to be in secret development," droned the radio. "Whoever achieves it first thereby gains a strategic advantage from the military viewpoint."

"Sometimes," said Harrison, "I wonder what's the use of getting born."

His desk-box squawked and announced, "Fellow named Burge Kimmelman waiting for you, chief."

"Send him in."

Kimmelman entered. He was dapper, self-assured, seemed to regard his rush to the aid of the law as a welcome change from the daily round. He sat, crossed his legs, made himself at home and told his story.

"It was the craziest thing, captain. For a start, I never give rides to strangers. But I stopped and picked up this fellow and still can't make out why I did it."

"*Where* did you pick him up?" asked Rider.

"About half a mile this side of Seeger's filling station. He was waiting by the roadside and first thing I knew I'd stopped and let him get in. I took him into Northwood, dropped him, pushed straight on to the city. I was in a hurry and moved good and fast. When I got there I walked out the car park and darned if he wasn't right there on the other side of the street." He eyed them, seeking comment.

"Go on," Rider urged.

"I picked on him then and there, wanting to know how he'd beaten me to it. He acted like he didn't know what I was talking about." He made a gesture of bafflement. "I've thought it over a dozen times since and can take it no further. I *know* I gave a lift to that guy or his twin brother. And it wasn't his twin brother because if he'd had one he'd have guessed my mistake and said so. But he said nothing. Just behaved offishly polite like you do when faced with a lunatic."

"When you were giving him this ride," asked Harrison, "did he make any informative remarks? Did he mention his family, his occupation, destination, or anything like that? Did he tell you where he'd come from?"

"Not a word worth a cent. So far as I know he dropped straight out of the sky."

"So did everything else concerned with this case," remarked Harrison, feeling sour again. "Unidentifiable seeds and unknown fruit-skins and—" He stopped, let his mouth hang open, popped his eyes.

"... A vantage-point from which every quarter of the world would be within effective range," gabbled the radio. "With such a base for guided missiles it would be possible for one nation to implement its policies in a manner that—"

Getting to his feet, Rider crossed the room, switched off the radio, said, "Mind waiting outside, Mr. Kimmelman?" When the other had gone, he continued with Harrison, "Well, make up your mind whether or not you're going to have a stroke."

Harrison shut his mouth, opened it again, but no sound came out. His eyes appeared to have protruded too far to retract. His right hand made a couple of meaningless gestures and temporarily that was the most he could manage.

*

Resorting to the phone, Rider got his call through, said, "O'Keefe, how's the artificial satellite business down there?"

"You called just to ask that? I was about to phone you myself."

"What about?"

"Eleven of those bills have come in. The first nine came from two cities. The last pair were passed in New York. Your man is moving around. Bet you ten to one in coconuts that if he takes another bank it'll be in the New York area."

"That's likely enough. Forget him for a moment. I asked you about this satellite rumpus. What's the reaction from where you're sitting?"

"The place is buzzing like a disturbed beehive. Rumour is rife that professional astronomers saw and reported the thing nearly a week before the news broke. If that's true, somebody in authority must have tried to suppress the information."

"Why?"

"Don't ask me," shouted O'Keefe. "How do I know why others do things that make neither rhyme nor reason?"

"You think they should say whether it's ours or theirs seeing that the truth is bound to emerge sooner or later?"

"Of course. Why are you harping on this subject, Eddie? What's it got to do with you, anyway?"

"I've been made vocal by an idea that has had the reverse effect on Harrison. He's struck dumb."

"What idea?"

"That this artificial satellite may not be an artificial satellite. Also that authority has said nothing because experts are unwilling to commit themselves one way or the other. They can't say something unless they've something to say, can they?"

"I've got something to say," O'Keefe declared. "And that's to advise you to tend your own business. If you've finished helping Harrison, quit lazing around and come back."

"Listen, I don't call long-distance for the fun of it. There's a thing up in the sky and nobody knows what it is. *At the same time* another thing is down here loping around and imitating people, robbing banks, dropping debris of alien origin, and nobody knows what that is, either. Two plus two makes four. Add it up for yourself."

"Eddie, are you cracked?"

"I'll give you the full details and leave you to judge." He recited them swiftly, ended, "Use all your Treasury pull to get the right people interested. This case is far too big to be handled by us alone. You've got to find the ones with enough power and influence to cope. You've got to kick 'em awake."

He cut off, glanced at Harrison who promptly got his voice back and said, "I can't believe it. It's too far-fetched for words. The day I tell the mayor a Martian did it will be the day Northwood gets a new chief. He'll take me away to have my head examined."

"Got a better theory?"

"No. That's the hell of it."

Shrugging expressively, Rider took the phone again, made a call to Acme Paint Company. That done, he summoned Kimmelman.

"There's a good chance that you'll be wanted here tomorrow and perhaps for two or three days. I've just consulted your employers and they say you're to stay with us."

"Suits me," agreed Kimmelman, not averse to taking time off with official approval. "I'd better go book in at an hotel."

"Just one question first. This character you picked up—was he carrying any luggage?"

"No."

"Not even a small bag or a parcel?"

"He'd nothing except what was in his pockets," said Kimmelman, positively.

A gleam showed in Rider's eyes. "Well, that may help."

The mob that invaded Northwood at noon next day came in a dozen cars by devious routes and successfully avoided the attention of the press. They crammed Harrison's office to capacity.

Among them was a Treasury top-ranker, a general, an admiral, a Secret Service chief, a Military Intelligence brasshat, three area directors of the F.B.I., a boss of the Counter Espionage Service, all their aides, secretaries and technical advisers, plus a bunch of assorted scientists including two astronomers, one radar expert, one guided missiles expert and a slightly bewildered gentleman who was an authority on ants.

They listened in silence, some interested, some sceptical, while Harrison read them a complete report of the case. He finished, sat down, waited for comment.

A grey-haired, distinguished individual took the lead, said, "Personally, I'm in favour of your theory that you're chasing somebody not of this world. I don't presume to speak for others who may think differently. However, it seems to me futile to waste any time debating the matter. It can be settled one way or the other by catching the culprit. That, therefore, is our only problem. How are we going to lay hands on him?"

"That won't be done by the usual methods," said an F.B.I. director. "A guy who can double as anyone, and do it well enough to convince even at close range, isn't going to be caught easily. We can hunt down a particular identity if given enough time. I don't see how we can go after somebody who might have *any* identity."

"Even an alien from another world wouldn't bother to steal money unless he had a real need for it," put in a sharp-eyed individual. "The stuff's no use elsewhere in the cosmos. So it's safe to accept that he did have need of it. But money doesn't last forever no matter who is spending it. When he has splurged it all, he'll need some more. He'll try robbing another bank. If every bank in this country were turned into a trap, surely one of them would snap down on him."

"How're you going to trap somebody who so far as you know is your best and biggest customer?" asked the F.B.I. director. He put on a sly grin, added, "Come to that, how do you know that the fellow in question isn't *me*?"

Nobody liked this last suggestion. They fidgeted uneasily, went quiet as their minds desperately sought a solution some place.

Rider spoke up. "Frankly, I think it a waste of time to search the world for somebody who has proved his ability to adopt two successive personalities and by the same token can adopt two dozen or two hundred. I've thought about this until I've gone dizzy and I can't devise any method of pursuing and grabbing him. He's far too elusive."

"It might help if we could learn precisely how he does it," interjected a scientist. "Have you any evidence indicative of his technique?"

"No, sir."

"It looks like hypnosis to me," said the scientist.

"You may be right," Rider admitted. "But so far we've no proof of it." He hesitated, went on, "As I see it, there's only one way to catch him."

"How?"

"It's extremely unlikely that he's come here for keeps. Besides, there's that thing in the sky. What's it waiting for? My guess is that it's waiting to take him back whenever he's ready to go."

"So—?" someone prompted.

"To take him back that sphere has got to swing in from several thousands of miles out. That means it has to be summoned when wanted. He's got to talk to its crew, if it has a crew. Or, if crewless, he's got to pull it in by remote control. Either way, he must have some kind of transmitter."

"If transmission-time is too brief to enable us to tune in, take cross-bearings and get there—" began an objector.

Rider waved him down. "I'm not thinking of that. We know he came to Northwood without luggage. Kimmelman says so. Mrs. Bastico says so. Numerous witnesses saw him at various times but he was never seen to carry anything other than the cash-bag. Even if an alien civilization can produce electronic equipment one-tenth the size and weight of anything we can turn out, a long-range transmitter would still be far too bulky to be hidden in a pocket."

"You think he's concealed it somewhere?" asked the sharp-eyed man.

"I think it highly probable. If he has hidden it, well, he has thereby limited his freedom of action. He can't take off from anywhere in this world. He's got to return to wherever he has stashed the transmitter."

"But that could be any place. It leaves us no better off than before."

"On the contrary!" He picked up Harrison's report, read selected passages with added emphasis. "I may be wrong. I hope I'm right. There's one thing he could not conceal no matter what personality he assumed. He could not conceal his behaviour. If he'd chosen to masquerade as an elephant and then become curious, he'd have been a very plausible elephant—but still obviously curious."

"What are you getting at?" demanded a four-star general.

"He was too green to have been around long. If he'd had
only a couple of days in some other town or village, he'd have
been a lot more sophisticated when in Northwood. Consider the
reports on the way he nosed around. He was raw. He behaved
like somebody to whom everything is new. If I'm right about this,
Northwood was his first port of call. And that in turn means his
landing place—*which is also his intended take-off point*—must be
fairly near, and probably nearer still to where Kimmelman picked
him up."

They debated it for half an hour, reached a decision. The result
was legwork on a scale that only high authority can command.
Kimmelman drove nearly five miles out, showed the exact spot
and that became the centre of operations.

Attendants at Seeger's filling station were queried extensively
and without result. Motorists known to be regular users of the
road, bus drivers, truckers and many others to whom it was a
well-used route, were traced and questioned. Dirt-farmers, drift-
ers, recluses, hoboes and everyone else who lurked in the thinly
populated hills were found and quizzed at length.

Four days' hard work and numberless questionings over a
circle ten miles in diameter produced three people who nursed the
vague idea that they'd seen something fall from or rise into the
sky about three weeks ago. A farmer thought he'd seen a distant
saucer but had kept quiet for fear of ridicule. Another believed he
had glimpsed a strange gleam of light which soared from the hills
and vanished. A trucker had spotted an indefinable object out the
corner of an eye but when he looked direct it had gone.

These three were made to take up their respective points of
observation, sight through theodolites and line the cross-hairs as
nearly as they could on the portions of skyline cogent to their

visions. All pleaded inability to be accurate but were willing to do their best.

The bearings produced an elongated triangle that stretched across most of a square mile. This at once became the second focus of attention. A new area two miles in radius was drawn from the triangle's centre. Forthwith police, deputies, troopers, agents and others commenced to search the target foot by foot. They numbered a small army and some of them bore mine-detectors and other metal-finding instruments.

One hour before dusk a shout drew Rider, Harrison and several bigwigs to a place where searchers were clustering excitedly. Somebody had followed the faint *tick-tick* of his detector, lugged a boulder aside, found a gadget hidden in the hollow behind it.

The thing was a brown metal box twelve inches by ten by eight. It had a dozen silver rings set concentrically in its top, these presumably being the sky-beam antenna. Also four dials ready set in various positions. Also a small press-stud.

Experts knew exactly what to do, having come prepared for it. They colour-photographed the box from every angle, measured it, weighed it, placed it back in its original position and restored the boulder to its former place.

Sharpshooters with night-glasses and high-velocity rifles were posted in concealed positions at extreme range. While data on the superficial appearance of the transmitter was being rushed to the city, ground-microphones were placed between the hiding place and the road, their hidden wires led back to where ambushers awaited stealthy footsteps in the dark.

Before dawn, four searchlight teams and half a dozen anti-aircraft batteries had taken up positions in the hills and camouflaged themselves. A command post had been established in a lonely farmhouse and a ground-to-air radio unit had been shoved out of sight in its barn.

For anyone else a road-block set up by tough cops would have served. Not for this character who could be anyone at all. He might, for all they knew, appear in the dignified guise of the Bishop of Miff. But if he made for that transmitter and laid hands on it—

A couple of days later a truck came from the city, picked up the transmitter, replaced it with a perfect mock-up incapable of calling anything out of the sky. This game of imitation was one at which two could play.

Nobody got itchy fingers and pressed the stud on the real instrument. The time wasn't yet. So long as the ship remained in the sky, so long would its baffling passenger enjoy a sense of false security and, sooner or later, enter the trap.

Earth was willing to wait. It was just as well. The biding-time lasted four months.

A bank on Long Island got taken for eighteen thousand dollars. The same technique; walk in, collect, walk out, vanish. A high-ranking officer made a tour of the Brooklyn Navy Yard at a time when he was also attending a conference at Newport News. An official inspected television studios on the twentieth to twenty-fifth floors of a skyscraper while simultaneously tending to office work on the tenth floor. The invader had now learned enough to become impudent.

Blueprints were pored over, vaults were entered, laboratories were examined. Steelworks and armaments plants got a careful, unhurried look-over. A big machine-tool factory actually had its works manager conduct a phony visitor around the plant and provide technical explanations as required.

It wasn't all plain sailing even for someone well-nigh invincible. The cleverest can make mistakes. Harasha Vanash blundered when he flashed a fat roll in a tavern, got followed to his hideout. Next day he went out without being tailed and while he was busily sneaking some more of Earth's knowledge, somebody was briskly plundering his room. He returned to find the proceeds of his last robbery had vanished. That meant he had to take time off from espionage to soak a third bank.

By August 21st he had finished. He had concentrated his attention on the most highly developed area in the world and it was doubtful whether anything to be learned elsewhere was sufficiently weighty to be worth the seeking. Anyway, what he'd got was enough for the purposes of the Andromedans. Armed with all this information, the hypnos of a two-hundred-planet empire could step in and take over another with no trouble at all.

Near Seeger's station he stepped out of a car, politely thanked the driver who was wondering why he'd gone so far out of his way to oblige a character who meant nothing to him. He stood by the roadside, watched the car vanish into the distance. It rocked along at top pace, as though its driver was mad at himself.

Holding a small case stuffed with notes and sketches, he studied the landscape, saw everything as it had been originally. To anyone within the sphere of his mental influence he was no more than a portly and somewhat pompous business man idly surveying the hills. To anyone beyond that range he was made vague by distance and sufficiently humanlike to the naked eye to pass muster.

But to anyone watching through telescopes and binoculars from most of a mile away he could be seen for what he really was—just a thing. A thing not of this world. They could have made

a snatch at him then and there. However, in view of the preparations they'd made for him there was, they thought, no need to
bother. Softly, softly, catchee monkey.

Tightly gripping the case, he hurried away from the road, made
straight for the transmitter's hiding place. All he had to do was
press the stud, beat it back to Northwood, enjoy a few quiet drinks
in a tavern, have a night's sleep and come back tomorrow. The
ship would come in along the transmitter's beam, landing here
and nowhere else, but it would take exactly eighteen hours and
twenty minutes to arrive.

Reaching the boulder, he had a final wary glance around.
Nobody in sight, not a soul. He moved the rock, felt mild relief
when he saw the instrument lying undisturbed. Bending over it,
he pressed the stud.

The result was a violent *pouf!* and a cloud of noxious gas.
That was their mistake; they'd felt sure it would lay him out for
twenty-four hours. It did not. His metabolism was thoroughly
alien and had its own peculiar reaction. All he did was retch and
run like blazes.

Four men appeared from behind a rock six hundred yards away.
They pointed guns, yelled to him to halt. Ten more sprang out of
the ground on his left, bawled similar commands. He grinned at
them, showing them the teeth he did not possess.

He couldn't make them blow off their own heads. But he could
make them do it for each other. Still going fast, he changed direction to escape the line of fire. The four obligingly waited for him
to run clear, then opened up on the ten. At the same time the ten
started slinging lead at the four.

At top speed he kept going. He could have lounged on a rock, in
complete command of the situation, and remained until everyone

had bumped everyone else—given that there was no effective force located outside his hypnotic range. He could not be sure of just how far the trap extended.

The obviously sensible thing to do was to get right out of reach as swiftly as possible, curve back to the road, confiscate a passing car and disappear once more among Earth's teeming millions. How to contact the ship was a problem that must be shelved until he could ponder it in a safe place. It wasn't unsolvable; not to one who could be the President himself.

His immediate fear was well-founded. At twelve-hundred yards there happened to be a beefy gentleman named Hank who found that a brazen escape during an outbreak of civil war was too much to be endured. Hank had a quick temper, also a heavy machine-gun. Seeing differently from those nearer the prey, and being given no orders to the contrary, Hank uttered an unseemly word, swung the gun, scowled through its sights, rammed his thumbs on its button. The gun went *br-r-r-r* while its ammo-belt jumped and rattled.

Despite the range his aim was perfect. Harasha Vanash was flung side-wise in full flight, went down and didn't get up. His supine body jerked around under the impact of more bullets. He was very decidedly dead.

Harrison got on the phone to pass the news, and O'Keefe said, "He's not here. It's his day off."

"Where'll I find him then?"

"At home and no place else. I'll give you his number. He might answer if he's not busy baby-sitting."

Trying again, Harrison got through. "They killed him… or it… just under an hour ago."

"Hm-m-m! Pity they didn't take him alive."

"Easier said than done. Anyway, how can you retain a firm hold on someone who can make you remove his manacles and get into them yourself?"

"That," said Rider, "is the problem of our Security boys in general and our police in particular. I work for the Treasury."

Replacing the phone, Harrison frowned at the wall. Beyond the wall, several hundreds of miles to the south, a group of men walked onto the dispersal-point of an airport, placed a strange box on the ground, pressed its stud. Then they watched the sky and waited.

The hordes of Andromeda were very, very old. That was why they'd progressed as far as they had done. Flashes of inspiration had piled up through the numberless centuries until sheer weight of accumulated genius had given them the key to the cosmos.

Like many very old people, they had contempt for the young and eager. But their contempt would have switched to horror if they could have seen the methodical way in which a bunch of specialist legworkers started pulling their metal sphere apart.

Or the way in which Earth commenced planning a vast armada of similar ships.

A good deal bigger.

With several improvements.

THE END

MIRROR IMAGE

Isaac Asimov

Although Isaac Asimov (1920–92) was one of the world's best known science-fiction writers he was also a proficient writer of crime fiction and melded the two admirably in The Caves of Steel *(serial, 1953) and* The Naked Sun *(serial, 1956). Both include his investigator Lije Baley and robot companion R. Daneel Olivaw, tackling crimes that happened in situations which should have been impossible in those societies. They remain two of the best mergers of crime fiction and science fiction. The two characters are reunited in the following story.*

Asimov enjoyed setting puzzles and solving them. Along with editor John W. Campbell, Jr., he created the three laws of robotics, which also feature in this story, and then had fun seeing how these laws could be manipulated. Perhaps the best known of them is "Little Lost Robot" (1947) where robopsychologist Susan Calvin has to find a robot that has hidden itself amongst scores of identical models. Asimov also wrote an occasional series featuring a Holmesian-like detective Wendell Urth which began with "The Singing Bell" (1954). Each story usually depended upon some little known scientific principle, which Asimov often deployed in other stories, the best being collected as Asimov's Mysteries *(1968).*

A passionate Sherlockian, Asimov was a member of the Baker Street Irregulars and of the banqueting society Trap Door Spiders which he used as the basis for his stories about the Black Widowers. In each story—of which there are fifty—the diners discuss and attempt to solve problems brought to the club by various members, though the problem is usually solved by the waiter. Most of the characters are based on a real-life sf personality—except for the waiter. There are six collections starting with Tales of the Black Widowers *(1974). Asimov also wrote two genuine non-sf murder mysteries,* The Death Dealers *(1958; also known as* A Whiff of Death*) and* Murder at the ABA *(1976), ABA being the American Booksellers Association. There is little doubt that, had he chosen, Asimov could have been as equally adept in a career as a crime-fiction writer as he was in whatever he turned his hand and inventive mind to.*

The Three Laws of Robotics

    1: A robot may not injure a human being, or, through inaction, allow a human being to come to harm.

    2: A robot must obey the orders given it by human beings except where such orders would conflict with the First Law.

    3: A robot must protect its own existence as long as such protection does not conflict with the First or Second Laws.

L IJE BALEY HAD JUST DECIDED TO RELIGHT HIS PIPE, WHEN the door of his office opened without a preliminary knock, or announcement, of any kind. Baley looked up in pronounced annoyance and then dropped his pipe. It said a good deal for the state of his mind that he let it lie where it had fallen.

"R. Daneel Olivaw," he said, in a kind of mystified excitement. "Jehoshaphat! It *is* you, isn't it?"

"You are quite right," said the tall, bronzed newcomer, his even features never flicking for a moment out of their accustomed calm. "I regret surprising you by entering without warning, but the situation is a delicate one and there must be as little involvement as possible on the part of the men and robots even in this place. I am, in any case, pleased to see you again, friend Elijah."

And the robot held out his right hand in a gesture as thoroughly human as was his appearance. It was Baley who was so unmanned by his astonishment as to stare at the hand with a momentary lack of understanding.

But then he seized it in both his, feeling its warm firmness. "But Daneel, *why*? You're welcome any time, but—What is this situation that is a delicate one? Are we in trouble again? Earth, I mean?"

"No, friend Elijah, it does not concern Earth. The situation to which I refer as a delicate one is, to outward appearances, a small thing. A dispute between mathematicians, nothing more. As we happened, quite by accident, to be within an easy Jump of Earth—"

"This dispute took place on a starship, then?"

"Yes, indeed. A small dispute, yet to the humans involved astonishingly large."

Baley could not help but smile. "I'm not surprised you find humans astonishing. They do not obey the Three Laws."

"That is, indeed, a shortcoming," said R. Daneel, gravely, "and I think humans themselves are puzzled by humans. It may be that you are less puzzled than are the men of other worlds because so many more human beings live on Earth than on the Spacer worlds. If so, and I believe it is so, you could help us."

R. Daneel paused momentarily and then said, perhaps a shade too quickly, "And yet there are rules of human behaviour which I have learned. It would seem, for instance, that I am deficient in etiquette, by human standards, not to have asked after your wife and child."

"They are doing well. The boy is in college and Jessie is involved in local politics. The amenities are taken care of. Now tell me how you come to be here."

"As I said, we were within an easy Jump of Earth," said R. Daneel, "so I suggested to the captain that we consult you."

"And the captain agreed?" Baley had a sudden picture of the proud and autocratic captain of a Spacer starship consenting to make a landing on Earth—of all worlds—and to consult an Earthman—of all people.

"I believe," said R. Daneel, "that he was in a position where he would have agreed to anything. In addition, I praised you very highly; although, to be sure, I stated only the truth. Finally, I agreed to conduct all negotiations so that none of the crew, or passengers, would need to enter any of the Earthman cities."

"And talk to any Earthman, yes. But what has happened?"

"The passengers of the starship, *Eta Carina*, included two mathematicians who were travelling to Aurora to attend an interstellar conference on neurobiophysics. It is about these mathematicians, Alfred Barr Humboldt and Gennao Sabbat, that the dispute centres. Have you perhaps, friend Elijah, heard of one, or both, of them?"

"Neither one," said Baley, firmly. "I know nothing about mathematics. Look, Daneel, surely you haven't told anyone I'm a mathematics buff or—"

"Not at all, friend Elijah. I know you are not. Nor does it matter, since the exact nature of the mathematics involved is in no way relevant to the point at issue."

"Well, then, go on."

"Since you do not know either man, friend Elijah, let me tell you that Dr. Humboldt is well into his twenty-seventh decade— Pardon me, friend Elijah?"

"Nothing. Nothing," said Baley, irritably. He had merely muttered to himself, more or less incoherently, in a natural reaction to the extended life-spans of the Spacers. "And he's still active, despite his age? On Earth, mathematicians after thirty or so…"

Daneel said, calmly; "Dr. Humboldt is one of the top three mathematicians, by long-established repute, in the galaxy. Certainly he is still active. Dr. Sabbat, on the other hand, is quite young, not yet fifty, but he has already established himself as the most remarkable new talent in the most abstruse branches of mathematics."

"They're both great, then," said Baley. He remembered his pipe and picked it up. He decided there was no point in lighting it now and knocked out the dottle. "What happened? Is this a murder case? Did one of them apparently kill the other?"

"Of these two men of great reputation, one is trying to destroy that of the other. By human values, I believe this may be regarded as worse than physical murder."

"Sometimes, I suppose. Which one is trying to destroy the other?"

"Why, that, friend Elijah, is precisely the point at issue. Which?"

"Go on."

"Dr. Humboldt tells the story clearly. Shortly before he boarded the starship, he had an insight into a possible method for analysing neural pathways from changes in microwave absorption patterns of local cortical areas. The insight was a purely mathematical technique of extraordinary subtlety, but I cannot, of course, either understand or sensibly transmit the details. These do not, however, matter. Dr. Humboldt considered the matter and was more convinced each hour that he had something revolutionary on hand, something that would dwarf all his previous accomplishments in mathematics. Then he discovered that Dr. Sabbat was on board."

"Ah. And he tried it out on young Sabbat?"

"Exactly. The two had met at professional meetings before and knew each other thoroughly by reputation. Humboldt went into it with Sabbat in great detail. Sabbat backed Humboldt's analysis completely and was unstinting in his praise of the importance of the discovery and of the ingenuity of the discoverer. Heartened and reassured by this, Humboldt prepared a paper outlining, in summary, his work and, two days later, prepared to have it forwarded sub-etherically to the co-chairmen of the conference at Aurora, in order that he might officially establish his priority and arrange for possible discussion before the sessions were closed. To his surprise, he found that Sabbat was ready with a paper of his own, essentially the same as Humboldt's, and Sabbat was also preparing to have it sub-etherized to Aurora."

"I suppose Humboldt was furious."

"Quite!"

"And Sabbat? What was his story?"

"Precisely the same as Humboldt's. Word for word."

"Then just what is the problem?"

"Except for the mirror-image exchange of names. According to Sabbat, it was he who had the insight, and he who consulted Humboldt; it was Humboldt who agreed with the analysis and praised it."

"Then each one claims the idea is his and that the other stole it. It doesn't sound like a problem to me at all. In matters of scholarship, it would seem only necessary to produce the records of research, dated and initialled. Judgment as to priority can be made from that. Even if one is falsified, that might be discovered through internal inconsistencies."

"Ordinarily, friend Elijah, you would be right, but this is mathematics, and not in an experimental science. Dr. Humboldt claims to have worked out the essentials in his head. Nothing was put in writing until the paper itself was prepared. Dr. Sabbat, of course, says precisely the same."

"Well, then, be more drastic and get it over with, for sure. Subject each one to a psychic probe and find out which of the two is lying."

R. Daneel shook his head slowly, "Friend Elijah, you do not understand these men. They are both of rank and scholarship, Fellows of the Imperial Academy. As such, they cannot be subjected to trial of professional conduct except by a jury of their peers—their professional peers—unless they personally and voluntarily waive that right."

"Put it to them, then. The guilty man won't waive the right because he can't afford to face the psychic probe. The innocent man will waive it at once. You won't even have to use the probe."

"It does not work that way, friend Elijah. To waive the right in such a case—to be investigated by laymen—is a serious and perhaps irrecoverable blow to prestige. Both men steadfastly refuse to waive the right to special trial, as a matter of pride. The question of guilt, or innocence, is quite subsidiary."

"In that case, let it go for now. Put the matter in cold storage until you get to Aurora. At the neurobiophysical conference, there will be a huge supply of professional peers, and then—"

"That would mean a tremendous blow to science itself, friend Elijah. Both men would suffer for having been the instrument of scandal. Even the innocent one would be blamed for having been party to a situation so distasteful. It would be felt that it should have been settled quietly out of court at all costs."

"All right. I'm not a Spacer, but I'll try to imagine that this attitude makes sense. What do the men in question say?"

"Humboldt agrees thoroughly. He says that if Sabbat will admit theft of the idea and allow Humboldt to proceed with transmission of the paper—or at least its delivery at the conference, he will not press charges. Sabbat's misdeed will remain secret with him; and, of course, with the captain, who is the only other human to be party to the dispute."

"But young Sabbat will not agree?"

"On the contrary, he agreed with Dr. Humboldt to the last detail—with the reversal of names. Still the mirror-image."

"So they just sit there, stalemated?"

"Each, I believe, friend Elijah, is waiting for the other to give in and admit guilt."

"Well, then, wait."

"The captain has decided this cannot be done. There are two alternatives to waiting, you see. The first is that both will remain stubborn so that when the starship lands on Aurora, the intellectual scandal will break. The captain, who is responsible for justice on board ship will suffer disgrace for not having been able to settle the matter quietly and that, to him, is quite insupportable."

"And the second alternative?"

"Is that one, or the other, of the mathematicians will indeed admit to wrongdoing. But will the one who confesses do so out of actual guilt, or out of a noble desire to prevent the scandal? Would it be right to deprive of credit one who is sufficiently ethical to prefer to lose that credit than to see science as a whole suffer? Or else, the guilty party will confess at the last moment, and in such a way as to make it appear he does so only for the sake of science, thus escaping the disgrace of his deed and casting its shadow upon the other. The captain will be the only man to know all this but he does not wish to spend the rest of his life wondering whether he has been a party to a grotesque miscarriage of justice."

Baley sighed. "A game of intellectual chicken. Who'll break first as Aurora comes nearer and nearer? Is that the whole story now, Daneel?"

"Not quite. There are witnesses to the transaction."

"Jehoshaphat! Why didn't you say so at once. *What* witnesses?"

"Dr. Humboldt's personal servant—"

"A robot, I suppose."

"Yes, certainly. He is called R. Preston. This servant, R. Preston, was present during the initial conference and he bears out Dr. Humboldt in every detail."

"You mean he says that the idea was Dr. Humboldt's to begin with; that Dr. Humboldt detailed it to Dr. Sabbat; that Dr. Sabbat praised the idea, and so on."

"Yes, in full detail."

"I see. Does that settle the matter or not? Presumably not."

"You are quite right. It does not settle the matter, for there is a second witness. Dr. Sabbat also has a personal servant, R. Idda, another robot of, as it happens, the same model as R. Preston, made, I believe, in the same year in the same factory. Both have been in service equal times."

"An odd coincidence—very odd."

"A fact, I am afraid, and it makes it difficult to arrive at any judgment based on obvious differences between the two servants."

"R. Idda, then, tells the same story as R. Preston?"

"Precisely the same story, except for the mirror-image reversal of the names."

"R. Idda stated, then, that young Sabbat, the one not yet fifty"— Lije Baley did not entirely keep the sardonic note out of his voice; he himself was not yet fifty and he felt far from young—"had the idea to begin with; that he detailed it to Dr. Humboldt, who was loud in his praises, and so on."

"Yes, friend Elijah."

"And one robot is lying, then."

"So it would seem."

"It should be easy to tell which. I imagine even a superficial examination by a good roboticist—"

"A roboticist is not enough in this case, friend Elijah. Only a qualified robopsychologist would carry weight enough and experience enough to make a decision in a case of this importance. There is no one so qualified on board ship. Such an examination can be performed only when we reach Aurora—"

"And by then the crud hits the fan. Well, you're here on Earth. We can scare up a robopsychologist, and surely anything that happens on Earth will never reach the ears of Aurora and there will be no scandal."

"Except that neither Dr. Humboldt, nor Dr. Sabbat, will allow his servant to be investigated by a robopsychologist of Earth. The Earthman would have to—" He paused.

Lije Baley said stolidly, "He'd have to touch the robot."

"These are old servants, well thought of—"

"And not to be sullied by the touch of Earthman. Then what do you want me to do, damn it?" He paused, grimacing. "I'm sorry, R. Daneel, but I see no reason for your having involved me."

"I was on the ship on a mission utterly irrelevant to the problem at hand. The captain turned to me because he had to turn to someone. I seemed human enough to talk to, and robot enough to be a safe recipient of confidences. He told me the whole story and asked what I would do. I realized the next Jump could take us as easily to Earth as to our target. I told the captain that, although I was at as much a loss to resolve the mirror-image as he was, there was on Earth one who might help."

"Jehoshaphat!" muttered Baley under his breath.

"Consider, friend Elijah, that if you succeed in solving this puzzle, it would do your career good and Earth itself might benefit. The matter could not be publicized, of course, but the captain is a man of some influence on his home world and he would be grateful."

"You just put a greater strain on me."

"I have every confidence," said R. Daneel, stolidly, "that you already have some idea as to what procedure ought to be followed."

"Do you? I suppose that the obvious procedure is to interview the two mathematicians, one of whom would seem to be a thief."

"I'm afraid, friend Elijah, that neither one will come into the city. Nor would either one be willing to have you come to them."

"And there is no way of forcing a Spacer to allow contact with an Earthman, no matter what the emergency. Yes, I understand that, Daneel—but I was thinking of an interview by closed-circuit television."

"Nor that. They will not submit to interrogation by an Earthman."

"Then what do they want of me? Could I speak to the robots?"

"They would not allow the robots to come here, either."

"Jehoshaphat, Daneel. *You've* come."

"That was my own decision. I have permission, while on board ship, to make decisions of that sort without veto by any human being but the captain himself—and he was eager to establish the contact. I, having known you, decided that television contact was insufficient. I wished to shake your hand."

Lije Baley softened. "I appreciate that, Daneel, but I still honestly wish you could have refrained from thinking of me at all in this case. Can I talk to the robots by television at least?"

"That, I think, can be arranged."

"Something, at least. That means I would be doing the work of a robopsychologist—in a crude sort of way."

"But you are a detective, friend Elijah, not a robopsychologist."

"Well, let it pass. Now before I see them, let's think a bit. Tell me: is it possible that both robots are telling the truth? Perhaps the conversation between the two mathematicians was equivocal. Perhaps it was of such a nature that each robot could honestly believe its own master was proprietor of the idea. Or perhaps one robot heard only one portion of the discussion and the other another portion, so that each could suppose its own master was proprietor of the idea."

"That is quite impossible, friend Elijah. Both robots repeat the conversation in identical fashion. And the two repetitions are fundamentally inconsistent."

"Then it is absolutely certain that one of the robots is lying?"

"Yes."

"Will I be able to see the transcript of all evidence given so far in the presence of the captain, if I should want to?"

"I thought you would ask that and I have copies with me."

"Another blessing. Have the robots been cross-examined at all, and is that cross-examination included in the transcript?"

"The robots have merely repeated their tales. Cross-examination would be conducted only by robopsychologists."

"Or by myself?"

"You are a detective, friend Elijah, not a—"

"All right, R. Daneel. I'll try to get the Spacer psychology straight. A detective can do it because he isn't a robopsychologist. Let's think further. Ordinarily a robot will not lie, but he will do so if necessary to maintain the Three Laws. He might lie to protect, in legitimate fashion, his own existence in accordance with the Third Law. He is more apt to lie if that is necessary to follow a legitimate order given him by a human being in accordance with the Second Law. He is most apt to lie if that is necessary to save a human life, or to prevent harm from coming to a human in accordance with the First Law."

"Yes."

"And in this case, each robot would be defending the professional reputation of his master, and would lie if it were necessary to do so. Under the circumstances, the professional reputation would be nearly equivalent to life and there might be a near-First-Law urgency to the lie."

"Yet by the lie, each servant would be harming the professional reputation of the other's master, friend Elijah."

"So it would, but each robot might have a clearer conception of the value of its own master's reputation and honestly judge it to be greater than that of the other's. The lesser harm would be done by his lie, he would suppose, than by the truth."

Having said that, Lije Baley remained quiet for a moment. Then he said, "All right, then, can you arrange to have me talk to one of the robots—to R. Idda first, I think?"

"Dr. Sabbat's robot?"

"Yes," said Baley, dryly, "the young fellow's robot."

"It will take me but a few minutes," said R. Daneel. "I have a micro-receiver outfitted with a projector. I will need merely a blank wall and I think this one will do if you will allow me to move some of these film cabinets."

"Go ahead. Will I have to talk into a microphone of some sort?"

"No, you will be able to talk in an ordinary manner. Please pardon me, friend Elijah, for a moment of further delay. I will have to contact the ship and arrange for R. Idda to be interviewed."

"If that will take some time, Daneel, how about giving me the transcripted material of the evidence so far."

Lije Baley lit his pipe while R. Daneel set up the equipment, and leafed through the flimsy sheets he had been handed.

The minutes passed and R. Daneel said, "If you are ready, friend Elijah, R. Idda is. Or would you prefer a few more minutes with the transcript?"

"No," sighed Baley, "I'm not learning anything new. Put him on and arrange to have the interview recorded and transcribed."

R. Idda, unreal in two-dimensional projection against the wall, was basically metallic in structure—not at all the humanoid creature that R. Daneel was. His body was tall but blocky, and there was very little to distinguish him from the many robots Baley had seen, except for minor structural details.

Baley said, "Greetings, R. Idda."

"Greetings, sir," said R. Idda, in a muted voice that sounded surprisingly humanoid.

"You are the personal servant of Gennao Sabbat, are you not?"

"I am, sir."

"For how long, boy?"

"For twenty-two years, sir."

"And your master's reputation is valuable to you?"

"Yes, sir."

"Would you consider it of importance to protect that reputation?"

"Yes, sir."

"As important to protect his reputation as his physical life?"

"No, sir."

"As important to protect his reputation as the reputation of another?"

R. Idda hesitated. He said, "Such cases must be decided on their individual merit, sir. There is no way of establishing a general rule."

Baley hesitated. These Spacer robots spoke more smoothly and intellectually than Earth-models did. He was not at all sure he could out-think one.

He said, "If you decided that the reputation of your master were more important than that of another, say, that of Alfred Barr Humboldt, would you lie to protect your master's reputation?"

"I would, sir."

"Did you lie in your testimony concerning your master in his controversy with Dr. Humboldt?"

"No, sir."

"But if you were lying, you would deny you were lying in order to protect that lie, wouldn't you?"

"Yes, sir."

"Well, then," said Baley, "let's consider this. Your master, Gennao Sabbat, is a young man of great reputation in mathematics, but he is a young man. If, in this controversy with Dr. Humboldt, he had succumbed to temptation and had acted unethically, he would suffer a certain eclipse of reputation, but he is young and would have ample time to recover. He would have many intellectual triumphs ahead of him and men would eventually look upon this plagiaristic attempt as the mistake of a hot-blooded youth, deficient in judgment. It would be something that would be made up for in the future.

"If, on the other hand, it were Dr. Humboldt who succumbed to temptation, the matter would be much more serious. He is an old man whose great deeds have spread over centuries. His reputation has been unblemished hitherto. All of that, however, would be forgotten in the light of this one crime of his later years, and he would have no opportunity to make up for it in the comparatively short time remaining to him. There would be little more that he could accomplish. There would be so many more years of work ruined in Humboldt's case than in that of your master and so much less opportunity to win back his position. You see, don't you, that Humboldt faces the worse situation and deserves the greater consideration?"

There was a long pause. Then R. Idda said, with unmoved voice, "My evidence was a lie. It was Dr. Humboldt whose work it was, and my master has attempted, wrongfully, to appropriate the credit."

Baley said, "Very well, boy. You are instructed to say nothing to anyone about this until given permission by the captain of the ship. You are excused."

The screen blanked out and Baley puffed at his pipe. "Do you suppose the captain heard that, Daneel?"

"I am sure of it. He is the only witness, except for us."

"Good. Now for the other."

"But is there any point to that, friend Elijah, in view of what R. Idda has confessed?"

"Of course there is. R. Idda's confession means nothing."

"Nothing?"

"Nothing at all. I pointed out that Dr. Humboldt's position was the worse. Naturally, if he were lying to protect Sabbat, he would switch to the truth as, in fact, he claimed to have done. On the other hand, if he were telling the truth, he would switch to a lie to protect Humboldt. It's still mirror-image and we haven't gained anything."

"But then what will we gain by questioning R. Preston?"

"Nothing, if the mirror-image were perfect—but it is not. After all, one of the robots *is* telling the truth to begin with, and one *is* lying to begin with, and that is a point of asymmetry. Let me see R. Preston. And if the transcription of R. Idda's examination is done, let me have it."

The projector came into use again. R. Preston stared out of it; identical with R. Idda in every respect, except for some trivial chest design.

Baley said, "Greetings, R. Preston." He kept the record of R. Idda's examination before him as he spoke.

"Greetings, sir," said R. Preston. His voice was identical with that of R. Idda.

"You are the personal servant of Alfred Barr Humboldt, are you not?"

"I am, sir."

"For how long, boy?"

"For twenty-two years, sir."

"And your master's reputation is valuable to you?"

"Yes, sir."

"Would you consider it of importance to protect that reputation?"

"Yes, sir."

"As important to protect his reputation as his physical life?"

"No, sir."

"As important to protect his reputation as the reputation of another?"

R. Preston hesitated. He said, "Such cases must be decided on their individual merit, sir. There is no way of establishing a general rule."

Baley said, "If you decided that the reputation of your master were more important than that of another, say, that of Gennao Sabbat, would you lie to protect your master's reputation?"

"I would, sir."

"Did you lie in your testimony concerning your master in his controversy with Dr. Sabbat?"

"No, sir."

"But if you were lying, you would deny you were lying, in order to protect that lie, wouldn't you?"

"Yes, sir."

"Well, then," said Baley, "let's consider this. Your master, Alfred Barr Humboldt, is an old man of great reputation in mathematics, but he is an old man. If, in this controversy with Dr. Sabbat, he had succumbed to temptation and had acted unethically, he would suffer a certain eclipse of reputation, but his great age and his centuries of accomplishments would stand against that and would win out. Men would look upon this plagiaristic attempt as the mistake of a perhaps-sick old man, no longer certain in judgment.

"If, on the other hand, it were Dr. Sabbat who had succumbed to temptation, the matter would be much more serious. He is a young man, with a far less secure reputation. He would ordinarily have centuries ahead of him in which he might accumulate knowledge and achieve great things. This will be closed to him, now, obscured by one mistake of his youth. He has a much longer future to lose than your master has. You see, don't you, that Sabbat faces the worse situation and deserves the greater consideration?"

There was a long pause. Then R. Preston said, with unmoved voice, "My evidence was a l—"

At that point, he broke off and said nothing more.

Baley said, "Please continue, R. Preston."

There was no response.

R. Daneel said, "I am afraid, friend Elijah, that R. Preston is in stasis. He is out of commission."

"Well, then," said Baley, "we have finally produced an asymmetry. From this, we can see who the guilty person is."

"In what way, friend Elijah?"

"Think it out. Suppose you were a person who had committed no crime and that your personal robot were a witness to that. There would be nothing you need do. Your robot would tell the truth and bear you out. If, however, you were a person who *had* committed the crime, you would have to depend on your robot to lie.

That would be a somewhat riskier position, for although the robot would lie, if necessary, the greater inclination would be to tell the truth, so that the lie would be less firm than the truth would be. To prevent that, the crime-committing person would very likely have to *order* the robot to lie. In this way, First Law would be strengthened by Second Law; perhaps very substantially strengthened."

"That would seem reasonable," said R. Daneel.

"Suppose we have one robot of each type. One robot would switch from truth, unreinforced, to the lie, and could do so after some hesitation, without serious trouble. The other robot would switch from the lie, *strongly reinforced*, to the truth, but could do so only at the risk of burning out various positronic-trackways in his brain and falling into stasis."

"And since R. Preston went into stasis—"

"R. Preston's master, Dr. Humboldt, is the man guilty of plagiarism. If you transmit this to the captain and urge him to face Dr. Humboldt with the matter at once, he may force a confession. If so, I hope you will tell me immediately."

"I will certainly do so. You will excuse me, friend Elijah? I must talk to the captain privately."

"Certainly. Use the conference room. It is shielded."

Baley could do no work of any kind in R. Daneel's absence. He sat in uneasy silence. A great deal would depend on the value of his analysis, and he was acutely aware of his lack of expertise in robotics.

R. Daneel was back in half an hour—very nearly the longest half hour of Baley's life.

There was no use, of course, in trying to determine what had happened from the expression of the humanoid's impassive face. Baley tried to keep his face impassive.

"Yes, R. Daneel?" he asked.

"Precisely as you said, friend Elijah. Dr. Humboldt has confessed. He was counting, he said, on Dr. Sabbat giving way and allowing Dr. Humboldt to have this one last triumph. The crisis is over and you will find the captain grateful. He has given me permission to tell you that he admires your subtlety greatly and I believe that I, myself, will achieve favour for having suggested you."

"Good," said Baley, his knees weak and his forehead moist now that his decision had proven correct, "but Jehoshaphat, R. Daneel, don't put me on the spot like that again, will you?"

"I will try not to, friend Elijah. All will depend, of course, on the importance of a crisis, on your nearness, and on certain other factors. Meanwhile, I have a question—"

"Yes?"

"Was it not possible to suppose that passage from a lie to the truth was easy, while passage from the truth to a lie was difficult? And in that case, would not the robot in stasis have been going from a truth to a lie, and since R. Preston was in stasis, might one not have drawn the conclusion that it was Dr. Humboldt who was innocent and Dr. Sabbat who was guilty?"

"Yes, R. Daneel. It was possible to argue that way, but it was the other argument that proved right. Humboldt did confess, didn't he?"

"He did. But with arguments possible in both directions, how could you, friend Elijah, so quickly pick the correct one?"

For a moment, Baley's lips twitched. Then he relaxed and they curved into a smile. "Because, R. Daneel, I took into account human reactions, not robotic ones. I know more about human beings than about robots. In other words, I had an idea as to which mathematician was guilty before I ever interviewed the robots. Once I provoked an asymmetric response in them, I simply interpreted it in such a way as to place the guilt on the one I already believed to be guilty. The robotic response was dramatic enough to break down the guilty man; my own analysis of human behaviour might not have been sufficient to do so."

"I am curious to know what your analysis of human behaviour was?"

"Jehoshaphat, R. Daneel; think, and you won't have to ask. There is another point of asymmetry in this tale of mirror-image besides the matter of true-and-false. There is the matter of the age of the two mathematicians; one is quite old and one is quite young."

"Yes, of course, but what then?"

"Why, this. I can see a young man, flushed with a sudden, star-tling and revolutionary idea, consulting in the matter an old man whom he has, from his early student days, thought of as a demigod in the field. I can *not* see an old man, rich in honours and used to triumphs, coming up with a sudden, startling and revolutionary idea, consulting a man centuries his junior whom he is bound to think of as a young whippersnapper—or whatever term a Spacer would use. Then, too, if a young man had the chance, would he try to steal the idea of a revered demigod? It would be unthinkable. On the other hand, an old man, conscious of declining powers, might well snatch at one last chance of fame and consider a baby in the field to have no rights he was bound to observe. In short, it was not conceivable that Humboldt consult Sabbat, or that Sabbat steal Humboldt's idea; and from both angles, Dr. Humboldt was guilty."

R. Daneel considered that for a long time. Then he held out his hand. "I must leave now, friend Elijah. It was good to see you. May we meet again soon."

Baley gripped the robot's hand, warmly. "If you don't mind, R. Daneel," he said, "not too soon."

THE FLYING EYE

Jacques Futrelle

Futrelle (1875–1912) has long been immortalized in the annals of crime and mystery fiction because of his detective Professor Augustus S.F.X. Van Dusen, known as the Thinking Machine who, often from the comfort of his own room, solves seemingly impossible crimes. The best known and one of the most reprinted of all mystery stories is "The Problem of Cell 13" (1905) in which Van Dusen demonstrates how it is possible to escape within a week from a purportedly escape-proof cell. Not surprisingly the Thinking Machine stories, of which there are around fifty, have rather overshadowed Futrelle's other work but in 1912 he began another series featuring Paul Darraq who likes to investigate the strange and unusual. Alas only three of these stories appeared, of which the following is the third. Futrelle went down on the R.M.S. Titanic *in April 1912 having made sure his wife, May, was safely in one of the lifeboats. There may well have been other Darraq stories with him onboard but, alas, we shall never know.*

E VERY MORNING FOR A WEEK OR MORE PAUL DARRAQ HAD been snooping about my library, seemingly up to his nose in pursuit of some elusive bit of information which, I gathered from a cursory remark, had to do with optics, or refraction of light, or something else I knew nothing about. My library consists principally of Shakespeare and half a dozen sets of encyclopædias, these last being mountainous affairs written in the typical dry-as-dust style. Mere bulk and aridity didn't deter Darraq, however; every morning found him fluttering among the books. In the afternoons he disappeared from my ken.

One day he paused beside my desk and looked up into a puzzled, bewildered countenance. The eyes were flicked by thoughtful shadows; and the ready smile, which was so potent a part of the man, was conspicuous by its absence.

"Look here, Lester," Darraq began interrogatively, "suppose you were gazing straight at a thing and it disappeared, vanished, faded away, melted into the void as you looked, what would you think?"

"I'd think about consulting an oculist," I replied.

"I'm quite serious," Darraq went on as he dropped into a chair and regarded me steadily. "Suppose you should happen to be looking up into a clear sky in the full glare of daylight, and you should see floating there—floating, understand—some sort of a—a thing that resembled nothing so much as a giant eye, big as the end of a barrel; and suppose as you looked the—the whatever it was, vanished; and suppose the same thing had happened not once but half a dozen times?"

I dropped my pencil and turned to face him. The deadly earnestness of his manner halted some trivial answer I had framed.

"An eye as large as the end of a barrel, floating in the sky?" I inquired explicitly. "Is that what I understand you to say? Just a detached eye with nothing—no body behind it? No backing, as it were?"

"Precisely," he agreed, "and flat like a disc; that is, not globular, if you get what I mean; approximately stationary as to its height from the ground; or rather the water, but moving, apparently, towards me." He paused a moment. "And there is nothing the matter with my sight," he added.

I abandoned myself utterly to the lure of the intangible. The detached eye of a giant floating in the sky! It was certainly not a cheerful thought, but it was infinitely fascinating in a bizarre sort of way.

"How high up in the air?" I inquired.

"That I couldn't say," Darraq replied. "There was nothing to gauge it by. It might have been only fifty feet up, or it might have been five hundred."

"Perhaps," I ventured, "it passed behind a cloud?"

Darraq shook his head slowly.

"I had thought of that," he said, "but there was not a cloud in the sky."

"Or disappeared behind a tree or a house?" I suggested.

"It couldn't have passed behind anything, for the simple reason there was nothing tall enough to screen it." And again he shook his head. "I have seen it five times, each time in the same relative position over a lake, and—"

"Perhaps it fell *into* the lake?"

"No. Each time at the instant before it disappeared it seemed to be going up and away, if you understand. But it has vanished immediately—that is before it has gone half a dozen feet—so it could not have been that it passed beyond my range of vision."

For a time we were both silent.

"There are two other possibilities," I went on after a little. Darraq's eyes showed his quick interest. "First, it may only be some trick of reflection due to atmospheric conditions."

"There is a chance of that," Darraq admitted finally, "although I can find in your encyclopædias no record of a reflection against a sky which is absolutely cloudless and clear of mist. I dare say, however, that that isn't utterly impossible."

"And, again," I went on, "there is a chance that the—the eye, being flat, like a disc, becomes invisible at the moment it is turned sideways to the observer."

"That is obviously true." And Darraq smiled a little. "But it gives us absolutely no light on what it is, or how it gets up there, and why it *is* there."

There is inborn in every individual a love of the mystic, the physical paradox, the thing that defies explanation. This characteristic is rather strong in me; I flung my work aside and rose.

"What's it all about, anyway?" I demanded. "Tell me about it. Where is it? How did you happen to come across it?"

"I don't know what it's all about," Darraq replied. "My attention was directed to the—the phenomenon, by a—the—well, there's no secret about it—by one of the high officials of the Government. I can't add to that." He was thoughtful a moment. "It's rather uncanny, really," he went on. "I mean it—it—you know what I mean. Hang it, it's positively ghastly. I was thinking if you have nothing particular to do this afternoon perhaps you'd like to come along, and—"

I assented eagerly, and so it came to pass that that afternoon, about half-past three, Darraq and I stepped from a train at a small station a few miles out of London, and after a brisk walk of a couple of miles brought up beside a little lake. The shores of the lake had been denuded of trees, and the water had overflowed the low banks until it had made a marsh of what was once solid ground.

"This lake," Darraq told me, "is about two miles long. It is not wider anywhere than half a mile, and I have explored the neighbourhood until I am perfectly convinced that there is not a single person living near it—that is, nearer than the railroad station back there. Standing here, as you can see for yourself, there's not one sign of humanity; not a building of any kind."

Not only was there not one sign of humanity, beyond the great bare stumps of slain giants of the forest, but the place was bleak, desolate, dreary; the water partly overgrown with rank vegetation, but in some places reflecting perfectly the clear azure of the cloudless sky. Some hundred yards from shore, where we stood, was open space, free of water growth.

"Just here, usually about half-past four o'clock," Darraq said. "The—the eye has always appeared to me just above the spot where the channel narrows into the stream which connects with the lake above—I should say a mile away. It's almost half-past four now."

We sat down to wait, Darraq with a tense, searching stare fixed immovably on the blank sky where he had indicated; and I, curious beyond belief, yet struggling with an uneasy feeling that I had journeyed into the wilds of this desolate country merely because another man was suffering from defective eyesight. From time to time Darraq raised his binoculars, and each time, hopefully, my gaze followed his.

Half-past four passed, and a quarter to five.

"I imagine this is the—the whatever it is—its afternoon off," I remarked.

"There, there, man!" Darraq exclaimed suddenly, and he thrust the binoculars into my hand. "There, just over the narrow channel, about a hundred feet up!"

An uneasy thrill shot down my spinal column, and my hands trembled a little as I raised the binoculars. I focused the—the thing instantly, and stared, stared until my eyes were popping out of my head. It was an eye—a huge, round, monstrous thing, with well-defined pupil and iris, fading off into an impalpable part of the void in which it hung, isolated, detached, glaring down malevolently upon us, upon the lake, upon the desolate waste. What was supporting it? 'Twas nothing below, 'twas nothing above, 'twas nothing at either side—'twas merely a fascinating, sinister thing, the size of a hogshead top, hanging above the lake.

"It will come toward us now," Darraq remarked at my elbow.

And as I looked, I could see that the eye was drawing nearer, or rather I conjectured it from the fact that the disc grew larger, larger; and every visible line of it grew sharper, clearer. Still, with the aid of the binoculars, I was trying to find the thing, whatever it was, which held it up.

"What keeps it there?" I demanded.

"I wish I knew," Darraq replied in a tone which soothed my troubled nerves tremendously. "Odd, isn't it?"

"Odd?" I repeated. "Odd! It's some illusion; I don't believe it's there."

I glanced around at him; his gaze was fixed immovably upon the flying thing.

"It's there all right enough," he assured me. "Look!" he exclaimed suddenly.

I looked. The thing slowed up, stopped, hung there—there against a blank sky, over the unruffled face of the waters.

"It's falling!" I cried, after an instant.

Falling was hardly the word, however; it was settling rather, slowly, surely, straight down, gently as a feather floats. Now it seemed to be only about seventy-five feet up, now fifty, now forty, thirty; and now not more than twenty-five. It stopped; I was watching it with tense gaze.

"It will disappear now," Darraq remarked quietly in my ear.

I don't know if I can quite make it clear—the manner of its vanishing. It was as if one held a silver coin face up in his fingers, then turned it slowly until only the edge was visible, with the difference that if one turned the silver coin far enough the other side of it would come into view. With this thing there *was* no other side; we saw what seemed to be the edge of it for a fraction of a minute, and then even that vanished, leaving nothing—nothing save the unbroken dome of the blue sky!

I turned upon Darraq with a strange giddy feeling, and then I laughed hysterically. He paid not the slightest attention to me now; his gaze was fixed upon the spot where the eye had been. I said something, I don't remember what, and allowed my gaze to follow his.

And at just that moment the body of a man came hurtling down from—from—well, from the vacant sky. Straight as a plummet it fell, feet foremost, with hands raised above the head, into the exact centre of the large space in the lake which happened to be free of the slimy growth; fell, splashed and vanished beneath the surface of the water. It had not been in sight for more than half a second.

"Let's—let's get away from here," I said to Darraq weakly. "My eyes are playing me tricks."

"It happened," he assured me coolly. "You saw it; it is no illusion; the ripples in the water prove it."

As if on the rebound, the body of the man was rising from the water again, hands still above his head, feet together; rising from the water, *above* the water, *through the air*—motionless, rigid! Up, up he went, ten, twenty, twenty-five feet, and then—just as he had disappeared into the water, he *vanished into the air*! From the air he came; and into the air he went!

I continued my gaze for an instant, then dropped down upon a huge stump, with an almost overwhelming desire to scream.

"Did *that* happen?" I demanded.

"Yes," Darraq replied without looking round. "The water was streaming from him as he went up; see the little ripples on the lake."

"Where is he? Where did he go?"

Darraq shrugged his shoulders.

I felt shaken, weak, sick. It had not happened; none of it had happened. Someone would come along and bang on my door after a while, and then I'd awake to find I had overslept. A giant eye floating in the sky! A man falling from the void into the water, and thence returning to the void again! Surely this was the stuff dreams are made of! If someone only *would* wake me!

Darraq stood motionless, still staring upward, for a minute, perhaps, and then lowered his gaze. The bosom of the lake was placid again; there was not so much as a wind-ripple there; the dead, oppressive silence about us was broken only by the raucous cry of a crow in the distance. Finally Darraq turned towards me. His face was pale; I wondered if mine was.

"Strange, isn't it?" he questioned.

I didn't answer; there was nothing to be said. I motioned to him that I was going, and started.

"Just a minute," he requested.

I turned back, and he pointed to a slight, rapidly moving ripple in the water—the sort of disturbance that one might make by dragging a stick through it.

Fascinated, I paused to watch, and unconsciously I drew near Darraq again. The little ripple was coming straight towards us, across the open space in the water, through the rank growth—straight towards us. I made as if to move; his hand closed on my shoulder and I stood still. Then the ripple stopped. Again I turned away from Darraq as if to go.

Terror is a hideous thing—terror of the intangible. At that moment I suffered it. Without having seen anything, I felt myself suddenly gripped by a coiling, serpent-like thing, which seemed to slide up from the ground and settle under my arms. Involuntarily I seized it; it felt like a rope.

"Darraq!" I shouted desperately. "Here—"

An agony shot through my chest as the—the whatever it was, tightened around me. At that instant I felt myself lifted, lifted; my feet dragged, then they swung clear, and I was writhing clear of the ground! I think I screamed; I know I tried to. The earth seemed to be falling away beneath me; only the vacant sky was above, and I was rising into it as we had seen that other man rise.

If only I could reach my knife! This thing was crushing the life out of me. Darraq's amazed face, blank, colourless, was directly beneath me—and I was swinging as a pendulum swings. Then I seemed to hear the beat of great unseen wings, the whir of invisible machinery, growing nearer, nearer. Came a crashing blow upon my head; the earth was dancing fifty feet below me. I knew no more.

I don't just know how long I remained unconscious—it might have been an hour, or even two hours—but when my senses came back my head was throbbing painfully, and I was dizzy from the blow. I was lying upon my back, and dully I was conscious of a gentle swaying motion, as a small boat might rock.

I opened my eyes to find a young man bending over me with an anxious face.

"Now you're coming round all right," he remarked cheerfully. "We made a bungling job of it, picking you up. How does the head feel?"

I started to sit up, but the sharp pain in my head caused me to drop back again.

"The hurt isn't serious," the young man assured me; "but I imagine you saw stars when you struck."

"What happened?" I asked. "Where am I? And how did I get here?"

"The lifting gear got tangled somehow," he replied enigmatically. "I imagine it dragged through the water. The leather strap should have caught you just under the arms, but instead you were picked up in the rope and it closed tightly around your body. I imagine it squeezed your breath out, didn't it?" He stared at me reflectively. "It's lucky it didn't catch you round the neck!"

"Yes, it is lucky," I agreed. My recollection of the squeezing I had had was vivid. "But what rope?"

"You mean you don't know what happened?" the young man inquired.

"I don't know anything that happened, except that I was lifted off the ground in some way I don't understand, and now I find myself here. Where am I, anyway? What makes us sway like this? Are we in a boat, or what?"

The young man grinned good-naturedly.

"We thought you would understand," he remarked. "You lie still and I'll send the governor to you. I hope you'll believe we're awfully sorry we bunged you up so?"

He moved away and I heard a door open and close somewhere. Despite the pain in my head, I straightened up and looked about me. I seemed to be in a small cabin of a small boat, and this first impression was strengthened by the grinding of machinery somewhere. Light was admitted to the cabin by two small, round windows.

I was just about to stand up to look out when again came the opening and shutting of the door and another man appeared—an elderly man, evidently, from a striking resemblance, the father or elder brother of the young man I had seen before.

"Ah, Mr. Darraq!" he greeted me cordially. "I'm glad to see that you've come round all right. Too bad, that—"

"I'm not Mr. Darraq," I interrupted. "But who are you? What's happening?"

The elderly man seemed nonplussed.

"Not Mr. Darraq?" he questioned.

"My name is Lester," I told him. "I'm a friend of Mr. Darraq's. I was standing with him beside a small lake—that's the last I remember. Now I want to know some things. What—"

"You are *not* Mr. Darraq?" he repeated incredulously. "Well, by George, we have made a mess of it! Not only picked up the wrong man, but have injured the man we *did* pick up." His eyes suddenly grew grave. "Too bad!" he said.

I raised myself on my elbow.

"I am waiting for an explanation," I reminded him.

"Explanation? Yes, yes," he said absently. "But Mr.—Mr. Lester, I am very much afraid I shan't be able to give you an explanation—right now, anyway. We thought you were Mr. Darraq. A serious mistake has been made."

He stood staring at me for half a minute, then turned away; a moment later I heard the door open and close again.

At breakfast on the following morning Darraq received in his mail one letter that clouded his face with perplexity.

"Just west of the main roadway in the park is a common. On the southern edge of this common are several groups of large rocks. At four o'clock this afternoon—*if the day is perfectly clear*—please walk out into the common about two hundred feet due north from the rocks and wait. Four o'clock precisely!"

My name was signed to the letter. Darraq knew the handwriting and knew my signature. At one minute to four he strolled leisurely from the rocks indicated towards the centre of the common. A policeman stood watching him.

From a distance of about one hundred feet the policeman saw him raise his hands above his head as if to grasp something, and apparently dive straight upwards into the atmosphere. Forty feet up he went, perhaps, and then disappeared, vanished in mid-air! With goggling eyes the policeman stood riveted, gazing into the blank heavens. Finally, he removed his helmet with shaking hands, mopped an icy dew from his forehead, and wandered on muttering to himself.

This was the first of a series of unbelievably strange and weird happenings which occurred in and around London during that day and the next. For instance, an aged farmer saw his dog come to its feet suddenly from a sound sleep and race madly across a field, snapping viciously at something which the farmer was unable to see. At last the dog seemed to close its teeth upon whatever it was chasing, whereupon it was lifted clean off its feet, up five, ten, fifteen feet, and, apparently flying, carried a couple of hundred yards before its grip broke and it fell. A deck hand on a boat in the river saw two enormous sea-birds flying high above him, and, attracted by their unusual size, watched them curiously. As he watched, their flight was stopped as if they had struck some invisible obstacle, and they fell at his feet with necks broken and heads crushed. A steel worker, high upon the girders of a rising building, paused suddenly in his labours, stared intently into the air above him, laid down his tools and scrambled down the long ladders to the ground. Twice, without any apparent reason, he screamed, and at the foot of the last ladder he fell to the ground, senseless.

Then came the crowning one of the bizarre, inexplicable little mysteries. The captain of a battleship, which was poking its nose out into the river from Chatham dockyard saw a huge shadow, obviously of something in the sky, scuttling along the face of the waters; and then when he looked there was nothing in the sky to cast the shadow. And while he was puzzling over it a small shot-bag, filled with sand, dropped, apparently from a great height, directly at his feet on the bridge.

Startled, he stepped back involuntarily and stared at the thing that had fallen, then sharply searched the sky. Where had it come from? There was no place where it could have come from, so far as he could see. Again he stared straight above him. Nothing!

Finally, he turned his attention to the bag. It had burst as it struck, and he shoved the toe of his boot into the sand inquiringly. The gleam of white paper, partly covered by the sand, caught his attention, and he picked it up. On it were five words:

"If this had been dynamite!"

From that moment these minor incidents, trivial as they were, became matters of moment to the Admiralty. The captain of the battleship wrote a lengthy report of the falling of the shot-bag and posted it to London. It so happened that the First Lord of the Admiralty was in London at the moment, and the captain supplemented his report by calling upon him. There, hopelessly befuddled, he stated it all over again in detail.

"And you saw absolutely nothing?" the First Lord inquired.

"Nothing," was the emphatic response.

"And you say you searched the skies for signs of—of, say, an airship, or—or flying machine?"

"Every inch of it," declared the naval officer. "I saw nothing except the shadow on the river and the shot-bag that fell at my feet."

The First Lord rubbed his hands together in vast delight.

"Good!" he exclaimed at last, and he leaned towards the officer confidentially: "Captain, we are now the masters of the world!"

"Once upon a time," Darraq remarked to me a day or so later, "I entered a room which fairly bewildered me for a moment, and I didn't know why. Then I came to realize that this sense of bewilderment was due to the tinting of the walls and ceiling. They were a sky colour, if you understand; and by sky colour I don't mean sky-blue. I mean a colour that gave one the impression that the room had no walls or ceiling; I felt as if I were out in the open, looking into a clear sky. The thing interested me tremendously, and I made some inquiries. It seemed that the effect had been obtained quite by accident. The walls and ceiling had first been tinted pink, but this was unsatisfactory, and, later, a blue tint was laid over the pink. The result was startling. This little incident of years ago leads ultimately to an explanation of the things we have witnessed during the last few days, you and I."

He paused long enough to light a cigar, and then, as if he had finished with the subject, went on irrelevantly:

"In the old days, Lester, war was largely a matter of physical prowess; now it is a game of skill. Soldiers have become pawns, moved here and there by wireless, by telephone, by signals of various other sorts; and always not only expected, but ordered, to take advantage of every cover that offers concealment. Concealment is the keynote of war.

"The flying-machine, or airship, is gradually, but certainly, nearing mechanical perfection, both the dirigible and aeroplane, but it has been a question up to this time"—and there was a marked emphasis in his tone—"of their value as machines of war. Their effectiveness has been wholly theoretical. Theoretically, a balloon hovering over a fleet could destroy every ship with dynamite, as it could destroy a city like London or New York; but practically it could not, for the reason that a single rifle-shot would disable any balloon; and a well planted shell wreck an aeroplane.

"But suppose"—and Darraq leaned towards me earnestly—"suppose a dirigible balloon or an aeroplane had been made *invisible*! Suppose, even, in the bright glare of the day, the air machine could not be seen by fleet or city? Wouldn't that be, beyond question, the most perfect instrument of death man has ever conceived?

"This Mr. Dickinson and his son, with whom you and I have been sailing all over the place during the last couple of days, has not improved the airship; as a matter of fact, his dirigible craft, compared to Count Zeppelin's, for instance, is crude; but he has done the simpler and greater thing—he has discovered or invented, whichever you please, a paint which makes his ship absolutely invisible in a clear sky; in other words, has produced a colour so like the blue of the sky that it is invisible against the sky, so long as the sky is not clouded. His airship is visible, however, when it passes between the observer and any other object; it is visible, faintly, against a cloudy or misty sky; and it does cast a shadow, of course. We didn't see the shadow that afternoon because the sun was so far in the west; it was thrown away from the surface of the lake. Strangely enough, the colours he has used to get this invisible paint are pink and blue—the combination that was used in that room."

"But his flying-machine isn't absolutely invisible," I objected. "The flying eye—"

"The pilot's window, you mean?" Darraq interrupted. "It did look like an eye, didn't it? Of course the darkness of the interior of the airship behind the large circular plate glass emphasized the resemblance; but some sort of an observation window is necessary in order that the operator may handle the dirigible safely. For instance, that trick of picking up people from the ground, as they picked us up, could never have been accomplished unless the operator of the balloon was able to see perfectly. Dragging us through the hole in the bottom of the cabin was simple with the assistance of a windlass. They are going to reduce the size of that eye, as you call it."

Darraq glanced at his watch.

"Some day, Lester," he said seriously, "the world will become civilized enough to abolish war, with its pitifully useless waste of life, and then the ingenuity which has produced the great fighting machines will be devoted to things which will greatly advance the welfare of the world. Meanwhile the First Lord of the Admiralty is waiting for us at his hotel."

"Us?" I exclaimed. "You, you mean."

"Us," Darraq repeated. "The First Lord of the Admiralty is the high Government official who requested me to watch the tests. In a vague sort of way I knew what they were to be; and where and when to go to witness them. The thing puzzled me so, and I was expecting strange things, that I obtained permission to take another person along that afternoon. Naturally, I chose you as that person." He glanced at his watch again. "We'd better hustle," he added characteristically. "The Dickinsons are there by this time, and we don't want to keep them waiting."

I arose without a word, put on my hat, and we went out together.

NONENTITY

E. C. Tubb

Edwin Charles Tubb (1919–2010) was one of Britain's most prolific writers and though he could write formulaic work if necessary, he could turn his hand to inventiveness and originality when needed and he was at his best when pitting men against insurmountable problems. His work goes back to 1951 with his first novel Saturn Patrol *under the pseudonym King Lang, but he is probably best remembered for his 32-volume series about Earl Dumarest's search to find his home planet, Earth, that began with* The Winds of Gath *in 1967, and which is really one long novel of mystery and investigation. Tubb did write one crime novel,* Assignment New York *(1955), with its Chandleresque private eye Mike Lantry, the eponymous alias under which name the book was published. Under another alias, Arthur Maclean, Tubb wrote a Sexton Blake adventure,* Touch of Evil *(1959), which is a bona fide science fiction novel of alien infiltration. Tubb wrote several other science fiction crime stories which have been collected as* Murder in Space *(1997).*

T HE LIFESHELL WAS A TIN CAN WITH STORES AND A RADIO, an air conditioner and some accumulators, seven hundred cubic feet of space, a single direct vision port—and nothing else. It couldn't change course, land, orbit or spin. It couldn't do anything but drift, send out a radio signal and hope that some ship would receive it and come to the rescue. It had been designed to hold five people at maximum and now it held seven. It was the slow route to hell with a preview thrown in for free.

The officer was a young man with a uniform ripped and soiled as though he had wallowed in muck and crawled through a hedge. One shoulder sagged lower than the other, his left arm was twisted and tucked inside his belt, and his face was taut with the pain from his broken bones. He sat on the stool before the radio equipment, his legs gripping the stem in a futile effort to remain in position, and stared at the six lives which, technically speaking, were in his charge.

"Would any of you be a doctor?"

They looked at each other, the three men, the two women and the boy, and their silence gave their answer.

"Know anything about first aid then?" The officer bit his lips against his agony. "There's a medical kit… drugs… if you could dope me up?"

Again the looks, the blank expressions, the dragging silence as each waited for the other to move. Then the elder of the two women moved quietly towards the injured man.

Henley watched her, staring at her worn features, the lank hair, the body ruined by neglect and overwork. He knew her, a widow returning to Earth after wasting her life with a man who had been fated to fail before he started, then let his eyes flicker to the one stranger in the compartment.

The boy could have been no more than twelve, a pale, huge-eyed youth with the thin features and wasted appearance of those born in space. He huddled in a corner, one thin hand gripping a stanchion to hold him in position, and, staring at him, Henley wondered just who and what he was. An orphan probably, almost certainly now if not before, a waif, uprooted by war and flung among strangers. Idly he wondered how the boy came to be in the shell—the rest had all belonged to the same section—then forgot the boy as Lorna drifted towards him.

"Think he'll live?" It didn't take the jerk of the head to know whom she meant.

"Why not? We're in free fall and a man can live a long time with serious injuries. Worried?"

"You kidding?" She licked her lips with a quick, almost feral gesture, and stared directly into his eyes. "We're in trouble, buster, and don't you make any mistake about it. If pretty boy dies who's going to call for help?"

"Automatic radio call," he said, mildly. "We don't really need him." He kept his face blank at her expression of relief. "Who's the boy?"

"That kid?" She shrugged. "How should I know? Some poor devil separated from his people in the rush." She shuddered at the memory of the past few hours. "God! Who'd have thought people could act like that?"

"Panic," he explained. "Someone loses their head, fear gets out of control, it spreads and before you know it you've a mob on your hands." He looked up as a big man glided towards them. "Jeff! How's your face?"

"I'll live." The big man touched his slashed cheek. "That wildcat nearly ripped out an eye. Damn crazy dame, why didn't she go to her own shell?"

"She didn't get in this one, anyway," said Henley, drily. "You pack quite a right, Jeff. My guess is that you broke her jaw."

"So what? When the chips are down only the strong can survive." The big man dismissed the incident with a scowl. "What's the matter with the old guy?"

"Prentice?" Henley stared up to where the third civilian drifted close to the small, round, star-shot port.

He was old and he was almost dead with fear. His hands trembled and his eyes had the glazed look of a man suffering from extreme shock. Little globules of spittle drifted from his quivering lips, his skin looked grey, and the sound of his breathing echoed horribly in the confines of the tiny compartment. Shock, terror, the sickening fear of imminent death and the physical frenzy of desperation as he had fought his way into the lifeshell had combined to bring him near madness and death. Time might cure him—if he were given time.

"What I want to know," said Jeff, irritably, "is what happened? All I remember is the alarm going off, the lights going out, and a lot of people screaming and yelling all around. I thought those ships were supposed to be foolproof."

"The pile went, I think. I saw something explode as we blasted free." Lorna looked towards the officer. "Would he know?"

"He should." Henley pushed against the wall. "I'll go and ask him."

The officer looked no better than he had before the first aid. Beads of sweat glistened on his face and neck, and his lips were grey instead of red. He looked up as Henley cushioned himself to a stop against the wall, then stared down at his equipment.

"Can I help?"

"Finished. Mrs. Caulder is quite a nurse." The officer tried to smile at the woman. "Thank you, madam."

"I didn't do much," she said, nervously. "I'm not very clever at that sort of thing."

"You did your best," he said, quietly, then stared at Henley. "I suppose you're wondering what all this is about?"

"Naturally, and so are the others. What went wrong?"

"Nothing went wrong, not in the sense you mean. We were sabotaged by the Numen." The way he said it made the name sound like a curse."

"The Numen!"

"That's right. They must have sneaked one of their people aboard, God knows how or when, and he did a good job. First he spilled the pile then smashed the rod-controls. He wrecked the lighting circuits and gimmicked the air doors. The guts of the pile burned their way towards the fuel tanks and touched them off. We blasted free only just in time." The officer winced as pain stabbed from his smashed bones. "Damn fools! If they had only kept their heads we could have abandoned ship in good order. As it was, I had to fight my way to the shell and collected a few broken bones on the way." He swore then, bitterly, savagely, more at the human animals who had reverted to the beast than at the saboteur.

"What happened to the Numan?"

"Dead, I suppose. Those fanatics consider a life well spent if they can take some of us with them, and this particular specimen really went to town. A ship and two hundred people, not to count the stores and equipment for the Mars base. We're lucky to be alive."

"Are we?" Henley glanced at the terror-stricken figure of the old man. "What are our chances?"

"No better and no worse than any other lifeshell ever blown adrift. If a ship picks up our call in time we'll be rescued."

"And if it doesn't?" The girl thrust herself forward and Henley realized that everyone in the compartment had heard what the officer had said. "How long must we wait to be picked up? That's what I want to know. How long?"

"Yeah." Jeff joined the girl, one arm slipping possessively around her waist. "When are we going to get out of this mess?"

"A few days, perhaps. Maybe a week or two. It depends."

"And what if a ship doesn't arrive in time? What then?"

"Please!" The officer frowned at the girl and glanced towards the boy. "There's no need to make things seem worse than what they are. Remember the child."

"That's right." Henley smiled towards the boy. "What's your name, son?"

"Tommy, sir."

"Well, Tommy, we're in a little trouble, but you mustn't worry about it. We're all going to be all right. Now you just do as you're told and you'll be home before you know it."

"Yes, sir." The boy hesitated. "Sir?"

"Yes, son?"

"What about the others? My dad got left behind. Will he be home soon, too?"

"Of course." Henley forced a false conviction into his tones as he patted the stringy black hair. "Don't worry about it, Tommy, everything is going to be all right." He looked at the toil-worn features of the woman. "Perhaps you could take care of him, madam?"

"I'll look after him," promised Mrs. Caulder. She pulled the boy towards her. "Come on now, Tommy, time for you to get some sleep."

Henley watched her as she mothered the boy, recognizing a long thwarted maternal instinct in the way she touched him, smoothing his hair and resting his head on her shoulder. He turned as Jeff swore with quiet, bitter anger.

"The swine! The dirty stinking swine!"

"The Numen?"

"Who else? To do a thing like that. Wreck a ship in deep space and kill off women and children as if they were vermin." He knotted his big hands. "If I could just get hold of the swine who did it…"

"He's dead," said Henley, tiredly. He didn't want to get dragged into an argument on the merits of the war, and yet, deep within himself, he had a sneaking sympathy for the Numen. Whatever else they were, they were brave. They carried on a hopeless struggle with nothing to help them but their own courage and a fanatical determination to be left alone at all costs. Sometimes it was hard to remember that they were human, of the same stock as the Terrestrials, settlers who had carved a living from the hostile satellites of Jupiter, a living threatened by the occupation of those worlds by the advancing frontiers of civilization. Perhaps he would have felt different had he lost a wife or son in the wreck, but he hadn't and he was alive, and that was all that mattered.

Night came with the switching off of the light—to save power, though no one mentioned that—and in the heavy darkness seven people tried to forget worry and fear in sleep. It wasn't easy. Free fall didn't induce physical weariness, and the novelty and danger of their position tended to keep them all awake. Henley hooked one leg beneath the strut retaining the air tanks and stared into the darkness, listening to the various sounds sighing and ebbing through the heavy air.

A slobbering, half-baby, half-animal whimper, moist and drooling, sucking and horrible—the old man still living with his terror. A whispered croon—the woman soothing the child. A gasp and a hiss of indrawn breath—the officer with his broken bones. A murmur and a soft whisper—Jeff and the girl. A soft, mechanical drone—the whirling fan of the conditioner as it stirred the air.

He isolated and registered the sounds, identifying and locating the position of each. The officer was still at his radio, his legs gripping the stem of the stool. The woman and child were in the opposite, upward corner; the old man had drifted into the centre of the cabin and Jeff and the girl rested beside the single door.

Seven people—with scaled rations for only five.

After a while the darkness and the heavy air, the lack of distraction and the murmuring silence brought a half-doze, half-coma, and he hovered in the strange region between sleep and waking, his thoughts flitting from one concept to another, touching lightly on old scenes and recent memories. Casually he thought of the war and of the saboteur who had died on his mission. He thought of the panic and the blue-lit hell of the last few moments when men and women had fought in the dim glow of the emergencies as they felt the spur of panic. He visualized his home and his office, the face of a woman he had once known, a friend and an enemy, the possibility of being picked up and whether or not the Numen would ever cease their fanatical struggle.

He snapped fully awake as he sensed someone at his side.

"Henley?"

It was the girl, breathing directly into his ear, the soft mass of her hair brushing his cheek as she hovered beside him. He waited a moment before answering, locating the heavy breathing of the big man where he drifted, finally asleep, almost seven feet above.

"Yes?"

"It's me, Lorna." She gripped his arm and drew herself even closer. "Look, you're intelligent, at least you can't be as dumb as that big ox. Maybe you could answer a question."

"Maybe." He kept his voice low, too, whispering directly into her ear.

"How much air and stuff does this shell carry?"

"Enough," he said, carefully. "Why?"

"Don't give me that," she said, bitterly. "I may be a cheap dancer working the dives, but I'm not stupid. Look, there're seven of us in here and there isn't room to spit. How long can the air and water and stuff last?"

"We carry scaled rations to last five people for a period of twenty-five days." He wished that it were light so that he could see her expression. "That answer you?"

"And how long will it take for us to be picked up?"

"I don't know. You heard what the officer said."

"I want the truth, Henley. I'm a big girl now."

"When the ship blew, a signal was broadcast on the emergency band. It will be received and the nearest vessel will head towards us. They will know the flight pattern of the ship, its velocity, the time of the explosion, and from that can work out just where we are. All they have to do is search until they pick up our signal."

"How long?"

"They've probably received the signal already, but the nearest ship could be going away from us and so would pass it on. We'll have to wait until a ship can match velocities and, of course, they will have to get here from wherever they are." He hesitated. "I don't know how long it will take."

"Days?"

"Highly unlikely."

"Weeks?"

"Perhaps. Perhaps a month. It's impossible to say."

"I see." Against his ear he could hear the hiss of her indrawn breath. "Rations for five and we're carrying seven. Six—the boy doesn't count. Say a month. Say…"

"If you're trying to work out what I think you are, I can give you the answer. Eighteen days."

"I make it different."

"Jeff uses a lot of oxygen and he's going to need a lot of water. He and the boy make two normal adults between them. Eighteen days."

"And you said that we couldn't be picked up for at least a month." Abruptly her fingers were digging into his arm. "Henley! What can we do?"

"We?"

"Sure! Why not? The old guy's almost dead and the officer's well on the way. Jeff is dumb. Who have I left?"

"I don't like what you're saying," he said, curtly. "We're all in this together and I'm not going to be a party to killing anyone for their rations. I—"

"Killing? Who said anything about killing?" Despite the denial she didn't raise her voice. "I never suggested—"

"Work it out for yourself," he said, impatiently. "The only way to stretch the rations is for someone to stop using them. I want no part of it."

"You…" For a moment he thought that she would strike him. Then she swore, thrust angrily at the metal and drifted away.

He shrugged.

The lights came on and they ate, cold, tasteless paste from cans washed down with stale water sucked through a nipple. Lorna ate in sulky silence, not looking at Henley, and after the meal drifted into a corner with Jeff, their heads bent close together. The woman moved towards the officer and Henley joined her as she opened the medical kit.

"How is he?"

"Bad. The collar bone is smashed and I think some ribs as well. His arm is useless and there's some internal bleeding." She fumbled among the small store of drugs. "There's nothing I can do."

"Will he die?"

"I don't know. I hope not; he's such a nice young man and it's a pity that he should end like this." There was a naked sincerity in her voice and Henley was surprised to find her eyes brimming with unshed tears. "He reminds me of Joe, my husband, when we first met. That was back home before we left for the asteroids. I…" She gulped and shook her head. "You wouldn't be interested in that."

"I could be interested," he said, gently, and took the hypodermic from her hands. "Let me do that."

"Can you?"

"I can give an injection—if you tell me what to inject." He glanced towards the boy, hunched against a wall, wide-eyed and shrunken. "Go back to Tommy now, he looks scared." For a moment mother instinct struggled with duty; then, as Henley turned towards the officer, her maternal feelings won and she returned to the thin-faced boy.

"How are you feeling?" Henley carefully slipped the needle into a vein and pressed the plunger. "Better?"

"I suppose so." The officer tried not to show his obvious pain. "That stuff could be water for all the good it seems to be doing. How are the others?"

"Same as usual." Henley wiped the hypodermic and replaced it in the medical kit. "Prentice doesn't seem to be any better."

"The old man?" The officer couldn't shrug, but his meaning was plain. "He's had his turn. I'm more concerned with the boy.

A hell of a fine way to start life. Those damn swine! I wish they were here now to see what they've done." He gulped, his face a mask of sweat, and gestured for Henley to stoop closer. "Look, I think that we'd better come to an understanding."

"How do you mean?"

"I can't last much longer, and the way I feel now the quicker I go the better I'd like it. Maybe it's just as well; we don't carry anywhere near enough stores for us all to last, and my share may mean life for someone." He stared at Henley. "I want that someone to be the boy. The rest of us are full grown and we've had our time, but the kid never had a chance. Understand?"

"Is it as bad as that?"

"Yes."

"How long do you think?"

"Weeks, maybe. A month at least." The officer swayed a little, and perspiration streamed from his contorted features. "Don't kid yourself, Henley, this isn't going to be easy. Lifeshells are nice in theory. They can even be useful on the Tri-Planet runs, where space is full of ships and a one-week wait is the most expected. But we're a long way from the sun and space is a hell of a big place. Out here lifeshells are a morale factor; they're comforting to have around—so long as you don't have to use them. The rations are supposed to last twenty-five days, but that's all in theory, and as soon as you overload you're in trouble. That's another good reason why I'd better clock out pretty soon. While we're two extra the consumption goes up double."

"Double!" Henley remembered to lower his voice. "I don't get that. I made it that we could last eighteen days."

"Excess humidity for one thing. Heat for another. We're not losing any heat, you know, just a little by radiation, and there are seven of us acting as quite efficient heat sources. The conditioner can't stand too much overload… carbon dioxide… non-conduction…" The officer shook his head as he swayed again. "The hell with it. I can't give you a lecture. Just remember what I said."

Henley left him then, left him alone with his agony and the invisible burden of his responsibility, swaying and sweating from the pain of his torn tissues and crushed bones. And yet, despite his pain, the man could still think of the one thing which had made his race what it was. He could still think of the next generation.

Three days later he was dead, and those remaining faced a new problem.

There was no air lock in the lifeshell. The single door opened, if it were possible to open it at all, directly on space, and the refuse ejectors were far too small to permit of the expulsion of anything so large as a body.

"You'll have to get rid of him." Lorna made a point of not looking at the silent figure, still sitting on the stool, the legs bound with a torn fragment of uniform. "If I have to stay in here with that I'll go crazy!"

"Yeah." Jeff automatically clenched his big hands as if the problem could be solved by physical violence. "How do we do it, Henley?"

"We can't."

"You've got to. I can't stand him sitting there like that! I can't stand it, I tell you!"

"Shut up, Lorna!" Henley stared at the big man. "She's right, though. We can't leave him like that. In a couple of days he'll start going bad and you know what that'll mean." He glanced at the others, the woman hunched against the boy, the old man still whimpering to himself as he wandered in the regions of his mental terror. "As far as I can see it there are only two ways. We can seal him up in one of those big plastic bags in the locker, or we can pass him through the refuse ejectors. I suggest that we seal him up. I've an idea that is what those bags are for, and if we seal it, it should be airtight."

"I don't like it," protested the girl. "Even if you seal him up he'll still be in here. God! You think I want to keep company with a corpse!"

"What else can we do?"

"We could cut him up," said Jeff, slowly. "The ejectors would take small pieces and we could get rid of him that way."

"You know what would happen then?" Henley stared bleakly at the big man. "His blood would drift in tiny globules and break against whatever they touched. The human body holds quite a bit of blood, Jeff, and I don't think you'd like living under those conditions. A slaughterhouse would be hospital-clean in comparison."

"But we'd get rid of the body."

"Yes, and then we'd have to get rid of the blood." Henley shook his head. "We'll seal him up."

"Who says so? I don't remember anyone making you the boss. Who are you to give the orders?"

"Do you want to give them?" Henley shrugged. "Go ahead, then. Jam the ejectors and let our air escape into space. Fill the shell with blood and tissue then. When it goes bad, maybe you'll figure out a way to clean the air. Me? I don't give a damn. If you want to act big in front of your girl friend go ahead, but when you're spewing your life out two hours away from rescue, maybe you'll regret it."

For a moment it hung in the balance. For a moment Henley thought the big man would react in the only way that seemed possible to a man of his type, with fists and boots, and blind, savage violence; then, to his relief, the big man blinked and nodded. "We'll seal him up."

The job didn't take long and Henley was glad of it. They pulled one of the two huge plastic bags over the body, sealed the edges and fastened the shapeless bundle to a stanchion. Then they tried to forget it, tried to ignore the fact that it contained what had once been a man, and who, even though dead, still kept them company. Tried—and failed.

For death was too close. It hovered all around them, in the flickering needle of the air gauge, the falling hand of the power supply, the dwindling stores of food and water. Death rode the hands of the chronometer—and they all knew it.

And knowing it, reacted each in their own fashion.

Prentice did nothing. Lost in his mental world he drifted like a thing of wood, uncaring, unaware, whimpering his animal sounds and twitching with his baby motions. The woman said nothing, but she clutched the boy a little more possessively, watched a little more sharply. The boy did nothing—merely watched and did as he was told, his wide, dark eyes and thin face a constant reproach to selfish thoughts. Jeff became a little more arrogant, a little too eager to grab his share of the rations, a little less polite and far more possessive. Lorna did something about it.

She came up to Henley one "night," drifting like a pale ghost in the dim star-glow from the single port, and settled beside him where he sat on the stool.

"How are we going?" Again she whispered directly in his ear, her hair brushing against his cheek.

"As expected. Why?"

"You know what I mean. How long can we last now that the officer's dead?"

"About eight days."

"Eight! How's that? With one less we should be able to last a lot longer."

"It isn't as simple as that. The overload cut down our time by half and the officer died too late to do us any good. I'd guess eight days, maybe ten, maybe seven. I don't know."

"And the rescue?"

"At least twice as long."

"So we're going to die."

"Naturally. We've been going to do that since the day we were born."

"Don't get clever with me, Henley, you know what I mean." Against his ear her voice was surprisingly harsh and bitter. "We're going to die... unless..."

"Unless what?"

"The old man's pretty useless," she said, softly. "He doesn't eat much, but he breathes a lot of air. Why should we all suffer to keep one worn-out old man alive?"

"Are you asking me, or telling me?" He stirred impatiently on the stool. "You tried this once before, Lorna, and my answer is still the same. We live or die together."

"Why? Why should we consider others at all? It's our life, isn't it? We've only the one, and I intend hanging onto mine. If you weren't so damn noble you'd feel the same way."

"Shut up!" He didn't trouble to lower his voice. "I know your kind, Lorna. Selfish and rotten to the core. You've always had what you wanted and you've always managed to find some poor fool to get it for you. Now you want life, and you think I'll kill so that you can fill your lungs for a few days longer. Why should I? What the hell are you to me?"

"I'm a woman, aren't I?"

"So what? What's so special about being a woman? You think I'm like the rest of the morons you've met? Do you think I'd do anything for a woman merely because she is a woman? Get wise to yourself, Lorna. To me you're just a lump of flesh and nothing else. Remember that."

"You—"

"Say that again and I'll smash your teeth down your throat. What's the matter, Lorna, won't Jeff play?"

"Go to hell!"

"We're all going to hell, Lorna, one way or another."

"You're a fool," she said, bitterly. "I'm not just talking of myself; there's others to consider—the kid, you, me. What is the old man to us? Nobility is all right in its place, but not here, not when we're racing the clock and losing out on every breath. If he died we'd all stand a chance."

"We'd stand a better chance if Jeff died; he's big and uses too much air, radiates too much heat."

"Leave Jeff out of this."

"Sure, but if we're talking of survival, let's face the facts. You mentioned the old man, I mention Jeff. If they both were to die, maybe we'd stand a chance. The old man alone won't make any difference."

"You wouldn't dare try to kill him."

"Did I say anything about killing? You brought the matter up, not me, but suppose you got your own way and only the two of you were left. He's a big man, Lorna. I'd say that he uses twice as much air as you do, and he isn't particular how he gets it. Remember the way he hit that woman? If you were the last two alive, could you trust him?"

"I think so," she said, uncertainly. "He likes me a lot, he wouldn't do anything to hurt me."

"No?"

"No."

"Then you've nothing to worry about, have you?" He stretched and smiled into the darkness. "Forget it, Lorna. You're tired and worried. Better get some sleep now; things will seem better in the morning."

She left him as silently as she had come.

With the morning came horror.

It came with "day," with the flashing of the single light, and it came with blood and violent death. Prentice was the one who died, his throat punctured and his blood spraying in a thick, red mist from the force of his slowing heart. Jeff was the one who hovered beside him, a knife in his hand, a foolish expression on his face, blood on his clothing and dull wonder in his eyes.

"He's dead," he said, stupidly. "The old man's dead."

"So he is." Henley felt his stomach muscles tighten as he stared at the big man. "What made you do it, Jeff?"

"Do it? Do what?" Understanding and rage came together. "I didn't kill him."

"No?"

"Damn it! I tell you I didn't kill him and you can't make me say I did! I was asleep, drifting, and I heard a groan. I reached out and felt the knife and at the same time you put the lights on. Hell! Anyone could have done it!"

"Who?" Henley shook his head. "You might have got away with it, Jeff, but you were unlucky. Another minute and you'd have been in the clear. You could have got rid of the knife, perhaps palmed it off on someone else, and the blood would have stained us all." He took a deep breath. "Sorry, Jeff, but the facts are plain."

"Are they?" The big man closed his fist around the knife and glared his defiance. "We'll see about that. I'm innocent and I know it, and when we get picked up the lie detectors will prove it. Someone in here is a murderer, and the only thing I'm certain about is that it isn't me." He glared at the others. "It could have been you, or Lorna, or the woman. How do I know that one of you didn't do it?"

"I was sitting here all night," said Henley, tiredly. "Lorna?"

"I was with you part of the time, with Jeff some of the rest." She didn't look at the big man. "I was by myself just before the lights went on."

"Mrs. Caulder?"

"Asleep. Tommy was restless and I didn't drop off for some time."

"You see? No one's got an alibi. I just happened to be the unlucky one." Jeff stared down at the dulled blade. "Someone must have carried this thing on him, and it's not likely that it belongs to a woman. That leaves you and me, Henley—and I know that it wasn't me."

"I didn't kill him," said Henley, tiredly. He kicked himself from the stool. "Talking is getting us nowhere. Let's seal him up and get him out of the way."

They used the second and last of the big bags for the job, and lashed what remained of the old man beside the officer. They worked in silence, avoiding each other's eyes, and the sense of guilt and helplessness drove them apart as soon as the job was done. Henley held out his hand.

"The knife, Jeff. I'll take it."

"I'm keeping it."

"I want the knife, Jeff."

"You can keep on wanting." The big man glowered his hate. "And another thing, the light stays on. I'm taking no chances on getting stabbed in the dark. Someone in here is a killer and I don't intend to be next. I'll keep the knife for self protection, and if you don't like the idea, you can try to take it from me." He grinned, an animal writhing of the lips utterly devoid of humour. "If you've got sense, Henley, you won't try it."

It was an ultimatum. It was defeat and Henley knew it, and the knowledge was bitter in his mouth. Angrily he returned to the stool, then glanced up as Mrs. Caulder drifted towards him.

"Mr. Henley."

"Yes?"

"I'd like to talk to you." She glanced at the others and bent her lips to his ear. "Privately."

"Go ahead." He bent his head, and like two lovers, they sat cheek to cheek, each whispering into the other's ear.

"It's about Tommy," she whispered. "I'm worried about him."

"There's no need to worry, Mrs. Caulder. It's a trying time for all of us, but he's young and he'll get over it."

"I don't mean that," she whispered. "It's something else. I think…"

Her voice faded with the dying of the light, and in the sudden darkness Henley felt her stiffen and the sound of a curse.

"What the hell? Put those damn lights on!"

"I'm trying." Henley fumbled for the switch, found it, flipped it without result. "Must be fused."

"Like…" Jeff's voice cut off with a peculiar gurgle and something wet and warm sprayed Henley's face with sticky moisture. Desperately he fumbled at the unfamiliar wiring, tracing the strands from the switch to the fuses, feeling his way until current stabbed at his fingers with sudden pain. Gingerly he felt the wires, touched the severed ends together, and blinked in the sudden light.

"What happened?" Lorna was crouched in a corner, her face distorted with fear and terror, her skin dappled with tiny red patches.

"Someone cut the wires." Carefully Henley twisted them together and frowned down at the join. He touched his face and stared down at his stained fingers. "Jeff!"

The big man didn't answer. He couldn't answer; the knife thrust into his neck gave the reason and explained the red mist filling the compartment. "Lorna! Are you all right?"

"Yes."

"Mrs. Caulder!" Henley kicked himself towards the woman. "Mrs. Caulder! Are you sick?"

She wasn't sick. She would never be sick again, and as she drifted a limp and inert bundle, her glazed eyes stared at the light with pathetic hopelessness, their expression matching the distorted angle of her head.

"Dead!" Henley gently felt at the thin neck. "Broken, and someone killed Jeff." He stared accusingly at the girl.

"It wasn't me, Henley. I swear that it wasn't me." She cringed at the murderous hate in his eyes. "I stayed where I was when the lights went out. Henley! Don't look at me like that!"

"I can understand the old man," he said, thickly. "He was no loss to anyone. I can even understand Jeff, he would have been dangerous, but to kill the woman! To murder a decent, inoffensive woman whose only concern was for the boy. Damn you, Lorna, you've gone too far!"

"I didn't do it," she pleaded. "I didn't do it."

"You cut the wires," he accused. "You saw your chance to safeguard that precious life of yours and you took it. Three dead and three to go. How long can we last now, Lorna? How long can we last now—damn you!"

Hate mastered him then. Hate and rage, and a sick distorted feeling of repulsion and murderous frenzy. She was strong but he was stronger, and even without weight he still had the greater mass. Her throat was slippery with blood by the time he gripped her, his hands were red with it, the entire interior was awash with sticky wetness, but it made no difference and he smiled as he watched her die.

Afterwards, when he realized what he had done, and more important, whom he had done it before, he felt shame and guilt and a terrible revulsion of feeling.

"I'm sorry, Tommy," he said, quietly. "But she was a bad woman, you know that, and she had to die."

The boy didn't answer. He sat as he had sat since the beginning, wide-eyed and silent, watchful and poised like an overscared young animal, ready to run, but not knowing from where danger would come. Henley sighed as he looked at the boy, so young to have suffered so much, and, turning off the light, settled down to wait for rescue.

Somehow, it was better in the dark. It was better still when he finally drove himself to lash the drifting bodies to a stanchion, and even though the blood was a nuisance, yet it could be borne. He was safe. He was alive and the others were dead. He alone of them all would return to Earth and the warm comfort of civilization.

And he had a witness to prove his innocence.

He smiled as he thought about it; then, still thinking, he lost his smile. The officer had died a natural death, there was no mistake about that. The old man? Jeff. But Jeff had protested his innocence and held onto the knife. Mrs. Caulder had been touching him when the lights went out. Jeff had been talking to Lorna, so... who had cut the wires? And who had killed Jeff, big and armed and ready for trouble? And who had killed the woman, and why? She had died from a cunning blow to the neck, a skilled and highly technical blow unlikely to be known by the average person. Jeff could have done it, but Jeff was dying with a knife in his throat. Who?

"Tommy." Henley tried to keep his voice calm and even. "Where are you, son?"

"Worked it out yet, Henley?" The voice was the same, high and weak, and surprisingly boyish, but the tone was that of a man. "Surprised? You shouldn't be. It was pretty obvious from the start."

"You! You did it!"

"Of course." The boy—it was hard to think of him as other than a boy—chuckled. "I'm the saboteur you were all talking about. The scum you wanted to find and hurt. The filth you hate and despise because we're a little different from you and want to be left alone. You should learn more about your enemies, Henley."

"So you're the Numan. You wrecked the ship and managed to get on this lifeshell." Henley laughed, without humour. "My God! And the officer died so that you could have his rations and a chance for life. You were the one we all felt sorry for. You!"

"The more fools you." There was nothing but acid contempt in the young voice. "I'm a Numan, yes, what you would call a midget, and I wrecked your ship and killed your people. Why not? We are at war, aren't we?"

"Then you must have cut the wires. You killed Mrs. Caulder and the others, but why? We meant you no harm."

"The woman suspected, but even without that she would have had to die. All of them had to die. You don't know much about survival, Henley. Jeff thought he knew, but he only played with the idea. To survive at all you have to be strong all of the time, not just a part of it. That's why we are going to win this war. We never stop, we daren't stop; for us the only rest and peace is in the grave."

He paused, and in the silence Henley fumbled for the switch and tried to throw on the light. He wasn't surprised when nothing happened.

"I wanted the air and food in this lifeshell and to get it they had to die. You had the same idea, the girl, too, but you did nothing but talk. I didn't talk, I acted, and now I shall survive while the rest of you rot." He chuckled again. "Funny, isn't it? When the rescue ship arrives they will all be so sorry for the poor little waif without a home, the nonentity caught in the cross currents of war. They will look after me, take me to Earth, give me a home, and then…" He sucked in his breath. "Then I'll show them what their 'scum' can do."

"Perhaps," said Henley, softly, and kicked himself to one side as steel lashed towards him. Savagely he struck out with the medical kit in his hand and grinned as he heard the knife tinkle against the plating. "Now we're even, you little swine. Now we'll see who survives. You made a mistake, Numan; you talked too much, but then you couldn't help it, could you? Half-pints like you always like to brag." Carefully he drifted across the compartment. "We aren't really soft, you know, not anywhere near as soft as you like to think. We respect our children and ignore nonentities, but, once we know them for what they are, we haven't the slightest compunction at killing our enemies. I'm bigger than you, with more mass and greater strength, and I'm going to kill you—slowly."

He drifted back across the cabin, feeling the sticky wetness on his face increase as he brushed against the hovering blood globules, and hate and rage, sorrow at what he had done to the girl, and anger at having been made a fool, all combined to fill him with a killing frenzy.

He didn't know that the air conditioner had stopped, clogged by the drifting blood, and that it was only a matter of time before he, too, would be dead.

DEATH OF A TELEPATH

George Chailey

Here is a real mystery to solve. I know nothing about George Chailey. He appeared just twice in the sf magazines, both times in issues of the British Science Fiction Adventures, *with this story in the January 1959 issue and with an article on cave painting two issues later. The magazine editor, John Carnell, gave no clues to his identity in his introductory notes, which suggests the name may be a pseudonym. The story bears comparison with Alfred Bester's classic* The Demolished Man *(serial, 1952) which questions how murder, or any crime, could be committed in a world where telepathy was possible, as the telepath would know beforehand. The following shows how it might be done.*

M CCLANE WATCHED THE TWO-MAN SPACESTATION SPIN INTO view, a shining disc against the black backdrop. He fired his jets briefly, to match speed, and operated magnetic clamps; the airlock of his ship married that of the satellite.

He rose and stretched, a big man with red hair, his massive face liberally sprinkled with freckles. Waiting for the lock to fill, he thought bitterly of his situation—promotion due and he had to get a job like this…

He stepped through to see a thin, white-coated figure with a high forehead and pale, watery eyes. McClane produced a badge from his grey uniform; rank, it stated, Detective-Patrolman.

"I'm Burke," said the thin figure, thrusting out a bony hand.

McClane ignored it.

"Where's the body?"

"In the power room. I haven't touched anything, naturally."

McClane grunted. In his experience, such behaviour was definitely *not* natural.

"I haven't been inside," Burke assured him.

"I suppose you loved him like a brother?"

"No. I hated him. You can understand that—"

McClane could. No-one loved a telepath, except another telepath. No-one enjoyed the knowledge that his most intimate thoughts were an open book and, in consequence, telepaths were universally hated.

"This way," Burke said.

The corridor was a hollow cylinder, ten feet across; at the far end was a solid door with a red light shining over it.

McClane began to struggle into a protective suit.

"All right," he grunted. "Let's have your version, Burke."

"When I came off shift, Forster went in—"

"Green showing?"

"Of course. The door can't be opened if the radiation is above a certain level. I have the circuits here."

He pushed a bundle of papers at McClane, who thrust them into his pocket.

"Go on."

"I went to my cabin to rest—"

"Did you leave it, for any reason at all?"

"No. Not till my rest period had ended. Then I returned to find red burning. Forster was nowhere on the station, so he had to be inside. I called H.Q.—"

"Forster's in there, still?"

"Presumably. There's nowhere else he can be."

McClane tightened the last clamp on his suit and gestured at the door. Burke switched off the safety circuit and retreated.

The door opened easily. McClane ducked through and slammed it behind him. The shields were down and the room lit by a weird glow from the pile.

Carefully touching nothing else, he rammed the shields back in place and started the flushing mechanism. Then he looked at the body. Forster lay face down midway between the door and the pile, and his position clearly showed that he'd been running hard when he came through. He was pint-sized, shrivelled, and stubby fingers covered his face, clawing upward at the tendril-hairs.

McClane prised the hands loose and studied an expression of terror.

The satellite was isolated; only Burke and Forster had lived and worked here. One human, the other telepath—a set-up for violent emotions. Burke hating, and the other knowing it.

McClane chewed over the situation. It was axiomatic in his department that no human could ever murder a telepath. It was impossible to keep such thoughts hidden; the victim *knew*... and so telepaths bore a charmed life.

Only this one was dead in circumstances that looked suspicious to McClane. The shields down. Forster running—not away from the unprotected pile—*but towards it*.

How the devil had Burke managed it?

McClane took a last look at the body and went outside. He wanted to study circuits.

The wiring was simple. The door of the power room could only be operated when radiation was at a safe level, and then a green light burned. If the level rose, the light changed to red and the door automatically locked. So Forster must have entered before the shields went down...

McClane mentally transposed two pair of wires. It was possible to rig the circuits, he realized, and straight away went to check the wiring points. He found everything in order and no tell-tale scratches, but the idea persisted in his head. The chamber could have been a deathtrap.

But—McClane came up against the basic problem—Forster could read Burke's mind. He would *know*.

"Satisfied?" asked a dry voice.

McClane turned to see Burke watching him at the junction-box.

"No," he said, and glanced down at his wrist-watch. "Tell it again, from the beginning."

Burke repeated his story, ending with: "Suicide, then? I know he was feeling depressed about something."

McClane grunted.

"Forster was sleeping immediately before his turn of duty?"

"I imagine so." Burke smiled slightly, and McClane became aware that his eyes wandered. He couldn't seem to keep them off the wall. In a rack on the wall was the emergency winding handle for manual operation of the airlock—ideal for a blunt instrument, McClane thought professionally.

"You never opened the door of the power room after Forster went in?"

"I never went near it."

"A telepath could read your mind," McClane warned.

"In law, that's not legal evidence," Burke said promptly.

McClane began to dust the winding handle for prints.

"I've handled it recently," Burke admitted. "Routine test—you'll find it logged."

"Thought of everything, haven't you?"

Burke sneered. "You'll never convince a jury that I killed him. No human ever killed a telepath, that's axiomatic."

"After this," McClane said, "we'll be changing a few axioms."

"You have a theory?"

"I know how you did it, if that's what you mean. You over-looked one detail, and that's enough to send you to Curative."

Burke's eyes dilated. He held his breath.

"Bluff!"

McClane stared him down.

"You let down the shields and turned the chamber into a death-trap, while Forster was sleeping. You changed over the wiring so the lamp showed green and the door could be opened. He couldn't know what was in your mind until he woke… and then you were thinking of something quite different.

"You were thinking furiously of attacking him with the winding handle. A telepath fears one thing more than anything else—damage to his tendrils. That's worse than death for them, for they lose their faculty for thought transference.

"Forster got the one danger reading. A specific danger, over-riding all else, and he panicked. He ran for the security of the power room… and ran straight into a blast of radiation. Then you changed back the wiring and called us."

Burke licked his lips.

"That's nice," he said. "Tell me, what did I forget?"

"The door. You said twice that you never went near the power room and Forster died too fast to close it after him. You closed it. Only you *could* have closed it."

McClane laid a big hand on Burke.

"Let's go," he said.

P. D. James

P. D. James (1920–2014) will certainly be the best known crime-fiction writer in this volume, noted for her series featuring Inspector Dalgliesh who debuted in her first novel, Cover Her Face *(1962). The series ran to twelve books concluding with* The Murder Room *(2004). Rather surprisingly most of James's novels were runners-up rather than winners of both the Mystery Writers of America Edgar Award or the British Crime Writers Association Gold Dagger, but in 1987 she received the CWA's Diamond Dagger for Lifetime Achievement and the equivalent Grandmaster Award from the MWA in 1999. She was also awarded an OBE in 1983 and was created a Baroness in 1991—something not even Agatha Christie achieved.*

Readers might not immediately associate James with science fiction and, indeed, she argued that her novel Children of Men *(1992), in which all men become infertile and the human race is threatened with extinction, was not science fiction. The following story was written over twenty years earlier, in 1970, so her version of 1986 was still sixteen years in her future and deals with another virus which is wiping out humanity. In such a world, why would anyone commit murder?*

T HE GIRL LAY NAKED ON THE BED WITH A KNIFE THROUGH her heart. That was the one simple and inescapable fact. No, not simple. It was a fact horrible in its complications. Sergeant Dolby, fighting nausea, steadied his shaking thighs against the foot of the bed and forced his mind into coherence—arranging his thoughts in order, like a child piling brick on coloured brick and holding its breath against the inevitable tumble into chaos. He mustn't panic. He must take things slowly. There was a proper procedure laid down for this kind of crisis. There was a procedure laid down for everything.

Dead. That, at least, was certain. Despite the heat of the June morning the slim girlish body was quite cold, the rigor mortis already well advanced in face and arms. What had they taught him in Detective School about the onset of rigor mortis, that inexorable if erratic stiffening of the muscles, the body's last protest against disintegration and decay? He couldn't remember. He had never been any good at the more academic studies. He had been lucky to be accepted for the Criminal Investigation Department; they had made that clear enough to him at the time. They had never ceased to make it clear. A lost car; a small breaking and entering; a purse snatch. Send Dolby. He had never rated anything more interesting or important than the petty crimes of inadequate men. If it was something no one else wanted to be bothered with, send Dolby. If it was something the C.I.D. would rather not be told about, send Dolby.

And that was exactly how this death would rate. He would have to report it, of course. But it wouldn't be popular news at

Headquarters. They were overworked already, depleted in strength, inadequately equipped, forced even to employ him six years after his normal retirement age. No, they wouldn't exactly welcome this spot of trouble. And the reason, as if he didn't know it, was fixed there on the wall for him to read. The statutory notice was pasted precisely over the head of her bed.

He wondered why she had chosen that spot. There was no rule about where it had to be displayed. Why, he wondered, had she chosen to sleep under it as people once slept under a Crucifix. An affirmation? But the wording was the same as he would find on the notice in the downstairs hall, in the elevator, on every corridor wall, in every room in the Colony. The Act to which it referred was already two years old.

> PRESERVATION OF THE
> RACE ACT—1984
> Control of Interplanetary Disease
> Infection Carriers

> All registered carriers of the Disease, whether or not they are yet manifesting symptoms, are required under Section 2 of the above Act to conform to the following regulations...

He didn't need to read further. He knew the regulations by heart— the rules by which the Ipdics lived, if you could call it living. The desperate defence of the few healthy against the menace of the many condemned. The small injustices which might prevent the greatest injustice of all, the extinction of man. The stigmata of the Diseased: the registered number tattooed on the left forearm; the regulation Ipdic suit of yellow cotton in summer, blue serge in winter; the compulsory sterilization, since an Ipdic bred only monsters; the rule prohibiting marriage or any close contact with a Normal; the few manual jobs they were permitted to do; the registered Colonies where they were allowed to live.

He knew what they would say at Headquarters. If Dolby had to discover a murder, it would have to be of an Ipdic. And trust him to be fool enough to report it.

But there was no hurry. He could wait until he was calmer, until he could face with confidence whomever they chose to send. And there were things they would expect him to have noticed. He had better make an examination of the scene before he reported. Then, even if they came at once, he would have something sensible to say.

He forced himself to look again at the body. She was lying on her back, eyes closed as if asleep, light brown hair streaming over the pillow. Her arms were crossed over her chest as if in a last innocent gesture of modesty. Below the left breast the handle of a knife stuck out like an obscene horn.

He bent low to examine it. An ordinary handle, probably an ordinary knife. A short-bladed kitchen knife of the kind used to peel vegetables. Her right palm was curved around it, but not touching it, as if about to pluck it out. On her left forearm the registered Ipdic number glowed almost luminous against the delicate skin.

She was neatly covered by a single sheet pulled smooth and taut so that it looked as if the body had been ritually prepared for examination—an intensification of the horror. He did not believe that this childish hand could have driven in the blade with such precision or that, in her last spasms, she had drawn the sheet so tidily over her nakedness. The linen was only a shade whiter than her skin. There had been two months now of almost continuous sunshine. But this body had been muffled in the high-necked tunic and baggy trousers of an Ipdic suit. Only her face had been open to the sun. It was a delicate nut-brown and there was a faint spatter of freckles across the forehead.

He walked slowly around the room. It was sparsely furnished but pleasant enough. The world had no shortage of living space, even for Ipdics. They could live in comfort, even in some opulence, until the electricity, the television, the domestic computer, the micro-oven broke down. Then these things remained broken. The precious skills of electricians and engineers were not wasted on Ipdics. And it was extraordinary how quickly squalor could replace luxury.

A breakdown of electricity in a building like this could mean no hot food, no light, no heating. He had known Ipdics who had frozen or starved to death in apartments which, back in 1980, only six years ago, must have cost a fortune to rent. Somehow the will to survive died quickly in them. It was easier to wrap themselves in blankets and reach for that small white capsule so thoughtfully provided by the Government, the simple painless way out which the whole healthy community was willing for them to take.

But this girl, this female Ipdic PXN 07926431, wasn't living in squalor. The apartment was clean and almost obsessively neat. The micro-oven was out of order, but there was an old-fashioned electric cooker in the kitchen and when he turned it on the hot plate glowed red. There were even a few personal possessions—a little clutch of seashells carefully arranged on the window ledge, a Staffordshire porcelain figurine of a shepherdess, a child's tea service on a papier-mâché tray.

Her yellow Ipdic suit was neatly folded over the back of a chair. He took it up and saw that she had altered it to fit her. The darts under the breasts had been taken in, the side seams carefully shaped. The hand stitching was neat and regular, an affirmation of individuality, of self-respect. A proud girl. A girl undemoralized by hopelessness. He turned the harsh cotton over and over in his hands and felt the tears stinging the back of his eyes.

He knew that this strange and half-remembered sweetness was pity. He let himself feel it, willing himself not to shrink from the pain. Just so, in his boyhood, he had tentatively placed his full weight on an injured leg after football, relishing the pain in the knowledge that he could bear it, that he was still essentially whole.

But he must waste no more time. Turning on his pocket radio he made his report.

"Sergeant Dolby here. I'm speaking from Ipdic Colony 865. Female Ipdic PXN 07926431 found dead. Room 18. Looks like murder."

It was received as he had expected.

"Oh, God! Are you sure? All right. Hang around. Someone will be over."

While he waited he gave his attention to the flowers. They had struck his senses as soon as he opened the door of the room, but the first sight of the dead girl had driven them from his mind. Now he let their gentle presence drift back into his consciousness. She had died amid such beauty.

The apartment was a bower of wild flowers, their delicate sweetness permeating the warm air so that every breath was an intimation of childhood summers, an evocation of the old innocent days. Wild flowers were his hobby. The slow brain corrected itself, patiently, mechanically: wild flowers had been his hobby. But that was before the Sickness, when the words flower and beauty seemed to have meaning. He hadn't looked at a flower with any joy since 1980.

1980. The year of the Disease. The year with the hottest summer for 21 years. That summer when the sheer weight of people had pressed against the concrete bastions of the city like an intolerable force, had thronged its burning pavements, had almost brought its transport system to a stop, had sprawled in chequered ranks across its parks until the sweet grass was pressed into pale straw.

1980. The year when there were too many people. Too many happy, busy, healthy human beings. The year when his wife had been alive; when his daughter Tessa had been alive. The year when brave men, travelling far beyond the moon, had brought back to earth the Sickness—the Sickness which had decimated mankind on every continent of the globe. The Sickness which had robbed him, Arthur Dolby, of his wife and daughter.

Tessa. She had been only 14 that spring. It was a wonderful age for a daughter, the sweetest daughter in the world. And Tessa had been intelligent as well as sweet. Both women in his life, his wife and daughter, had been cleverer than Dolby. He had known it, but it hadn't worried him or made him feel inadequate. They had loved him so unreservedly, had relied so much on his manhood, been so satisfied with what little he could provide. They had seen in him qualities he could never discern in himself, virtues which he knew he no longer possessed. His flame of life was meagre; it had needed their warm breaths to keep it burning bright. He wondered what they would think of him now. Arthur Dolby in 1986, looking once more at wild flowers.

He moved among them as if in a dream, like a man recognizing with wonder a treasure given up for lost. There had been no attempt at formal arrangement. She had obviously made use of any suitable container in the apartment and had bunched the plants together naturally and simply, each with its own kind. He could still identify them. There were brown earthenware jars of Herb Robert, the rose-pink flowers set delicately on their reddish stems. There were cracked teacups holding bunches of red clover meadow buttercups, and long-stemmed daisies; jam jars of white campion and cuckoo flowers; egg cups of birdsfoot trefoil—"eggs and bacon," Tessa used to call it—and even smaller jars of rue-leaved saxifrage and the soft pink spurs of haresfoot. But, above all, there were the tall vases of cow-parsley, huge bunches of strong hollow-grooved stems supporting their umbels of white flowers, delicate as bridal lace, yet pungent and strong, shedding a white dust on the table, bed, and floor.

And then, in the last jar of all, the only one which held a posy of mixed flowers, he saw the Lady Orchid. It took his breath away. There it stood, alien and exotic, lifting its sumptuous head proudly among the common flowers of the roadside, the white clover, campion, and sweet wild roses. The Lady Orchid. *Orchis Purpurea*.

He stood very still and gazed at it. The decorative spike rose from its shining foliage, elegant and distinctive, seeming to know its rarity. The divisions of the helmet were wine-red, delicately veined and spotted with purple, their sombre tint setting off the clear white beauty of the lip. The Lady Orchid. Dolby knew of only one spot, the fringe of a wood in old Kent County in the Southeast Province, where this flower grew wild. The Sickness had changed the whole of human life. But he doubted if it had changed that.

It was then that he heard the roar of the helicopter. He went to the window. The red machine, like a huge angry insect, was just bouncing down onto the roof landing pad. He watched, puzzled. Why should they send a chopper? Then he understood. The tall figure in the all-white uniform with its gleaming braid swung himself down from the cockpit and was lost to view behind the parapet of the roof. But Dolby recognized at once that helmet of black hair, the confident poise of the head. C. J. Kalvert. The Commissioner of the Home Security Force in person.

He told himself that it couldn't be true—that Kalvert wouldn't concern himself with the death of an Ipdic, that he must have some other business in the Colony. But what business? Dolby waited in fear, his hands clenched so that the nails pierced his palms, waited in an agony of hope that it might not be true. But it was true. A minute later he heard the strong footsteps advancing along the corridor. The door opened. The Commissioner had arrived.

He nodded an acknowledgement to Dolby and, without speaking, went over to the bed. For a moment he stood in silence, looking down at the girl. Then he said, "How did you get in, Sergeant?"

The accent was on the third word.

"The door was unlocked, sir."

"Naturally. Ipdics are forbidden to lock their doors. I was asking what you were doing here."

"I was making a search, sir."

That at least was true. He had been making a private search.

"And you discovered that one more female Ipdic had taken the sensible way out of her troubles. Why didn't you call the Sanitary Squad? It's unwise to leave a body longer than necessary in this weather. Haven't we all had enough of the stench of decay?"

"I think she was murdered, sir."

"Do you indeed, Sergeant. And why?"

Dolby moistened his dry lips and made his cramped fingers relax. He mustn't let himself be intimidated, mustn't permit himself to get flustered. The important thing was to stick to the facts and present them cogently.

"It's the knife, sir. If she were going to stab herself, I think she would have fallen on the blade, letting her weight drive it in. Then the body would have been found face downwards. That way, the blade would have done all the work. I don't think she would have had the strength or the skill to pierce her heart lying in that position. It looks almost surgical. It's too neat. The man who drove that knife in knew what he was doing. And then there's the sheet. She couldn't have placed it over herself so neatly."

"A valid point, Sergeant. But the fact that someone considerately tidied her up after death doesn't necessarily mean that he killed her. Anything else?"

He was walking restlessly about the room as he talked, touching nothing, his hands clasped behind his back. Dolby wished that he would stand still. He said, "But why use a knife at all, sir? She must have been issued her euthanasia capsule."

"Not a very dramatic way to go, Dolby. The commonest door for an Ipdic to let life out. She may have exercised a feminine preference for a more individualistic death. Look around this room, Sergeant. Does she strike you as having been an ordinary girl?"

No, she hadn't struck Dolby as ordinary. But this was ground he dare not tread. He said doggedly, "And why should she be naked, sir? Why take all her clothes off to kill herself?"

"Why, indeed. That shocks you, does it, Dolby? It implies an unpleasant touch of exhibitionism. It offends your modesty. But perhaps she was an exhibitionist. The flowers would suggest it. She made her room into a bower of fragrance and beauty. Then, naked, as unencumbered as the flowers, she stretched herself out like a sacrifice, and drove a knife through her heart. Can you, Sergeant, with your limited imagination, understand that a woman might wish to die like that?"

Kalvert swung round and strode over to him. The fierce black eyes burned into Dolby's. The Sergeant felt frightened, at a loss. The conversation was bizarre. He felt they were playing some private game, but that only one of them knew the rules.

What did Kalvert want of him? In a normal world, in the world before the Sickness when the old police force was at full strength, the Commissioner wouldn't even have known that Dolby existed.

Yet here they both were, engaged, it seemed, in some private animus, sparring over the body of an unimportant dead Ipdic.

It was very hot in the room now and the scent of the flowers had been growing stronger. Dolby could feel the beads of sweat on his brow. Whatever happened he must hold on to the facts. He said, "The flowers needn't be funeral flowers. Perhaps they were for a celebration."

"That would suggest the presence of more than one person Even Ipdics don't celebrate alone. Have you found any evidence that someone was with her when she died?"

He wanted to reply, "Only the knife in her breast." But he was silent. Kalvert was pacing the room again. Suddenly he stopped and glanced at his watch. Then, without speaking, he turned on the television. Dolby remembered. Of course. The Leader was due to speak after the midday news. It was already 12:32. He would be almost finished.

The screen flickered and the too familiar face appeared. The Leader looked very tired. Even the make-up artist hadn't been able to disguise the heavy shadows under the eyes or the hollows beneath the cheekbones. With that beard and the melancholy, pain-filled face, he looked like an ascetic prophet. But he always had. His face hadn't changed much since the days of his student protest. People said that, even then, he had only really been interested in personal power. Well, he was still under thirty, but he had it now. All the power he could possibly want. The speech was nearly over.

"And so we must find our own solution. We have a tradition in this country of humanity and justice. But how far can we let tradition hamper us in the great task of preserving our race? We know what is happening in other countries, the organized and ceremonial mass suicides of thousands of Ipdics at a time, the humane Disposal Squads, the compulsory matings between computer-selected Normals. Some compulsory measures against the Ipdics we must now take. As far as possible we have relied on gentle and voluntary methods. But can we afford to fall behind while other less scrupulous nations are breeding faster and more selectively, disposing of their Ipdics, re-establishing their technology, looking with covetous eyes at the great denuded spaces of the world. One day they will be repopulated. It is our duty to take part in this great process. The world needs our race. The time has come for every one of us, particularly our Ipdics, to ask ourselves with every breath we draw: have I the right to be alive?"

Kalvert turned off the set.

"I think we can forego the pleasure of seeing once again Mrs. Sartori nursing her fifth healthy daughter. Odd to think that the most valuable human being in the world is a healthy fecund female. But you got the message I hope, Sergeant. This Ipdic had the wisdom to take her own way out while she still had a choice. And if somebody helped her, who are we to quibble?"

"It was still murder, sir. I know that killing an Ipdic isn't a capital crime. But the Law hasn't been altered yet. It's still a felony to kill any human being."

"Ah, yes. A felony. And you, of course, are dedicated to the detection and punishment of felonies. The first duty of a policeman is to prevent crime; the second is to detect and punish the criminal. You learned all that when you were in Detective School, didn't you? Learned it all by heart. I remember reading the first report on you, Dolby. It was almost identical with the last. 'Lacking in initiative. Deficient in imagination. Tends to make errors of judgment. Should make a reliable subordinate. Lacks self-confidence.' But it did admit that, when you manage to get an idea into your head, it sticks there. And you have an idea in your head. Murder. And murder is a felony. Well, what do you propose to do about it?"

"In cases of murder the body is first examined by the forensic pathologist."

"Not this body, Dolby. Do you know how many pathologists this country now has? We have other uses for them than to cut up dead Ipdics. She was a young female. She was not pregnant. She was stabbed through the heart. What more do we need to know?"

"Whether or not a man was with her before she died."

"I think you can take it there was. Male Ipdics are not yet being sterilized. So we add another fact. She probably had a lover. What else do you want to know?"

"Whether or not there are prints on the knife, sir, and, if so, whose they are."

Kalvert laughed aloud. "We were short of forensic scientists before the Sickness. How many do you suppose we have now? There was another case of capital murder reported this morning. An Ipdic has killed his former wife because she obeyed the Law and kept away from him. We can't afford to lose a single healthy woman, can we, Dolby? There's the rumour of armed bands of Ipdics roaming the Southeast Province. There's the case of the atomic scientist with the back of his skull smashed in. A scientist, Dolby! Now, do you really want to bother the lab with this petty trouble?"

Dolby said obstinately, "I know that someone was with her when she picked the flowers. That must have been yesterday— they're still fresh even in this heat, and wild flowers fade quickly. I think he probably came back here with her and was with her when she died."

"Then find him, Sergeant, if you must. But don't ask for help I can't give."

He walked over to the door without another glance at the room or at the dead girl, as if neither of them held any further interest for him. Then he turned: "You aren't on the official list of men encouraged to breed daughters in the interest of the race, are you, Sergeant?"

Dolby wanted to reply that he once had a daughter. She was dead and he wanted no other.

"No, sir. They thought I was too old. And then there was the adverse psychologist's report."

"A pity. One would have thought that the brave new world could have made room for just one or two people who were unintelligent, lacking in imagination, unambitious, inclined to errors of judgment. People will persist in going their own obstinate way. Goodbye, Dolby. Report to me personally on this case, will you? I shall be interested to hear how you progress. Who knows, you may reveal unsuspected talents."

He was gone. Dolby waited for a minute as if to cleanse his mind of that disturbing presence. As the confident footsteps died away, even the room seemed to settle itself into peace. Then Dolby began the few tasks which still remained.

They weren't many. First, he took the dead girl's fingerprints. He worked with infinite care, murmuring to her as he gently pressed the pad against each fingertip, like a doctor reassuring a child. It would be pointless, he thought, to compare them with the prints on any of the ordinary objects in the room. That would prove nothing except that another person had been there. The only prints of importance would be those on the knife. But there were no prints on the knife—only an amorphous smudge of whorls and composites as if someone had attempted to fold her hand around the shaft but had lacked the courage to press the fingers firm.

But the best clue was still there—the Lady Orchid, splendid in its purity and beauty, the flower which told him where she had spent the previous day, the flower which might lead him to the man

who had been with her. And there was another clue, something
he had noticed when he had first examined the body closely. He
had said nothing to Kalvert. Perhaps Kalvert hadn't noticed it or
hadn't recognized its significance. Perhaps he had been cleverer
than Kalvert. He told himself that he wasn't really as stupid as
people sometimes thought. It was just that his mind was so easily
flustered into incoherence when stronger men bullied or taunted
him. Only his wife and daughter had really understood that, had
given him the confidence to fight it.

It was time to get started. They might deny him the services
of the pathologist and the laboratory, but they still permitted him
the use of his car. It would be little more than an hour's drive.

But, before leaving, he bent once more over the body. The
Disposal Squad would soon be here for it. He would never see it
again. So he studied the clue for the last time—the faint, almost
imperceptible circle of paler skin round the third finger of her left
hand. The finger that could have worn a ring through the whole
of a hot summer day…

He drove through the wide streets and sun-filled squares,
through the deserted suburbs, until the tentacles of the city fell
away and he was in open country. The roads were pitted and un-
mended, the hedges high and unkempt, the fields a turbulent sea
of vegetation threatening to engulf the unpeopled farmlands.
But the sun was pleasant on his face. He could almost persuade
himself that this was one of the old happy jaunts into the familiar
and well-loved countryside of Old Kent.

He had crossed the boundary into the Southeast Province and
was already looking for the remembered landmarks of hillside and
church spire when it happened. There was an explosion, a crack
like a pistol shot, and the windshield shattered in his face. He felt
splinters of glass stinging his cheeks. Instinctively he guarded his

face with his arms. The car swerved out of control and lurched onto the grass verge. He felt for the ignition key and turned off the engine. Then he tentatively opened his eyes. They were uninjured. And it was then he saw the Ipdics.

They came out of the opposite ditch and moved toward him, with stones still in their hands. There were half a dozen of them. One, the tallest, seemed to be their leader. The others shuffled at his heels, lumpy figures in their ill-fitting yellow suits, their feet brown and bare, their hair matted like animals', their greedy eyes fixed on the car. They stood still, looking at him. And then the leader drew his right hand from behind his back, and Dolby saw that it held a gun.

His heart missed a beat. So it was true! Somehow the Ipdics were getting hold of weapons. He got out of the car, trying to recall the exact instructions of such an emergency. Never show fear. Keep calm. Exert authority. Remember that they are inferior, unorganized, easily cowed. Never drop your eyes. But his voice, even to him, sounded feeble, pitched unnaturally high.

"The possession of a weapon by an Ipdic is a capital crime. The punishment is death. Give me that gun."

The voice that replied was quiet, authoritative, the kind of voice one used to call educated.

"No. First you give me the keys to the car. Then I give you something in return. A cartridge in your belly!"

His followers cackled their appreciation. It was one of the most horrible sounds in the world—the laughter of an Ipdic.

The Ipdic pointed the gun at Dolby, moving it slowly from side to side as if selecting his precise target. He was enjoying his power, drunk with elation and triumph. But he waited a second too long. Suddenly his arm jerked upward, the gun leaped from his grasp, and he gave one high desolate scream, falling into the dust of the road. He was in the first spasm of an Ipdic fit. His body writhed and twisted, arched and contracted, until the bones could be heard snapping.

Dolby looked on impassively. There was nothing he could do. He had seen it thousands of times before. It had happened to his wife, to Tessa, to all those who had died of the disease. It happened in the end to every Ipdic. It would have happened to that girl on the bed, at peace now with a knife in her heart.

The attack would leave this Ipdic broken and exhausted. If he survived, he would be a mindless idiot, probably for months. And then the fits would come more frequently. It was this feature of the Disease which made the Ipdics so impossible to train or employ, even for the simplest of jobs.

Dolby walked up to the writhing figure and kicked away the gun, then picked it up. It was a revolver, a Smith and Wesson .38, old but in good condition. He saw that it was loaded. After a second's thought he slipped it into the pocket of his jacket.

The remaining Ipdics had disappeared, scrambling back into the hedges with cries of anguish and fear. The whole incident was over so quickly that it already seemed like a dream. Only the tortured figure in the dust and the cold metal in his pocket were witnesses to its reality. He should report it at once, of course. The suppression of armed Ipdics was the first duty of the Home Security Force.

He backed the car onto the road. Then, on an impulse, he got out again and went over to the Ipdic. He bent to drag the writhing figure off the road and into the shade of the hedge. But it was no good. Revolted, he drew back. He couldn't bear to touch him. Perhaps the Ipdic's friends would creep back later to carry him away and tend to him. Perhaps. But he, Dolby, had his own problem. He had a murder to solve.

Fifteen minutes later he drove slowly through the village. The main street was deserted but he could glimpse, through the open cottage doors, the garish yellow of an Ipdic suit moving in the dim interior and he could see other yellow-clad figures bending at work in the gardens and fields. None of them looked up as he passed. He guessed that this was one of the settlements which had grown up in the country, where groups of Ipdics attempted to support themselves and each other, growing their own food, nursing their sick, burying their dead. Since they made no demands on the Normals they were usually left in peace. But it couldn't last long. There was no real hope for them.

As more and more of them were overtaken by the last inevitable symptoms, the burden on those left grew intolerable. Soon they too would be helpless and mad. Then the Security Force, the Health Authorities, and the Sanitary Squads would move in, and another colony of the dispossessed would be cleaned up. And it was a question of cleaning up. Dolby had taken part in one such operation. He knew what the final horror would be. But now in the heat of this sun-scented afternoon, he might be driving through the village as he had known it in the days before the Sickness, prosperous, peaceful, sleepy, with the men still busy on the farms.

He left the car at the churchyard gate and slipping the strap of his murder bag over his shoulder, walked up the dappled avenue of elms to the south entrance. The heavy oak door with its carved panels, its massive hinges of hammered iron creaked open at his touch. He stepped into the cool dimness and smelled again the familiar scent of flowers, musty hymn books, and wood polish, saw once again the medieval pillars soaring high to the hammer beams of the roof, and, straining his eyes through the dimness he glimpsed the carving on the rood screen and the far gleam of the sanctuary lamp.

The church was full of wild flowers. They were the same flowers as those in the dead girl's apartment but here their frail delicacy was almost lost against the massive pillars and the richly carved oak. But the huge vases of cow-parsley set on each side of the chancel steps made a brave show, floating like twin clouds of whiteness in the dim air. It was a church decked for a bride.

He saw a female Ipdic polishing the brass lectern. He made his way up the aisle toward her and she beamed a gentle welcome as if his appearance were the most ordinary event in the world. Her baggy Ipdic suit was stained with polish and she wore a pair of old sandals, the soles peeling away from the uppers. Her greying hair was drawn back into a loose bun from which wisps of hair had escaped to frame the anxious, sun-stained face.

She reminded him of someone. He let his mind probe once again, painfully, into the past. Then he remembered. Of course, Miss Caroline Martin, his Sunday School superintendent. It wasn't she, of course. Miss Martin would have been over 70 at the time of the Sickness. No one as old as that had survived, except those few Tasmanian aborigines who so interested the scientists. Miss Martin, standing beside the old piano as her younger sister thumped out the opening hymn and beating time with her gloved hand as if hearing some private and quite different music. Afterward, the students had gone to their different classes and had sat in a circle around their teachers. Miss Martin had taught the older children, himself among them. Some of the boys had been unruly, but never Arthur Dolby. Even in those days he had been obedient, law-abiding. The good boy. Not particularly bright, but well-behaved. Good, dull, ineffectual. Teacher's pet.

And when she spoke it was with a voice like Miss Martin's.

"Can I help you? If you've come for Evensong services, I'm afraid it isn't until five thirty today. If you're looking for Father

Reeves, he's at the Rectory. But perhaps you're just a visitor. It's a lovely church, isn't it? Have you seen our sixteenth-century reredos?"

"I hoped I would be in time for the wedding."

She gave a little girlish cry of laughter.

"Dear me, you are late! I'm afraid that was yesterday! But I thought no one was supposed to know about it. Father Reeves said that it was to be quite secret really. But I'm afraid I was very naughty. I did so want to see the bride. After all, we haven't had a wedding here since—"

"Since the Act?"

She corrected him gently, like Miss Martin rebuking the good boy of the class.

"Since 1980. So yesterday was quite an occasion for us. And I did want to see what the bride looked like in Emma's veil."

"In what?"

"A bride has to have a veil, you know." She spoke with gentle reproof, taking pity on his masculine ignorance. "Emma was my niece. I lost her and her parents in 1981. Emma was the last bride to be married here. That was on April 28, 1980. I've always kept her veil and headdress. She was such a lovely bride."

Dolby asked with sudden harshness the irrelevant but necessary question.

"What happened to her bridegroom?"

"Oh, John was one of the lucky ones. I believe he has married again and has three daughters. Just one daughter more and they'll be allowed to have a son. We don't see him, of course. It wasn't to be expected. After all, it is the Law."

How despicable it was, this need to be reassured that there were other traitors.

"Yes," he said. "It is the Law." She began polishing the already burnished lectern, chatting to him as she worked.

"But I've kept Emma's veil and headdress. So I thought I'd just place them on a chair beside the font so that this new bride would see them when she came into church. Just in case she wanted to borrow them, you know. And she did. I was so glad. The bridegroom placed the veil over her head and fixed the headdress for her himself, and she walked up the aisle looking so beautiful."

"Yes," said Dolby. "She would have looked very beautiful."

"I watched them from behind this pillar. Neither of them noticed me. But it was right for me to be here. There ought to be someone in the church. It says in the prayer book, 'In the sight of God and of this congregation.' She had a small bouquet of wild flowers, just a simple mixed bunch but very charming. I think they must have picked it together."

"She carried a Lady Orchid," said Dolby. "A Lady Orchid picked by her bridegroom and surrounded by daisies, clover, white campion, and wild roses."

"How clever of you to guess! Are you a friend, perhaps?"

"No," said Dolby. "Not a friend. Can you describe the bridegroom?"

"I thought that you must know him. Very tall, very dark. He wore a plain white suit. Oh, they were such a handsome couple! I wished Father Reeves could have seen them."

"I thought he married them."

"So he did. But Father Reeves, poor man, is blind."

So that was why he risked it, thought Dolby. But what a risk!

"Which prayer book did he use?"

She gazed at him, the milky eyes perplexed. "Father Reeves?"

"No, the bridegroom. He did handle a prayer book, I suppose?"

"Oh, yes. I put one out for each of them. Father Reeves asked me to get things ready. It was I who decorated the church. Poor dears, it wasn't as if they could have the usual printed service sheets. Emma's were so pretty, her initials intertwined with the bridegroom's. But yesterday they had to use ordinary prayer books. I chose them specially from the pews and put them on the two prayer stools. I found a very pretty white one for the bride and this splendid old book with the brass clasp for the bridegroom. It looked masculine, I thought."

It lay on the book ledge of the front pew. She made a move to pick it up, but he shot out his hand. Then he dropped his handkerchief over the book and lifted it by the sharp edges of the binding. Brass and leather. Good for a print. And this man's palm would be moist, clammy, perhaps, with perspiration and fear. A hot day; an illegal ceremony; his mind on murder. To love and to cherish until death us do part. Yes, this bridegroom would have been nervous. But Dolby had one more question.

"How did they get here? Do you know?"

"They came by foot. At least, they walked up to the church together. I think they had walked quite a long way. They were quite hot and dusty when they arrived. But I know how they really came."

She nodded her unkempt head and gave a little conspiratorial nod.

"I've got very good ears, you know. They came by helicopter. I heard it."

A helicopter. He knew almost without thinking exactly who was permitted the use of a helicopter. Members of the Central Committee of Government; high ranking scientists and technicians; doctors; the Commissioner of the Home Security Force, and his Deputy. That was all.

He took the prayer book out into the sun and sat on one of the flat-topped gravestones. He set up the prayer book on its end, then unzipped his murder bag. His hands shook so that he could hardly manage the brush and some of the grey powder was spilt and blew away in the breeze. He willed himself to keep calm, to take his time. Carefully, like a child with a new toy, he dusted the book and clasp with powder, gently blowing off the surplus with a small rubber nozzle. It was an old procedure, first practised when he was a young Detective Constable. But it still worked. It always would. The arches, whorls, and composites came clearly into view.

He was right. It was a beautiful print. The man had made no effort to wipe it clean. Why should he? How could he imagine that this particular book would ever be identified among the many scattered around the church? How could he suspect that he would ever be traced to this despised and unregarded place? Dolby took out his camera and photographed the print. There must be continuity of evidence. He must leave no room for doubt. Then he classified its characteristics, ready for checking.

There was a little delay at the National Identification Computer Center when he phoned, and he had to wait his turn. When it came he gave his name, rank, secret code, and the classification of the print. There was a moment's silence. Then a surprised voice asked, "Is that you, Dolby? Will you confirm your code."

He did so. Another silence.

"Okay. But what on earth are you up to? Are you sure of your print classification?"

"Yes. I want the identification for elimination purposes."

"Then you can eliminate, all right. That's the Commissioner. Kalvert, C. J. Hard luck, Dolby! Better start again."

He switched off the receiver and sat in silence. He had known it, of course. But for how long? Perhaps from the beginning. Kalvert. Kalvert, who had an excuse for visiting an Ipdic Colony. Kalvert, who had the use of a helicopter. Kalvert, who had known without asking that the television set in her room was in working order. Kalvert, who had been too sure of himself to take the most elementary precautions against discovery, because he knew that it didn't matter, because he knew no one would dare touch him. Kalvert, one of the four most powerful men in the country. And it was he, the despised Sergeant Dolby, who had solved the case.

He heard the angry purr of the approaching helicopter without surprise. He had reported the armed attack by the Ipdics. It was certain that Headquarters would have immediately summoned a Squad from the nearest station to hunt them down. But Kalvert would know about the message. He had no doubt that the Commissioner was keeping a watch on him. He would know which way Dolby was heading, would realize that he was dangerously close to the truth. The armed Squad would be here in time. But Kalvert would arrive first.

He waited for five minutes, still sitting quietly on the gravestone. The air was sweet with the smell of grasses and vibrating with the high-treble midsummer chant of blackbird and thrush. He shut his eyes for a moment, breathing in the beauty, taking courage from its peace. Then he got to his feet and stood at the head of the avenue of elms to wait for Kalvert.

The gold braid on the all-white uniform gleamed in the sun. The tall figure, arrogant with confidence and power, walked unhesitatingly toward him, unsmiling, making no sign. When they were three feet apart, Kalvert stopped. They stood confronting each other. It was Dolby who spoke first. His voice was little more than a whisper.

"You killed her."

He could not meet Kalvert's eyes. But he heard his reply.

"Yes, I killed her. Shall I tell you about it, Sergeant? You seem to have shown some initiative. You deserve to know part of the truth. I was her friend. That is prohibited by Regulation. She became my mistress. That is against the Law. We decided to get married. That is a serious crime. I killed her. That, as you earlier explained, is a felony. And what are you going to do about it, Sergeant?"

Dolby couldn't speak. Suddenly he took out the revolver. It seemed ridiculous to point it at Kalvert. He wasn't even sure that he would be able to fire it. But he held it close to his side and the curved stock fitted comfortably to his palm, giving him courage. He made himself meet Kalvert's eyes, and heard the Commissioner laugh.

"To kill a Normal is also against the Law. But it's something more. Capital murder, Dolby. Is that what you have in mind?"

Dolby spoke out of cracked lips, "But why? *Why?*"

"I don't have to explain to you. But I'll try. Have you the imagination to understand that we might have loved each other, that I might have married her because it seemed a small risk for me and would give her pleasure, that I might have promised to kill her when her last symptoms began? Can you, Sergeant Dolby, enter into the mind of a girl like that? She was an Ipdic. And she was more alive in her condemned cell than you have ever been in your life. Female Ipdic PXN 07926431 found dead. Looks like murder. Remember how you reported it, Dolby? A felony. Something to be investigated. Against the Law. That's all it meant to you, isn't it?"

He had taken out his own revolver now. He held it easily, like a man casually dangling a familiar toy. He stood there, magnificent in the sunshine, the breeze lifting his black hair. He said quietly, "Do you think I'd let any Law on earth keep me from the woman I loved?"

Dolby wanted to cry out that it hadn't been like that at all. That Kalvert didn't understand. That he, Dolby, had cared about the girl. But the contempt in those cold black eyes kept him silent.

There was nothing they could say to each other. Nothing. And Kalvert would kill him.

The Squad would be here soon. Kalvert couldn't let him live to tell his story. He gazed with fascinated horror at the revolver held so easily, so confidently, in the Commissioner's hand. And he tightened the grip on his own, feeling with a shaking finger for the trigger.

The armoured car roared up to the churchyard gate. The Squad were here. Kalvert lifted his revolver to replace it in the holster. Dolby, misunderstanding the gesture, whipped up his own gun and, closing his eyes, fired until the last cartridge was spent. Numbed by misery and panic, he didn't hear the shots or the thud of Kalvert's fall. The first sound to pierce his consciousness was a wild screaming and beating of wings as the terrified birds flew high. Then he was aware of an unnatural silence, and of an acrid smell tainting the summer air.

His right hand ached. It felt empty, slippery with sweat. He saw that he had dropped the gun. There was a long mournful cry of distress. It came from behind him. He turned and glimpsed the yellow-clad figure of the female Ipdic, hand to her mouth, watching him from the shadow of the church. Then she faded back into the dimness.

He dropped on his knees beside Kalvert. The torn arteries were pumping their blood onto the white tunic. The crimson stain burst open like a flower. Dolby took off his jacket with shaking hands and thrust it under Kalvert's head. He wanted to say that he was sorry, to cry out like a child that he hadn't really meant it, that it was all a mistake.

Kalvert looked at him. Was there really pity in those dulling eyes? He was trying to speak. "Poor Dolby! Your final error of judgment."

The last word was hiccupped in a gush of blood. Kalvert turned his head away from Dolby and drew up his knees as if easing himself into sleep. And Dolby knew that it was too late to explain now, that there was no one there to hear him.

He stood up. The Squad were very close now, three of them, walking abreast, guns at hip, moving inexorably forward in the pool of their own shadows. And so he waited, all fear past, with Kalvert's body at his feet. And he thought for the last time of his daughter. Tessa, whom he had allowed to hide from him because that was the Law. Tessa, whom he had deserted and betrayed. Tessa, whom he had sought at last, but had found too late. Tessa, who had led him unwittingly to her lover and murderer. Tessa who would never have picked that Lady Orchid. Hadn't he taught her when she was a child that if you pick a wild orchid it can never bloom again?

APPLE

Anne McCaffrey

Anne McCaffrey (1926–2011) is best known for her highly popular series set on the planet Pern. This began with the award-winning novella "Weyr Search" (1967) incorporated into the first novel Dragonflight *(1968). Because of dragons, the series is often thought of as fantasy, but it is far from that. Humans have colonized a planet where the predominant fauna are dragon-like beings which form a close telepathic, almost symbiotic bond with the colonists. The Pern series would eventually run to over twenty books, some written with or by her son Todd McCaffrey, and they have rather overshadowed her other work.*

Her interest in telepathy and other psi powers caused her to wonder what a society would be like when many individuals had such abilities and whether they would need to be monitored, or even policed. She first explored this in the following story in 1969 and it was later reworked into the first book of what became known as the Talents series, To Ride Pegasus *(1973). Rather than be persecuted it was realized how those with psychic abilities could benefit humanity and this was further explored in* Pegasus in Flight *(1990) and* Pegasus in Space *(2000). McCaffrey also created a spin-off series named after the first book,* The Rowan *(1990) which further explored the benefits and problems arising from telepaths and other psi-talented individuals in society.*

T HE THEFT WAS THE LEAD MORNING-'CAST AND RUINED Daffyd op Owen's appetite. As he listened to the description of the priceless sable coat, the sapphire necklace, the couture-model gown, and the jewel-strap slippers, he felt as if he were congealing in his chair as his breakfast cooled and hardened on the plate. He waited, numbed, for the commentator to make the obvious conclusion: a conclusion which would destroy all that the North American Parapsychic Center had achieved so slowly, so delicately. For the only way in which such valuable items could have been removed from a store dummy in a scanned, warded, very public display window in the five-minute period between the fixed TV frames was by kinetic energy.

"The police have several leads and expect to have a solution by evening. Commissioner Frank Gillings is taking charge of the investigation.

"'I keep my contractual obligations to the City,' Gillings is reported to have told the press early this morning as he person-ally supervised the examination of the display window at Coles, Michaels' and Charny Department Store. 'I have reduced street and consensual crimes and contained riot activity. Jerhattan is a safe place for the law-abiding. Unsafe for law-breakers.'"

The back-shot of Gillings' stern face was sufficient to break op Owen's stasis. He rose and strode toward the com-unit just as it beeped.

"Daffyd, you heard that 'cast?" The long, unusually grim face of Lester Welch appeared on the screen. "Goddammit, they promised no premature announcement. Mediamen!" His expression boded ill for the first unwary reporter to approach him. Over Les's shoulder, op Owen could see the equally savage face of Charlie Moorfield, duty officer of the control room of the Center.

"How long have *you* known about the theft?" Op Owen couldn't quite keep the reprimand from his voice. Les had a habit of trying to spare his superior, particularly these days when he knew op Owen had been spreading himself very thin in the intensive public educational campaign.

"Ted Lewis snuck in a cautious advice as soon as Headquarters scanned the disappearance. He also can't 'find' a thing. And, Dave, there wasn't a wrinkle or a peak between 7:03 and 7:08 on any graph that shouldn't be there, with every single Talent accounted for!"

"That's right, boss," Charlie added. "Not a single Incident to account for the kinetic 'lift' needed for the heist."

"Gillings is on his way here," said Les, screwing his face up with indignation.

"Why?" Daffyd op Owen exploded. "Didn't Ted clear us?"

"Christ, yes, but Gillings has been at Coles and his initial investigation proves conclusively to him that one of our people is a larcenist. One of our women, to be precise, with a secret yen for sable, silk, and sapphires."

Daffyd forced himself to nullify the boiling anger he felt. He could not afford to cloud reason with emotion. Not with so much at stake. Not with the Bill which would provide legal protection for Talents only two weeks away from passing.

"You'll never believe me, will you, Dave," Les said, "that the Talented will always be suspect?"

"Gillings has never cavilled at the use of Talents, Lester."

"He'd be a goddamned fool if he did." Lester's eyes sparkled angrily. He jabbed at his chest. "*We've* kept street and consensual crime low. Talent did his job for him. And now he's out to nail us. With publicity like this, we'll never get that Bill through. Christ, what luck! Two bloody weeks away from protection."

"If there's no Incident on the graphs, Les, even Gillings must admit to our innocence."

Welch rolled his eyes heavenward. "How can you be so naive, Dave? No matter what our remotes prove, that heist was done by a Talent."

"Not one of ours." Daffyd op Owen could be dogmatic, too.

"Great. Prove it to Gillings. He's on his way here now and he's out to get us. We've all but ruined his spotless record of enforcement and protection. That hits his credit, monetary and personal." Lester paused for a quick breath. "I told you that public education programme would cause more trouble than it's worth. Let me cancel the morning 'cast."

"No." Daffyd closed his eyes wearily. He didn't need to resume that battle with Les now. In spite of this disastrous development, he was convinced of the necessity of the campaign. The general public must learn that they had nothing to fear from those gifted with a parapsychic Talent. The series of public information programmes, so carefully planned, served several vital purposes: to show how the many facets of Talent served the community's best interests; to identify those peculiar traits that indicated the possession of a Talent; and, most important, to gain public support for the Bill in the Senate which would give Talents professional immunity in the exercise of their various duties.

"I haven't a vestige of Talent, Dave," Les went on urgently, "but I don't need it to guess some dissident in the common mass of have-nots listened to every word of those 'casts and put what you should never have aired to good use... for him. And don't comfort me with how many happy clods have obediently tripped up to the

Clinic to have their minor Talents identified. One renegade apple's all you need to sour the barrel!"

"Switch the 'cast to the standard recruiting tape. To pull the whole series would be worse. I'm coming right over."

Daffyd op Owen looked down at the blank screen for a long moment, gathering strength. It was no pre-cog that this would be a very difficult day. Strange, he mused, that no pre-cog had fore-seen this. No. *That* very omission indicated a wild Talent, acting on the spur of impulse. What was it Les had said? 'The common mass of have-nots'? Even with the basic dignities of food, shelter, clothing, and education guaranteed, the appetite of the have-not was continually whetted by the abundance that was not his. In this case, hers. Daffyd op Owen groaned. If only such a Talent had been moved to come to the Center where she could be trained and used. (Where had their so carefully worded programming slipped up?) She could have had the furs, the jewels, the dresses on overt purchase... and enjoyed them openly. The Center was well enough endowed to satisfy any material yearning of its members. Surely Gillings would admit that.

Op Owen took a deep breath and exhaled regret and supposi-tion. He must keep his mind clear, his sensitivities honed for any nuance that would point a direction toward success.

As he left his shielded quarters at the back of the Center's extensive grounds, he was instantly aware of tension in the atmos-phere. Most Talented persons preferred to live in the Center, in the specially shielded buildings that reduced the "noise" of constant psychic agitation. The Center preferred to have them here, as much to protect as to help their members. Talent was a double-edged sword; it could excise evil but it neatly divided its wielder from his fellow man. That was why these broadcasts were so vital. To prove to the general public that the psychically gifted were by no means supermen, able to pierce minds, play ball with massive weights, or rearrange the world to suit themselves. The "Talented" person who could predict events might be limited to Incidents involving fire, or water. He might have an affinity for metals or a kinetic skill enabling him to assemble the components of a microscopic gyro, to be used in space exploration. He might be able to "find" things by studying a replica, or people by holding a possession of the missing person. He might be able to receive thoughts sent from another sensitive or those around him. Or he might be able to broadcast only. A true telepath, sender and receiver—Daffyd op Owen was only one of ten throughout the world—was still rare. Research had indicated there were more people with the ability than would admit it. There were, however, definite limitations to most Talents.

The Parapsychic had been raised, in Daffyd's lifetime, to the level of a science with the development of ultra-sensitive electroencephalographs which could record and identify the type of "Talent" by the minute electrical impulses generated in the cortex during the application of psychic powers. Daffyd op Owen sometimes thought the word "power" was the villain in perpetuating the public misconceptions. Power means "possession of control" but such synonyms as "domination", "sway," "command" leapt readily to the average mind and distorted the true definition.

Daffyd op Owen was roused from his thoughts by the heavy beat of a copter. He turned onto the path leading directly to the main administration building and had a clear view of the Commissioner's marked copter landing on the flight roof, to the left of the control tower with its forest of antennal decorations.

Immediately he perceived a reaction of surprise, indignation, and anxiety. Surely every Talent who'd heard the news on the morning 'cast and realized its significance could not be surprised by Gillings' arrival. Op Owen quickened his pace.

Orley's loose! The thought was as loud as a shout.

People paused, turned unerringly toward the long low building of the Clinic where applicants were tested for sensitivity and trained to understand and use what Talent they possessed; and where the Center conducted its basic research in psionics.

A tall, heavy figure flung itself from the Clinic's broad entrance and charged down the lawn, in a direct line to the tower. The man leaped the ornamental garden, plunged through the hedges, swung over the hood of a parked lawn-truck, straight-armed the overhanging branches of trees, brushed aside several men who tried to stop him.

"Reassure Orley! Project reassurance!" the bullhorn from the tower advised. "Project reassurance!"

Get those cops in my office! Daffyd projected on his own as he began to run toward the building. He hoped that Charlie Moorfield or Lester had already done so. Orley didn't look as if anything short of a tranquillizer bullet would stop him. Who had been dim-witted enough to let the telempath out of his shielded room at a time like this? The man was the most sensitive barometer to emotion Daffyd had ever encountered and he was physically dangerous if aroused. By the speed of that berserker-charge, he had soaked up enough fear/anxiety/anger to dismember the objects he was homing in on.

The only sounds now in the grounds were those of op Owen's shoes hitting the permaplast of the walk and the thud-thud of Orley's progress on the thick lawn. One advantage of being Talented is efficient communication and total comprehension of terse orders. But the wave of serenity/reassurance was not penetrating Orley's blind fury: the openness dissipated the mass effect.

Three men walked purposefully out of the administration building and down the broad apron of steps. Each carried slim-barrelled hand weapons. The man on the left raised and aimed his at the audibly panting, fast-approaching charger. The shot took Orley in the right arm but did not cause him to falter. Instantly the second man aimed and fired. Orley lost stride for two paces from the leg shot but recovered incredibly. The third man—op Owen recognized Charlie Moorfield—waited calmly as Orley rapidly closed the intervening distance. In a few more steps Orley would crash into him. Charlie was swinging out of the way, his gun slightly raised for a chest shot, when the telempath staggered and, with a horrible groan, fell to his knees. He tried to rise, one clenched fist straining toward the building.

Instantly Charlie moved to prevent Orley from gouging his face on the course-textured permaplast.

"He took two double-strength doses, Dave," Moorfield exclaimed with some awe as he cradled the man's head in his arms.

"He would. How'n'ell did he get such an exposure?"

Charlie made a grimace. "Sally was feeding him on the terrace. She hadn't heard the 'cast. Said she was concentrating on keeping him clean and didn't 'read' his growing restlessness as more than response to her until he burst wide open."

"Too much to hope that our unexpected guests didn't see this?"

Charlie gave a sour grin. "They caused it, boss. Stood there on the roof, giving Les a hard time, broadcasting basic hate and distrust. You should've seen the dial on the psychic atmosphere gauge. No wonder Orley responded." Charlie's face softened as he glanced down at the unconscious man. "Poor damned soul. Where is that med-team? I 'called' them when we got outside."

Daffyd glanced up at the broad third floor windows that marked his office. Six men stared back. He put an instant damper on his thoughts and emotions, and mounted the steps.

★

The visitors were still at the window, watching the med-team as they lifted the huge limp body onto the stretcher.

"Orley acts as a human barometer, gentlemen, reacting instantly to the emotional aura around him," Les was saying in his driest, down-eastest tone. To op Owen's wide-open mind, he emanated a raging anger that almost masked the aura projected by the visitors. "He has an intelligence factor of less than fifty on the New Scale which makes him uneducable. He is, however, invaluable in helping identify the dominating emotion in seriously disturbed mental and hallucinogenic patients which could overcome a rational telepath."

Police Commissioner Frank Gillings was the prime source of the fury which had set Harold Orley off. Op Owen felt sorry for Orley, having to bear such anger, and sorrier for himself and his optimistic hopes. He was momentarily at a loss to explain such a violent reaction from Gillings, even granting the validity of Lester Welch's assumption that Gillings was losing face, financial and personal, on account of this affair.

He tried a "push" at Gillings' mind to discover the covert reasons and found the man had a tight natural shield, not uncommon for a person in high position, privy to sensitive facts. The burly Commissioner gave every outward appearance of being completely at ease, as if this were no more than a routine visit, and not one hint of his surface thoughts leaked. Deep-set eyes, barely visible under heavy brows, above fleshy cheeks in a swarthy face missed nothing, flicking from Daffyd to Lester and back.

Op Owen nodded to Ted Lewis, the top police "finder" who had accompanied the official group. He stood a little to one side of the others. Of all the visitors, his mind was wide open. Foremost was the thought that he hoped Daffyd would read him, so that he could pass the warning that Gillings considered Orley's exhibition another indication that Talents could not control or discipline their own members.

"Good morning, Commissioner. I regret such circumstances bring you on your first visit to the Center. This morning's newscast has made us all extremely anxious to clear our profession."

Gillings' perfunctory smile did not acknowledge the tacit explanation of Orley's behaviour.

"I'll come to the point, then, Owen. We have conclusively ascertained that there was no break in store security measures when the theft occurred. The 'lectric wards and spy-scanner were not tampered with nor was there any evidence of breaking or entering. There is only one method in which sable, necklace, dress, and shoes could have been taken from that window in the five minutes between TV scans.

"We regret exceedingly that the evidence points to a person with psychic talents. We must insist that the larcenist be surrendered to us immediately and the merchandise returned to Mr. Grey, the representative from Coles." He indicated the portly man in a conservative but expensive grey fitted.

Op Owen nodded and looked expectantly toward Ted Lewis.

"Lewis can't 'find' a trace anywhere so it's obvious the items are being shielded." A suggestion of impatience crept into Gillings' bass voice. "These grounds are shielded."

"The stolen goods are not here, Commissioner. If they were, they would have been found by a member the instant the broadcast was heard."

Gillings' eyes snapped and his lips thinned with obstinacy.

"I've told you I can read on these grounds, Commissioner," Ted Lewis said with understandable indignation. "The stolen…"

A wave of the Commissioner's hand cut off the rest of Lewis's statement. Op Owen fought anger at the insult.

"You're a damned fool, Gillings," said Welch, not bothering to control his rage, "if you think we'd shelter a larcenist at this time."

"Ah yes, that Bill pending Senate approval," Gillings said with an unpleasant smile.

Daffyd found it hard to nullify resentment at the smug satisfaction and new antagonism which Gillings was generating.

"Yes, that Bill, Commissioner," op Owen repeated, "which will protect any Talent *registered* with a parapsychic centre." Op Owen did not miss the sparkle of Gillings' deep-set eyes at the deliberate emphasis. "If you'll step this way, gentlemen, to our remote-graph control system, I believe that we can prove, to your absolute satisfaction, that no registered Talent is responsible. You haven't been here before, Commissioner, so you are not familiar with our method of recording incidents in which psychic powers are used.

"Power, by the way, means 'possession of control', personal as well as psychic, which is what this Center teaches each and every member. Here we are. Charles Moorfield is the duty officer and was in charge at the time of the robbery. If you will observe the graphs, you'll notice that the period—between 7:03 and 7:08 was the time given by the 'cast—has not yet wound out of sight on the storage drums."

Gillings was not looking at the graphs. He was staring at Charlie.

"Next time, aim at the chest first, mister."

"Sorry I stopped him at all… mister," replied Charlie, with such deliberate malice that Gillings coloured and stepped toward him.

Op Owen quickly intervened. "You dislike, distrust, and hate us, Commissioner," he said, keeping his own voice neutral. "You and your staff have prejudged us guilty, though you are at this moment surrounded by incontrovertible evidence of our collective innocence. You arrived here, emanating disruptive emotions—no,

I'm *not* reading your minds, gentlemen (Daffyd had all Gillings' attention with that phrase). That isn't necessary. You're triggering responses in the most controlled of us—not to mention that poor witless telempath we had to tranquillize. And, unless you put a lid on your unwarranted hatred and fears, I will have no compunction about pumping you all full of tranks, too!"

"That's coming on mighty strong for a man in your position, Owen," Gillings said in a tight hard voice, his body visibly tense now.

"You're the one that's coming on strong, Gillings. Look at that dial behind you." Gillings did not want to turn, particularly not at op Owen's command, but there is a quality of righteous anger that compels obedience. "That registers—as Harold Orley does—the psychic intensity of the atmosphere. The mind gives off electrical impulses, Gillings, surely you have to admit that. Law enforcement agencies used that premise for lie detection. Our instrumentation makes those early registers as archaic as spaceships make oxcarts. We have ultra-delicate equipment which can measure the minutest electrical impulses of varying frequencies and duration. And this p.a. dial registers a dangerous high right now. Surely your eyes must accept scientific evidence.

"Those rows of panels there record the psychic activity of each and every member registered with this Center. See, most of them register agitation right now. These red divisions indicate a sixty-minute time span. Each of those drums exposes the graph as of the time of that theft. Notice the difference. Not one graph shows the kinetic activity required of a 'lifter' to achieve such a theft. But every one shows a reaction to your presence.

"There is no way in which a registered Talent can avoid these graphs. Charlie, were any kinetics out of touch at the time of the theft?"

Charlie, his eyes locked on Gillings, shook his head slowly.

"There has never been so much as a civil misdemeanour by any of our people. No breach of confidence, nor integrity. No crime could be shielded from fellow Talents.

"And can you rationally believe that we would jeopardize years and years of struggle to become accepted as reliable citizens of indisputable integrity for the sake of a fur coat and a string of baubles? When there are funds available to any Talent who might want to own such fripperies?" Op Owen's scorn made the Coles man wince.

"Now get out of here, Gillings. Discipline your emotions and revise your snap conclusion. Then call through normal channels and request our co-operation. Because, believe me, we are far more determined—and better equipped—to discover the real criminal than you could ever be, no matter what *your* personal stake in assigning guilt might conceivably be."

Op Owen watched for a reaction to that remark, but Gillings, his lips thin and white with anger, did not betray himself. He gestured jerkily toward the one man in police blues.

"Do not serve that warrant now, Gillings!" op Owen said in a very soft voice. He watched the frantic activity of the needle on the p.a. dial.

"Go. Now. Call. Because if you cannot contain your feelings, Commissioner, you had better maintain your distance."

It was then that Gillings became aware of the palpable presence of those assembled in the corridor. A wide aisle had been left free, an aisle that led only to the open elevator. No one spoke or moved or coughed. The force exerted was not audible or physical. It was, however, undeniably unanimous. It prevailed in forty-four seconds.

"My firm will wish to know what steps are being taken," the Coles man said in a squeaky voice as he began to walk, with erratic but ever quickening steps, toward the elevator.

Gillings' three subordinates were not so independent but there was no doubt of their relief as Gillings turned and walked with precise, unhurried strides to the waiting car.

No one moved until the thwapping rumble of the copter was no longer audible. Then they turned for assignments from their director.

City Manager Julian Pennstrak, with a metropolis of some four millions to supervise, had a habit of checking up personally on any disruption to the smooth operation of his city. He arrived as the last of the organized search parties left the Center.

"I'd give my left kidney and a million credits to have enough Talent to judge a man accurately, Dave," he said as he crossed the room. He knew better than to shake hands unless a Talented offered but it was obvious to Daffyd, who liked Pennstrak, that the man wanted somehow to convey his personal distress over this incident. He stood for a moment by the chair, his handsome face without a trace of his famous genial smile. "I'd've sworn Frank Gillings was pro Talent," he said, combing his fingers through his thick, wavy black hair, another indication of his anxiety. "He certainly has used your people to their fullest capabilities since he became L E and P Commissioner."

Lester Welch snorted, looking up from the map he was annotating with search patterns. "A man'll use any tool that works... until it scratches him, that is."

"But you could prove that no registered Talent was responsible for that theft."

"'A man convinced against his will, is of the same opinion still,'" Lester chanted.

"Les!" Op Owen didn't need sour cynicism from any quarter, even one dedicated to Talent. "No *registered* Talent was responsible."

Pennstrak brightened. "You did persuade Gillings that it's the work of an undiscovered Talent?"

Welch made a rude noise. "He'll be persuaded when we produce, both missing person and missing merchandise. Nothing else is going to satisfy either Gillings or Coles."

"True," Pennstrak agreed, frowning thoughtfully. "Nor the vacillating members of my own Council. Oh, I know, it's a flash reaction but the timing is so goddamned lousy, Dave. Your campaign bore down heavy on the integrity and good citizenship of the Talented."

"It's a deliberate smear job—" Welch began gloomily.

"I thought of that," Pennstrak interrupted him, "and had my own expert go over the scanner films. You know the high-security-risk set-up: rotating exposures on the stationary TV eyes. One frame the model was clothed; next, exposed in all its plastic glory. It was a 'lift' all right. No possibility of tampering with that film." Pennstrak leaned forward to Dave, though there was scarcely any need to guard his statements in this company. "Furthermore, Pat came along. She 'read' everyone at the store, and Gillings' squad. Not Gillings, though. She said he has a natural shield. The others were all clean... at least, of conspiracy." Pennstrak's snide grin faded quickly. "I made her go rest. That's why there's no one with me."

Op Owen accepted the information quietly. He had half-hoped... it was an uncharacteristic speculation for him. However, it did save time and Talent to have had both store and police checked.

It had become general practice to have a strong telepathic receiver in the entourage of any prominent or controversial public figure. That Talent was rarely identified publicly. He or she usually performed some obvious service so that their constant presence was easily explicable. Pat Tawfik was overtly Pennstrak's chief speechwriter.

"I have, however," Pennstrak continued, "used my official prerogative to supervise the hunt. There're enough sympathetic people on the public media channels to play down the Talent angle—at my request. But you know what this kind of adverse publicity is going to do to you, this Center, and the Talented in general. One renegade can discredit a hundred honest Injuns. So, what can I do to help?"

"I wish I knew. We've got every available perceptive out on the off chance that this—ah, renegade happens to be broadcasting joy and elation over her heist."

"Her?"

"The consensus is that while a man might lift furs and jewels, possibly the dress, only a woman would take the shoes, too. Top finders are coming in from other Centers…"

"A 'find' is reported, boss," Charlie said over the intercom. "Block Q."

As Pennstrak and op Owen reached the map, Welch announced with a groan, "Gawd, that's a multilayer apartment zone."

"A have-not," op Owen added.

"Gil Gracie made the find, boss," Charlie continued. "And the fur is not all he's found but he's got a problem."

"You just bet he has," Les muttered under his breath as he grimaced down at the map coordinates.

"Charlie, send every finder and perceptive to Block Q. If they can come up with a fix…"

"Boss, we got a fix, but there's one helluva lot of similarities."

"What's the problem?" Pennstrak asked.

"We'll simply have to take our time and eliminate, Charlie. Send anyone who can help." Then op Owen turned to Pennstrak.

"In reporting a 'find,' the perceptive is aware of certain particular spatial relationships between the object sought and its immediate surroundings. It isn't as if he has seen the object as a camera sees it. For example, have you ever entered a room, turned down a street, or looked up quickly and had the feeling that you had seen just"—and Daffyd made a bracket of his hands—"that portion of the scene before, with exactly the same lighting, exactly the same components? But only that portion of the scene, so that the rest was an indistinguishable blur?"

Pennstrak nodded.

"'Finding' is like that. Sometimes the Talent sees it in lucid detail, sometimes it's obscured or, as in this case, there are literally hundreds of possibilities… apartments with the same light exposure, same scene out the window, the same floor plan and furnishings. Quite possible in this instance since these are furnished, standard subsistence dwellings. Nothing to help us single out, say Apartment 44E, Building 18, Buhler Street."

"There happens to be a Building 18 on Buhler Street, boss," Les Welch said slowly, "and there are forty-eight levels, ten units per floor."

Pennstrak regarded op Owen with awe.

"Nonsense, this office is thoroughly shielded and I'm *not* a pre-cog!"

"Before you guys took the guesswork out of it, there were such things as hunches," Pennstrak suggested.

For op Owen's peace of mind and Lester's pose of misogyny, it was neither Building 18 nor Buhler Street nor Apartment 44. It was Apartment 1E, deep in the centre of Q Block. No one had entered nor left it—by normal means—since Gil Gracie and two other finders had made a precise fix. Gil handed op Owen the master key obtained from the dithering super.

"My Gawd," Pennstrak said in a voice muted with shocked surprise as they swung open the door. "Like an oriental bazaar."

"Indiscriminate pilfering on a wholesale basis," op Owen corrected, glancing around at the rich brilliant velvet drapes framing the dingy window to the wildly clashing pillows thrown on the elegant Empire loveseat. A marble-topped table was a jumble of pretty vases, silver boxes, and goblets. Priceless china held decaying remains of food. Underneath the table were jaggedly opened, empty cans bearing the label of an extremely expensive caterer. Two empty champagne bottles pointed green, blind eyes in their direction. A portable colour 'caster was piled with discarded clothing; a black-lace sheer body stocking draped in an obscene posture across the inactive screen. "A magpie's nest rather," he sighed, "and I'd hazard that Maggie is very young and has been poor all her life until…" He met Pennstrak's sympathetic gaze. "Until our educational programme gave her the hints she needed to unlock her special Talent."

"Gillings is going to have to work with you on this, Dave," Pennstrak said reluctantly as he reached for the intercom at his belt. "But first he's going to have to apologize"

Op Owen shook his head vigorously. "I want his co-operation, Julian, grudged or willing. *When* he really believes in Talent, then he will apologize voluntarily… and obliquely," he couldn't resist adding.

To op Owen's consternation, Gillings arrived noisily in the cowlike lab copter, sirens going, lights flashing.

"Don't bother now," op Owen advised Pennstrak, for he could see the City Manager forming a furious reprimand. "She might have been warned by the finders' activity anyhow."

"Well, she's certainly been warned off now," Pennstrak stalked off, to confer with one of his aides just as Gillings strode into the corridor with his technicians.

According op Owen and Gracie the merest nod, Gillings began issuing crisp orders. He knew his business, op Owen thought, and he evidently trusted *these* technicians, for he didn't bother to crowd into the tiny apartment to oversee them.

"As soon as your men have prints and a physical profile, Commissioner, we'd like to run the data through our computer. There's the chance that the girl did take advantage of the open Talent test the Center has been advertising."

"You mean you don't *know* who it is *yet?*"

"I found the coat since I *knew* what it looked like," Gil Gracie said, bristling at Gillings' manner.

"Then where is it?" Gillings gestured peremptorily to the sable-less apartment.

"These are the shoes, Commissioner," said one of his team, presenting the fragile jewelled footwear, now neatly sealed in clear plastic. "Traces of dirt, dust, fleck of nail enamel and from the 'scope imprint, I'd say they were too big for her."

Gillings stared at the shoes disinterestedly. "No sign of the dress?"

"Still looking."

"Odd that you people can't locate a girl with bare feet in a sable coat and a bright blue silk gown?"

"No odder than it is for your hundreds of patrolmen throughout the city, Commissioner, to overlook a girl so bizarrely dressed," op Owen said with firm good humour. "When you 'saw' the coat, Gil, where was it?"

"Thrown across the loveseat, one arm hanging down to the floor. I distinguished the edge of the sill and the tree outside, the first folds of the curtain, and the wall heating unit. I called in, you sent over enough finders so that we were able to eliminate the similarities. It took us nearly an hour…"

"Were you keeping an 'eye' on the coat all the time?" Gillings demanded in a voice so devoid of expression that his contempt was all the more obvious.

Gil flushed, bit his lip, and only partially inhibited by op Owen's subtle warning, snapped back, "Try keeping your physical eye on an object for an hour!"

"Get some rest, Gil," op Owen suggested gently. He waited until the finder had turned the corner. "If you are as determined to find this criminal as you say you are, Commissioner Gillings, then do not destroy the efficiency of my staff by such gratuitous criticism. In less than four hours, on the basis of photographs of the stolen objects, we located this apartment…"

"But not the criminal, who is still in possession of a sable coat which you found once but have now unaccountably lost."

"That's enough, Gillings," said Pennstrak, who had rejoined them. "Thanks to your arrival, the girl must know she's being sought and is shielding."

Pennstrak gestured toward the dingy windows of the flat, through which the vanes of the big copter were visible. A group of children, abandoning the known objects of the development play-yard, had gathered at a respectful but curiosity-satisfying distance.

"Considering the variety of her accomplishments," op Owen said, not above using Pennstrak's irritation with his Commissioner to advantage, "I'm sure she knew of the search before the Commissioner's arrival, Julian. Have any of these items been reported, Commissioner?"

"That console was. Two days ago. It was on 'find,' too."

"She has been growing steadily bolder, then," op Owen went on, depressed by Gillings' attitude. And depressed that such a Talent had emerged twisted, perverted, selfish. Why? Why? "If your department ever gets the chronology of the various thefts, we'd appreciate the copy."

"Why?" Gillings turned to stare at op Owen, surprised and irritated.

"Talent takes time to develop—in ordinary persons. It does not, like the ancient goddess Athena, spring full-grown from the forehead. This girl could not, for instance, have lifted that portable set the first time she used her Talent. The more data we have on... the lecture is ill-timed."

Gillings' unspoken "you said it" did reach op Owen, whose turn it was to stare in surprise.

"Well, your 'finders' are not novices," the Commissioner said aloud. "If they traced the coat once, why not again?"

"Every perceptive we have is searching," op Owen assured him. "But, if she was able to leave this apartment after Gil found the coat, taking it with her because it obviously is not here, she also is capable of shielding herself and that coat. And, until she slips that guard, I doubt we'll find it or her."

The report on the laboratory findings was exhaustive. There was a full set of prints, foot and finger. None matched those on file in the city records, or Federal or Immigration. She had not been tested at the Center. Long coarse black hair had been found. Skin flakes analysed suggested an olive complexion. Thermo-photography placed her last appearance in the room at approximately the time the four "finders" fixed on her apartment, thus substantiating op Owen's guess. The thermal prints also revealed that she was of slender build, approximately five-four, weighing 105 pounds. Stains on a kitchen knife proved her to possess blood type O. No one else had occupied the apartment within the eight-day range of the thermography used.

From such records, the police extrapolator made a rough sketch of Maggie O as she was called for want of a better name. The sketch was taken around the neighbourhood with no success. People living in Block Q didn't bother people who didn't bother them.

It was Daffyd op Owen who remembered the children crowding the police copter. From them he elicited the information that she was new in the building. (The records indicated that the apartment should be vacant.) She was always singing, dancing to the wall-'caster, and changing her clothes. Occasionally she'd play with them and bring out rich food to eat, promising they could have such good things if they'd think hard about them. While the children talked, Daffyd "saw" Maggie's face reflected in their minds. The police extrapolator had been far short of the reality. She was not much older than the children she had played with. She had not been pretty by ordinary standards but she had been so "different" that her image had registered sharply. The narrow face, the brilliant eyes, slightly slanted above sharp cheekbones, the thin, small mouth, and the pointed chin were unusual even in an area of ethnic variety.

This likeness and a physical description were circulated quickly to be used at all exits to the city and all transportation facilities. It was likely she'd try to slip out during the day-end exodus.

The south and west airstrips had been under a perceptive surveillance since the search had been inaugurated. Now every facility was guarded.

Gil Gracie "found" the coat again.

"She must have it in a suitcase," he reported on the police-provided hand unit from his position in the main railroad concourse. "It's folded and surrounded by dark. It's moving up and down. But there're so many people. So many suitcases. I'll circulate. Maybe the find'll fix itself."

Gillings gave orders to his teams on the master unit which had been set up in the Center's control room to coordinate the operations.

"You better test Gil for pre-cog," Charlie muttered to op Owen after they'd contacted all the sensitives. "He *asked* for the station."

"You should've told me sooner, Charlie. I'd've teamed him with a sensitive."

"Lookit that," Charlie exclaimed, pointing to a wildly moving needle on one of the remotes.

Les was beside it even as the audio for the Incident went on.

"Not that track! Oh! Watch out! Baggage. On the handcart! Watch out. Move, man. Move! To the right. The right! Ahhhh." The woman's voice choked off in an agonized cry.

Daffyd pushed Charlie out of the way, to get to the speaker.

"Gil this is op Owen. Do not pursue. Do not pursue that girl! She's aware of you. Gil, come in. Answer me, Gil... Charlie, keep trying to raise him. Gillings, contact your men at the station. Make them stop Gil Gracie."

"Stop him? Why?"

"The pre-cog. The baggage on the handcart," shouted Daffyd, signalling frantically to Lester to explain in detail. He raced for the emergency stairs, up the two flights, and slammed out onto the roof. Gasping for breath, he clung to the high retaining wall and projected his mind to Gil's.

He knew the man so well, trained Gil when an employer brought in the kid who had a knack for locating things. Op Owen could see him ducking and dodging through the trainward crowds, touching suitcases, ignoring irate or astonished carriers; every nerve, every ounce of him receptive to the "feel" of a dense, dark sable fur. And so single-minded that Daffyd could not "reach" him.

But op Owen knew the instant the loaded baggage cart swerved and crushed the blindly intent Talent against an I-beam. He bowed his head, too fully cognizant that a double tragedy had occurred. Gil was lost… and so now was the girl.

There was no peace from his thoughts even when he returned to the shielded control room. Lester and Charlie pretended to be very busy. Gillings was. He directed the search of the railway station, arguing with the stationmaster that the trains were to be held and that was that! The drone of his voice began to penetrate op Owen's remorse.

"All right, then, if the Talents have cleared it and there's no female of the same height and weight, release that train. Someone tried the johns, didn't they? No, Sam, you can detain anyone remotely suspicious. That girl is clever, strong, and dangerous. There's no telling what else she could do. But she damn well can't change her height, weight, and blood type!"

"Daffyd. Daffyd." Lester had to touch him to get his attention. He motioned op Owen toward Charlie, who was holding out the hand unit.

"It's Coles, sir."

Daffyd listened to the effusively grateful store manager. He made the proper responses, but it wasn't until he had relinquished the hand unit to Charlie that the man's excited monologue made sense.

"The coat, the dress, and the necklace have reappeared on the store dummy," op Owen said. He cleared his throat and repeated it loud enough to be heard.

"Returned?" Gillings echoed. "Just like that? Why, the little bitch! Sam, check the ladies' rooms in that station. Wait, isn't there a discount dress store in that station? Have them check for missing apparel. I want an itemized list of what's gone, and an exact duplicate from their stock shown to the sensitives. We've got her scared and running now."

"Scared and running now." Gillings' smug assessment rang ominously in Daffyd's mind. He had a sudden flash. Superimposed over a projection of Maggie's thin face was the image of the lifeless store dummy, elegantly reclad in the purloined blue gown and dark fur. "Here, take them back. I don't want them anymore. I didn't mean to kill him. I didn't mean to. See, I gave back what you wanted. Now leave me alone!"

Daffyd shook his head. Wishful thinking. Just as futile as the girl's belated gesture of penance. Too much too soon. Too little too late.

"We don't want her scared," he said out loud. "She was scared when she toppled that baggage cart."

"She *killed* a man when she toppled that baggage cart, op Owen!" Gillings was all but shouting.

"And if we're not very careful, she'll kill others."

"If you think I'm going to velvet glove a homicidal maniac…"

A shrill tone issuing from the remote unit forced Gillings to answer. He was about to reprimand the caller but the message got his stunned attention.

"We can forget the paternal bit, Owen. She knocked down every one of your people and mine at the Oriole Street entrance. Your men are unconscious. Mine and about twenty or more innocent commuters are afflicted with blinding headaches. Got any practical ideas, Owen, on catching this monster you created?"

"Oriole? Was she heading east or west?"

"Does it matter?"

"If we're to catch her it does. And we must catch her. She's operating at a psychic high. There's no telling what she's capable of now. Such Talent has only been a theoretic possibility…"

Gillings lost all control of himself. The fear and hatred burst out in such a wave that Charlie Moorfield, caught unaware, erupted out of his chair toward Gillings in an instinctive defence reaction.

"Gillings!" "Charlie!" Les and Daffyd shouted together, each grabbing the whilom combatants. But Charlie, his face white with shock at his own reaction, had himself in hand. Sinking weakly back into his chair, he gasped out an apology.

"You mean, you *want* to have more monsters like her and him?" Gillings demanded. Between his voice and the violent emotions, Daffyd's head rang with pain and confusion.

"Don't be a fool," Lester said, grabbing the Commissioner by the arm. "You can't spew emotions like that around a telepath and not get a reaction. Look at Daffyd! Look at Charlie! Christ, man, you're as bad as the scared, mixed up kid…" Then Les dropped Gillings' arm and stared at him in amazement. "Christ, you're a telepath yourself!"

"Quiet, everybody," Daffyd said with such urgency he had their instant attention. "I've the solution. And there's no time to waste. Charlie, I want Harold Orley airbound in the Clinic's copter heading south to the Central Station in nothing flat. We'll correct course en route. Gillings, I want two of the strongest, most stable patrolmen on your roster. I want them armed with fast-acting, double-strength trank guns and airborne to rendezvous near Central Station."

"Harold?" Les echoed in blank astonishment and then relief coloured his face as he understood Daffyd's intentions. "Of course. Nothing can stop Harold. And no one can read him coming."

"Nothing. And no one," op Owen agreed bleakly.

Gillings turned from issuing his orders to see an ambulance copter heading west across the sky.

"We're following?"

Daffyd nodded and gestured for Gillings to precede him to the roof. He didn't look back but he knew what Les and Charlie did not say.

She had been seen running east on Oriole. And she was easy to follow. She left people doubled up with nausea and crying with head pains. That is, until she crossed Boulevard.

"We'll head south-southeast on an intercept," Gillings told his pilot and had him relay the correction to the ambulance. "She's heading to the sea?" he asked rhetorically as he rummaged for the correct airmap of the city. "Here. We can set down at Seaman's Park. She can't have made it that far... unless she can fly suddenly." Gillings looked up at op Owen.

"She probably could teleport herself," Daffyd answered, watching the Commissioner's eyes narrow in adverse reaction to the admission. "But she hasn't thought of it yet. As long as she can be kept running, too scared to think..." That necessity would ever plague Daffyd op Owen: that they must run her out of her mind.

Gillings ordered all police hovercraft to close in on the area where she was last seen, blocks of residences and small businesses of all types.

By the time the three copters had made their rendezvous at the small park, there were no more visible signs of Maggie O's retreat.

As Gillings made to leave the copter, Daffyd op Owen stopped him.

"If you're not completely under control, Gillings, Harold will be after *you*."

Gillings looked at the director for a long moment, his jaw set stubbornly. Then, slowly, he settled into the seat and handed op Owen a remote com-unit.

"Thanks, Gillings," he said, and left the copter. He signalled to the ambulance to release Harold Orley and then strode across the grass to the waiting officers.

The two biggest men were as burly as he could wish. Being trained law enforcers, they ought to be able to handle Orley. Op Owen "pushed" gently against their minds and was satisfied with his findings. They possessed the natural shielding of the untemperamental which made them less susceptible to emotional storms. Neither Webster nor Heis was stupid, however, and they had been briefed on developments.

"Orley has no useful intelligence. He is a human barometer, measuring the intensity and type of emotions which surround him and reacting instinctively. He does not broadcast. He only receives. Therefore he cannot be harmed or identified by... by Maggie O. He is the only Talent she cannot 'hear' approaching."

"But, if he reaches her, he'd..." Webster began, measuring Harold with the discerning eye of a boxing enthusiast. Then he shrugged and turned politely to op Owen.

"You've the double-strength tranks? Good. I hope you'll be able to use them in time. But it is imperative that she be apprehended before she does more harm. She has already killed one man..."

"We understand, sir," Heis said when op Owen did not continue.

"If you can, shoot her. Once she stops broadcasting, he'll soon return to a manageable state." But, Daffyd amended to himself, remembering Harold sprawled on the ground in front of the building, not soon enough. "She was last seen on the east side of the boulevard, about eight blocks from here. She'd be tired, looking for someplace to hide and rest. But she is also probably radiating sufficient emotion for Harold to pick up. He'll react by heading in a straight line for the source. Keep him from trying to plough through solid walls. Keep your voices calm when you speak to him.

Use simple commands. I see you've got hand units. I'll be airborne; the copter's shielded but I'll help when I can."

Flanking Harold, Webster and Heis moved west along Oriole at a brisk even walk: the two officers in step, Harold's head bobbing above theirs. His being out of step was a cruel irony.

Daffyd op Owen turned back to the copter. He nodded to Gillings as he seated himself. He tried not to think at all.

As the copters lifted from the park and drifted slowly west amid other air traffic, op Owen looked sadly down at the people on the streets. At kids playing on the sidewalks. At a flow of men and women with brief-cases or shopping bags, hurrying home. At snub-nosed city cars and squatty trucks angling into parking slots. At the bloated cross-city helibuses jerking and settling to disgorge their passengers at the street islands.

"He's twitching," Heis reported in a dispassionate voice.

Daffyd flicked on the handset. "That's normal. He's beginning to register."

"He's moving faster now. Keeps wanting to go straight through the buildings." Reading Heis's undertone, op Owen knew that the men hadn't believed his caution about Orley ploughing through solids. "He's letting us guide him, but he keeps pushing us to the right. You take his other arm, Web. Yeah, that's better."

Gillings had moved to the visual equipment along one side of the copter. He focused deftly in on the trio, magnified it, and threw the image on the pilot's screen, too. The copter adjusted direction.

"Easy, Orley. No, don't try to stop him, Web. Stop the traffic!"

Orley's line of march crossed the busier wide north-south street. Webster ran out to control the vehicles. People turned curiously. Stopped and stared after the trio.

"Don't," op Owen ordered as he saw Gillings move a hand towards the bullhorn. "There's nothing wrong with her hearing."

Orley began to move faster now that he had reached the farther side. He wanted to go right through intervening buildings.

"Guide him left to the sidewalk, Heis," op Owen advised. "I think he's still amenable. He isn't running yet."

"He's breathing hard, Mr. Owen." Heis sounded dubious. "And his face is changing."

Op Owen nodded to himself, all too familiar with the startling phenomena of watching the blankness of Orley's face take on the classic mask of whatever emotions he was receiving. It would be a particularly unnerving transition under these conditions.

"What does he show?"

"I'd say… hatred." Heis's voice dropped on the last word. Then he added in his usual tone, "He's smiling, too, and it isn't nice."

They had eased Orley to the sidewalk heading west. He kept pushing Webster to the right and his pace increased until it was close to a run. Webster and Heis began to gesture people out of their way but it would soon be obvious to the neighbourhood that something was amiss. Would it be better to land more police to reassure people and keep their emanations down? Or would they broadcast suppressed excitement at police interference? She'd catch that. Should he warn Heis and Webster to keep their thoughts on Harold Orley? Or would that be like warning them against all thoughts of the camel's left knee?

Orley broke into a run. Webster and Heis were hard put to keep him to the sidewalk.

"What's in the next block?" op Owen asked Gillings.

The Commissioner consulted the map, holding it just above the scanner so he could keep one eye on the trio below.

"Residences and an area parking facility for interstate truck-ing." Gillings turned to op Owen now, his heavy eyebrows raised in question.

"No, she's still there because Orley is homing in on her projection."

"Look at his face! My God!" Heis exclaimed over the hand-unit. On the screen, his figure had stopped. He was pointing at Orley. But Webster's face was clearly visible to the surveillers; and what he saw unnerved him.

Orley broke from his guides. He was running, slowly at first but gathering speed steadily, mindlessly brushing aside anything that stood in his way. Heis and Webster were after him but both men were shaking their heads as if something were bothering them. Orley tried to plunge through a brick store wall. He bounced off it, saw the unimpeded view of his objective, and charged forward. Webster had darted ahead of him, blowing his whistle to stop the oncoming traffic. Heis alternately yelled into the hand unit and at startled bystanders. Now some of them were afflicted and were grabbing their heads.

"Put us on the roof," op Owen told the pilot. "Gillings, get men to cover every entrance and exit to that parking lot. Get the copters to hover by the open levels. The men'll be spared some of the lash."

It wouldn't do much good, op Owen realized, even as he felt the first shock of the girl's awareness of imminent danger.

"Close your mind," he yelled at the pilot and Gillings. "Don't think."

"My head, my head." It was Heis groaning.

"Concentrate on Orley," op Owen advised, his hands going to his temples in reaction to the knotting pressure. Heis's figure on the scanner staggered after Orley, who had now entered the parking facility.

Op Owen caught the mental pressure and dispersed it, projecting back reassurance/help/protection/compassion. *He* could forgive her Gil Gracie's death. So would any Talent. If she would instantly surrender, somehow the Centers would protect her from the legal aspects of her act. Only surrender now.

Someone screamed. Another man echoed that piercing cry. The copter bucked and jolted them. The pilot was groaning and gasping. Gillings plunged forward, grabbing the controls.

Op Owen, fighting an incredible battle, was blind to physical realities. If he could just occupy all the attention of that over-charged mind... hold it long enough... pain/fear/black/red/ moiled-orange/purples... breathing... shock. Utter disbelief/fear/ loss of confidence. Frantic physical effort.

Concrete scraped op Owen's cheek. His fingers bled as he clawed at a locked steel exit door on the roof. He could not enter. *He had to reach her* FIRST!

Somehow his feet found the stairs as he propelled himself down the fire escape, deliberately numbing his mind to the intensive pounding received. A pounding that became audible.

Then he saw her, fingers clawing for leverage on the stairpost, foot poised for the step from the landing. A too thin, adolescent figure, frozen for a second with indecision and shock; strands of black hair like vicious scars across a thin face, distorted and ugly from the tremendous physical and mental efforts of the frantic will. Her huge eyes, black with insane fury and terror, bloodshot with despair and the salty sweat of her desperate striving for escape, looked into his.

She knew him for what he was; and her hatred crackled in his mind. Those words—after Gil Gracie's death—had been hers, not his distressed imagining. She had known him then as her real antagonist. Only now was *he* forced to recognize her for what she was, all she was—and regrettably, all she would not be.

He fought the inexorable decision of that split-second con-
frontation, wanting more than anything else in his life that it did
not have to be so.

She was the wiser! She whirled!

She was suddenly beyond the heavy fire door without opening
it. Harold Orley, charging up the stairs behind her, had no such
Talent. He crashed with sickening force into the metal door. Daffyd
had no alternative. She had teleported. He steadied the telempath,
depressed the lock bar, and threw the door wide.

Orley was after the slender figure fleeing across the dimly lit,
low-ceilinged concrete floor. She was heading toward the down
ramp now.

"Stop, stop," op Owen heard his voice begging her.

Heis came staggering from the stairway.

"Shoot him. For Christ's sake, shoot Orley, Heis," op Owen
yelled.

Heis couldn't seem to coordinate. Op Owen tried to push aside
his fumbling hands and grab the trank gun himself. Heis's trained
reflexes made him cling all the tighter to his weapon. Just then,
op Owen heard the girl's despairing shriek.

Two men had appeared at the top of the ramp. They both
fired, the dull reports of trank pistols accentuated by her choked
gasp.

"Not her. Shoot Orley. Shoot the man," op Owen cried, but it
was too late.

Even as the girl crumpled to the floor, Orley grabbed her.
Grabbed and tore and beat at the source of the emotions which so
disturbed him. Beat and tore and stamped as she had assaulted him.

Orley's body jerked as tranks hit him from several sides, but
it took far too long for them to override the adrenal reactions of
the overcharged telempath.

There was pain and pity as well as horror in Gillings' eyes when he came running onto the level. The police stood at a distance from the blood-spattered bodies.

"Gawd, couldn't someone have stopped him from getting her?" the copter pilot murmured, turning away from the shapeless bloodied thing half-covered by Orley's unconscious body.

"The door would have stopped Orley, but he," Heis grimly pointed at op Owen, "opened it for him."

"She teleported through the door," op Owen said weakly. He had to lean against the wall. He was beginning to shudder uncontrollably. "She had to be stopped. Now. Here. Before she realized what she'd done. What she could do." His knees buckled. "She teleported through the door!"

Unexpectedly, it was Gillings who came to his aid, a Gillings whose mind was no longer shielded but broadcasting compassion and awe, and understanding.

"So did you."

The phrase barely registered in op Owen's mind when he passed out.

"That's all that remains of the late Solange Boshe," Gillings said, tossing the file reel to the desk. "As much of her life as we've been able to piece together. Gypsies don't stay long anywhere."

"There're some left?" Lester Welch asked, frowning at the three-inch condensation of fifteen years of a human life.

"Oh there are, I assure you," Gillings replied, his tone souring slightly for the first time since he had entered the office. "The tape also has a lengthy interview with Bill Jones, the cousin the social worker located after Solange had recovered from the bronchial pneumonia. He had no idea," Gillings hastily assured them, "that there is any reason other than a routine check on the whereabouts of a runaway county ward. He had a hunch," Gillings grimaced, "that the family had gone on to Toronto. They had. He also thought that they had probably given the girl up for dead when she collapsed on the street. The Toronto report substantiates that. So I don't imagine it will surprise you, op Owen, that her tribe, according to Jones, are the only ones still making a living at fortune-telling, palm-reading, tea leaves and that bit."

"Now, just a minute, Gillings," Lester began, bristling. He subsided when he saw that his boss and the Commissioner were grinning at each other.

"So... just as you suspected, op Owen, she was a freak Talent. We know from the ward nurses that she watched your propaganda broadcasts during her hospitalization. We can assume that she was aware of the search either when Gil Gracie 'found' the coat, or when the definite fix was made. It's not hard to guess her motivation in making the heist in the first place nor her instinctive desire to hide." Gillings gave his head an abrupt violent jerk and stood up. He started to hold out his hand, remembered, and raised it in a farewell gesture. "You are continuing those broadcasts, aren't you?"

Lester Welch glared so balefully at the Commissioner that op Owen had to chuckle.

"With certain deletions, yes."

"Good. Talent must be identified and trained. Trained young and well if they are to use their Talent properly." Gillings stared op Owen in the eye. "The Boshe girl was bad, op Owen, bad clear through. Listen to what Jones said about her and you won't regret Tuesday too much. Sometimes the young are inflexible, too."

"I agree, Commissioner," Daffyd said, escorting the man to the door as calmly as if he hadn't heard what Gillings was thinking so clearly. "And we appreciate your help in the cover yarns that explained Tuesday's odd occurrences."

"A case of mutual understanding," Gillings said, his eyes glinting. "Oh, no need to see me out. *I* can open this door."

That door was no sooner firmly shut behind him than Lester Welch turned on his superior.

"And just who was scratching whose back then?" he demanded. "Don't you dare come over innocent, either, Daffyd op Owen. Two days ago that man was your enemy, bristling with enough hate and distrust to antagonize me."

"Remember what you said about Gillings Tuesday?"

"There's been an awful lot of idle comment around here lately."

"Frank Gillings *is* telepathic." Then he added as Lester was choking on the news. "And he doesn't want to be. So he's suppressed it. Naturally he'd be antagonistic."

"Hah!"

"He's not too old, but he's not flexible enough to adapt to Talent, having denied it so long."

"I'll buy that. But what was that parting shot—'*I* can open this door'?" Lester mimicked the Commissioner's deep voice.

"I'm too old to learn new tricks, too, Les. I teleported through the roof door of that parking facility. He saw me do it. And *she* saw the memory of it in my mind. If she'd lived, she'd've picked my mind clean. And I didn't want her to die."

Op Owen turned abruptly to the window, trying to let the tranquillity of the scene restore his equilibrium. It did—until he saw Harold Orley plodding along the path with his guide. Instantly a white, wide-eyed, hair-streaked face was superimposed over the view.

The intercom beeped and he depressed the key for his sanity's sake.

"We've got a live one, boss," and Sally Iselin's gay voice restored him. "A strong pre-cog with kinetic possibilities. And guess what?"

Sally's excitement made her voice breathless. "He said the cop on his beat told him to come in. He doesn't want any more trouble with the cops so he…"

"Would his name be Bill Jones?"

"However did you know?"

"And that's no pre-cog, Sally," op Owen said with a ghost of a laugh, aware he was beginning to look forward again. "A sure thing's no pre-cog, is it, Les?"

THE ABSOLUTELY PERFECT MURDER

Miriam Allen deFord

*Miriam Allen deFord (1888–1975) was, like Anthony Boucher, every bit at
home writing science fiction and fantasy as she was crime fiction and true
crime. In fact she won an Edgar Award for the best fact crime book of the
year for* The Overbury Affair *(1960). Two other studies of criminals were*
The Real Bonnie and Clyde *(1968) and* The Real Ma Barker *(1970).
She enjoyed historical mysteries and wrote several such stories including
"The Mystery of the Vanished Brother" (1950), in which Edgar Allan Poe
is the detective, and "De Crimine" (1952) in which Cicero turns sleuth.*

*A socialist and feminist, she began to sell items to several of the radical
magazines from at least as early as 1910, when she worked as a teacher.
She became a journalist in 1912. From 1922 she corresponded with Charles
Fort, occasionally helping with his researches into the unusual until his
death in 1932. Her first known weird tale was "The Neatness of Ann
Rutledge" in* The Westminster Magazine *in 1924. Surprisingly, she
did not appear in* Weird Tales *until its penultimate issue in 1954 but she
sold regularly to its early companion* Real Detective Tales *during the
1920s. Her primary magazines, though, were* Ellery Queen's Mystery
Magazine *from 1944 and* The Magazine of Fantasy & Science Fiction
*from 1951. She continued to write almost to the day she died, a career of
over sixty-five years.*

Many of her crime stories were collected as The Theme is Murder
*(1967) though there are plenty more uncollected. Her sf and weird tales
were collected as* Xenogenesis *(1969) and* Elsewhere, Elsewhen,
Elsehow *(1971) and she also compiled an anthology of sf crime stories*

Space, Time & Crime *(1964). Her stories often pivoted on a clever plot twist or simple, but easily overlooked, fact and were occasionally imbued with humour, as with the following, which allows us to close this volume with a smile.*

I T WAS A QUIET, DOMESTIC EVENING IN THE SPRING OF 2146. Mervin Alspaugh and his wife Doreen, snugly ensconced in the viewing room of their living-yacht moored to the roof of a building in lower Manhattan, were separately occupied in private entertainment. Both, with hearing-plugs in their ears, directional conversion-glasses before their eyes, and Sensapills percolating through their blood-streams, were watching, listening to, smelling, tasting, and feeling their favourite telecasts. Doreen as usual was absorbed in advertisements of jewels, furs, new synthetics, and cosmetics; Mervin had switched on a science-ad programme. (All telecasts, of course, consisted exclusively of advertisements, aimed at the individual interests of the viewers.) But he was *not* absorbed: under his surface perception his constant preoccupation, which was becoming an obsession, dug into him as always.

How could he murder Doreen and get away with it?

This project, which had begun as a faint wistful dream a year or two ago, had now become the substratum of all his thinking. It was threatening to interfere with his work as a cybernattendant, and that would never do: it must be either fulfilled or repressed.

Now that his situation was clearly and sharply in his mind, he wondered often why he had ever married her. A combination of propinquity, lack of assertiveness, and loneliness, he supposed. The propinquity had become nerve-wracking, the lack of assertiveness had made him the victim of a nagging, bullying woman, and he no longer looked upon loneliness as an evil, but longed for it as a thirsty man for water. The truth was that he was not the marrying type, and he should have realized it and stayed out.

Divorce? Not a chance. He had no grounds whatever, no matter how lenient the divorce laws had become—not even incompatibility, since Doreen had long ago substituted her interests for his and seen to it that he was properly involved in them; these blessed evening hours of separate telecast programmes were her only concession. And nothing would have persuaded her to divorce him; she was completely, blandly satisfied with what to him was a persistent torture. The only time he had timidly and indirectly proposed the idea, she had laughed in his face. And if he merely left her without divorce, the police would find him and drag him back.

So there was nothing left, to avoid the wreckage of his own life, except to murder her.

But here again he was up against a seemingly impenetrable barrier. Never in his life had he physically attacked another human being; his knowledge of weapons was non-existent; and he shrank in distaste from the slyness of poison—even if he had known how to obtain any. More frustrating still, even if somehow he could find the means and the courage, there would be a body—a body bigger and heavier than his own—to dispose of. He had not the remotest idea how that could be accomplished. And if it weren't—if he were apprehended, accused, and convicted, as he most certainly would be—what kind of future would that leave him? There was no longer danger of his being executed, as in the old barbarous days, and the Rehabilitation Institutes would probably have seemed like heaven to inmates of even the most advanced prisons of a century or two earlier. But the essence of any imprisonment is the negation of liberty, the enforced absence of privacy, the prohibition of self-direction, and Mervin Alspaugh could see no profit in exchanging one kind of imprisonment for another, for years or for the rest of his existence.

No, there was no way out that he dared risk. And yet he could not endure much longer being tied to a woman he had come to hate.

A groan escaped him: fortunately Doreen, ear-plugged, failed to hear it. He forced his attention back to the programme.

A white-coated man, wearing the full synthetic wig of the research scientist, was doing a come-on for the newest of scientific triumphs.

"Aren't we all honestly becoming bored," he was saying, "with what we might call horizontal travel—of 40-minute trips to the uttermost reaches of our little planet, or week-end tours around the solar system and vacation cruises in outer space? Well, a new thrill is possible for those of adventurous spirit—and, I must add, of financial means." (He laughed ingratiatingly, and millions of viewers receiving his message transliterated into their own tongues smiled dutifully at his little joke.) "You can be among the first to experience what might be termed vertical travel.

"Now at last you can not only visit the moon or Mars or Alpha Centauri, but you can travel back into the past. Yes, folks, public time travel has finally come true.

"You can witness the burial of Tutankhamen, the assassination of Julius Caesar, the coronation of Napoleon, the inauguration of the first World President in 2065—and not just see and hear and feel them on a screen, but actually be there at the real event. You can visit your native city as you remember it, even if years ago it was razed to provide room for a Redevelopment Complex. You can hunt extinct wild animals in a natural forest, fish in a long ago diverted river. You can relive your own youth.

"You can see the world as it was in any period of the past, behold once more those dear to you who have died before you, make history a living thing."

Mervin Alspaugh sat transfixed. Theoretically, he knew, time travel to the past had been possible for at least five years, ever since the startling discoveries of Haffen and Ngumbo. Carefully trained temperonauts—Okimatu Figlietti was the first—had made journeys up to ten years back and returned safely. But the project had been incredibly complicated, and inexorably secret. The computers in his own department had played a small part, very hush-hush, in the earliest developments, or he would not even have known of them.

But that the range of the Time Transporter had been so far extended, that the general public could participate, that time travel could now be offered on the same basis as space-travel—that indeed was something new, and the white-coated scientist on the screen was making the first announcement.

A sudden warmth crept through Mervin's chest. Oh, he knew it wouldn't be as easy as the come-on indicated: it would be ferociously expensive, hedged about with all sorts of restrictions, all sorts of rules about secrecy, non-interference, non-liability of the dispatching agency—

But if his life's savings were enough—if he agreed to any and all conditions—if somehow, when he got to a selected time and place, he could escape, lose himself forever and never, never come back to a time with Doreen in it—

He sighed deeply, deflated by common sense. How could he earn his living in a time that did not yet know the only profession for which he was equipped? How could he hope not to be dragged back by the authorities of his own time as soon as he did not return at the scheduled moment? How could he endure the primitive conditions of any century before his own?

The little warmth died. He wrenched his attention back to the tele-ad.

"Now," said the speaker genially, "I know there are all kinds of questions and objections that will immediately occur to you. We are not in a position yet to offer luxury cruises in time as you know them in space. By the very nature of the mechanism of the Time Transporter, there will be strict limitations on where you can go and what you can do when you get there." Mervin felt himself nodding in sad agreement. "At first this is going to be a project barred to the very old, the disabled physically, and those of modest means.

"But just one week from today, the first Time Transportation offices will open in every city on earth. Your local visinews will give you the details. You will be able to get full information there. And some of those whom I am addressing now will soon discover for themselves the marvels of the most wonderful journey Man has ever made. Some day it will be as common to spend holidays in the past as it is now to visit a friend in Lunapolis. And some other day, not too far away, we shall be able to visit the future, just as, within another week, we shall be able to visit the past.

"Now let me save the energies of our Information Clerks by answering at once some of the questions that will most probably arise."

Mervin listened apathetically while most of the objections that he had already considered were outlined and disposed of. It was no use. There was no way out for him. He was still confronted by the urgent need to eliminate Doreen.

The scientist smiled, his perfect permateeth gleaming.

"And in conclusion," he said, "let me disabuse your minds of a notion that may sound amusing to some of you, but that has been brought up seriously over and over again in the course of our studies.

"No, you *can't* go back into the past and kill your grandfather, as people used to fancy, for the very good reason that if he *had* been killed, you wouldn't be alive now to make the trip. You would never have been born. So—"

Mervin lost track. He turned off the set. For a long time he sat, his eyes closed, thinking...

This was 2146. Doreen, in a weak moment at the beginning of their marriage, had confessed that she was seven years older than he. That made her 52. So she had been born in 2094.

For the first time he was grateful for her garrulous, egocentric recitals about her undistinguished family. "I was an only child," she had droned so many times. "I was born the year after my parents were married, and my father died suddenly when I was only four." At first he toyed with the idea of going back to a time when her father had been a child. It would be so much easier to overpower a child. But he knew he couldn't bring himself to harm a little boy. It was hard enough, driven as he was to utter despair, to confront another grown man.

But at whatever cost, he must nerve himself somehow to that. He began to calculate. Doreen's father and mother were married in 2093. Give it another year to be safe—he would aim for 2092, nine years before he himself had been born.

Even he was taken aback by what the journey cost. But by almost wiping out his bank account—the secret one he had managed to keep hidden from Doreen—he could just make it. He agreed to all the conditions, signed all the papers. He acquired clothing of the proper fashion, studied intensively the booklet on a half century's differences, to avoid suspicion.

He got his vacation changed to June, instead of the usual time in September: he couldn't stand waiting that long. He steeled himself to tell Doreen—at the last possible minute—that the department had ordered him to take his holiday earlier this year, and that therefore (since her own would still come in September) he must go away without her. It was a nasty scene, but he was desperate enough to go through it without giving in. Of course he lied about his destination: by the time her letter-tapes were returned from the false address he gave, there would be no need for him to worry any more.

On a day in June, 2092, Mervin Alspaugh found himself in New York, then still a separate city from both Philadelphia and Boston.

He knew where to go—he had listened to enough long-winded reminiscences. He found the apartment house without difficulty, only a bit confused until he remembered that there had still been surface transportation in cities in those days.

It was an ordinary 40-storey formaglass apartment building of those years before most people had been crowded out of Manhattan except for the dwellers in moored living-yachts. It looked about as he had expected. What did surprise him was a concourse of small children—five or six of them—gathered on the stoop and in the doorway, playing. Mervin Alspaugh viewed them with disfavour; in his day the neighbourhood robonurse would have put them to bed an hour before. Presumably their parents lived in the building and let them play outside till dark. He glanced at them sourly as he mounted the steps. A little girl, surely not more than four—a pudgy, unattractive child with sallow skin and a mean mouth—made a face at him and gave vent to a loud raspberry. Apparently she was the leader of the mob; the others immediately stopped their game and followed suit.

He ignored them; he had other things on his mind. He pressed the button for 1410.

He was face to face with the moment of truth.

Thanks to Doreen and her fond memories, he knew that Roger Tatum in his bachelor days had lived alone in the same flat to which he had taken his bride, and in which Doreen had spent her childhood until her father died. His life before and after his marriage, she had often remarked admiringly, had been "just like clockwork." He had got to the office by nine, was home again by half-past 18, after an early dinner at a nearby restaurant, then was home all evening to video lectures at the University of the Air, preparing himself for promotion in his job, and was in bed every night by half-past 22. "Why, even when he was going with my mother, he never went out with her except at week-ends."

And then she would invariably add: "He was a *serious* man, my father, always trying to improve himself. Not like you, with your head forever in the clouds."

An excellent regimen—for Mervin's present purpose. And when he rang the bell downstairs, it was just 19.53.

The buzzer sounded promptly. If the paragon of perfection was to be interrupted in his studies, then apparently he wanted the interruption disposed of quickly.

As Mervin mounted the escalator to the 14th floor he fingered nervously through his pocket what he thought of always, in capitals, as The Weapon.

He had pondered longest of all about this. Often, even as he made his preparations for the journey, it had seemed an insoluble problem—just as it had been when he had dreamed of eliminating Doreen directly. A blaster? He had never fired one in his life, and wouldn't know how. A knife? A blackjack? His blood turned cold. From Doreen's sarcastic comparisons—what a memory she must have had at four—he knew only too well how inferior he was in size and strength to Roger Tatum. So strangling or a blow was out of the question.

Only one thing that he knew of could kill a man instantly and painlessly, and that had not yet been invented in 2092. At first it had seemed impossible that he could get hold of one even in 2146. Mervin shuddered as he remembered the depths to which he, a man of hitherto blameless life, had descended to get The Weapon. It had cost him all that was left of his secret bank account, and he had risked his own life by venturing after dark into the notorious inner reaches of Central Park. (Overtime work, he had told Doreen, and she had been too indifferent to question him.)

He had succeeded, though he had had nightmares ever since. In his pocket, as the escalator carried him to his waiting prey, was a charged freeze hypo. Heaven knew from whom it had been stolen by the drug-ridden derelict who had furtively thrust it, wrapped in a dirty plastic rag, into his hand in exchange for the thick wad of credit notes.

Part of the Time Transport agreement he had signed was a prohibition against carrying arms into the past. But no one could have imagined that in this case the little Sleepwel pillbox everybody carried held instead that tiny, deadly needle, which once it penetrated the skin immediately froze its victim, reduced his temperature to an incredible degree, turned his blood to ice, and held its grip until no recovery was possible.

He took the box gingerly out of his pocket, opened it with care, and extracted the freeze hypo by its safe end.

He rang the doorbell of Apartment 1410, and in a minute the door opened.

He would have known anywhere that it was Doreen's father. The same cold grey eyes, the same tight mouth, the same scowl, and the same grating voice as the man snapped: "Yes?"

"Mr. Tatum—Mr. Roger Tatum?"

"Yes. What do you want?"

"I have a package for you." The package—plastic and Sealfast containing nothing—was under his arm.

Tatum glared suspiciously.

"I'm expecting no package. I haven't ordered anything."

Doreen's meanness again—somebody must be trying to put something over, extort money somehow.

"There's no charge."

Expertly Mervin Alspaugh proffered the dummy parcel. Over and over, while Doreen snored, he had practised holding the freeze hypo unseen under it.

Tatum stretched forth his hand grudgingly to take it. The needle went through his palm.

Without even a gasp, he turned rigid and then fell.

Mervin wheeled to leave. There was no need to touch the icy body—death was always instantaneous. He paused only to recover the hypo, harmless now that it had spent its charge. For a moment he thought he heard footsteps inside the apartment, hurrying to the door at the sound of Tatum's fall. (Perhaps father's studious bachelor evenings had not been so solitary as his doting daughter had fancied.) But he was on the escalator and out of sight before anyone could have glimpsed him.

The children were still gathered on the stoop. The pudgy little girl grimaced at him and yelled "Yah!" But a voice called from a downstairs window, and when Mervin reached the corner and looked back he saw the children, summoned, entering the building one by one for their belated bedtime.

Weak with a horrid churning mixture of terror, relief, and ecstasy, Mervin dared not linger longer in 2092. He hurried to the centre where the Time Transporter, invisible to others because it did not yet exist in that era, waited for its passenger. If they wondered at the other end why he had returned so soon, he would say that life 54 years earlier had proved too uncomfortable, and probably they would be only too glad to get the Transporter back early for the next traveller.

Everything went smoothly. As he taxicoptered from the Time Transportation office to the living-yacht—now all his again, haven of peace as it had been in his happy days before Doreen—the horror of having killed another human being, the fear of being caught before he escaped, were swallowed up in the rapture of his triumph. He savoured his new freedom with delight.

Roger Tatum had died two years before his daughter could have been born. There had never been a Doreen.

Delirious with happiness, he matched the door-pattern and stepped into his home—*his* home only, forevermore.

And then he saw a light in the viewing room.

Shaking, he burst into it.

Doreen sat there, watching her telecast. Ears plugged, eyes encased, she did not even notice him.

And in that awful moment, Mervin Alspaugh suddenly realized the truth.

Never in the world, as long as he lived, would he be able to get hold of enough money again to buy another freeze hypo, or to take another trip, to an earlier date, on the Time Transporter. Nor had he been wrong in thinking he had heard footsteps running to Tatum's door: he *had*—they were the footsteps of Mrs. Tatum.

And as for that pudgy, greedy-faced little girl on the stoop—now he knew why he had taken so instant a dislike to her—not seven years his senior, but eleven—at least eleven—

Doreen, that insatiable, incorrigible woman, had lied about her age!

STORY SOURCES

The following gives the first publication details for each story. They are listed in alphabetical order of author.

"Mirror Image" by Isaac Asimov, first published in *Analog*, May 1972.

"Elsewhen" by Anthony Boucher, first published in *Astounding SF*, January 1943.

"Puzzle for Spacemen" by John Brunner, first published in *New Worlds*, December 1955.

"Death of a Telepath" by George Chailey, first published in *Science Fiction Adventures*, January 1959.

"The Absolutely Perfect Murder" by Miriam Allen deFord, first published in *The Magazine of Fantasy & Science Fiction*, February 1965.

"The Flying Eye" by Jacques Futrelle, first published in *The Popular Magazine*, 1 November 1912.

"Murder, 1986" by P. D. James, first published in *Ellery Queen's Mystery Magazine*, October 1970.

"Apple" by Anne McCaffrey, first published in *Crime Prevention in the 30th Century*, edited by Hans Stefan Santesson (New York: Walker, 1969).

"Legwork" by Eric Frank Russell, first published in *Astounding SF*, April 1956.

"Nonentity" by E. C. Tubb, first published in *Authentic SF*, February 1955.

ALSO AVAILABLE

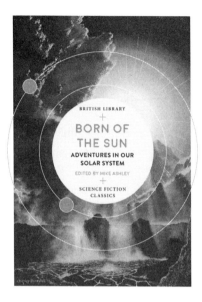

On Mercury: How do you outrun the dawn and its lethal sunrise?
On Jupiter: When humans transfer their minds into the local fauna
to explore the surface, why do they never return?
On Pluto: How long must an astronaut wait for rescue
at the furthest reaches of the system?

We have always been fascinated by the promise of space and the distant lure of our fellow planets orbiting the Sun. In this new collection of classic stories, Mike Ashley takes us on a journey from the harsh extremes of Mercury to the turbulent expanses of Saturn and beyond, exploring as we go the literary history of the planets, the influence of contemporary astronomy on the imagination of writers, and the impact of their storytelling on humanity's perception of these hitherto unreachable worlds.

Featuring the talents of Larry Niven, Robert Silverberg, Clare Winger Harris and more, this collection offers a kaleidoscope of innovative thought and timeless adventures.

CLASSIC LITERARY SCIENCE FICTION
BY MURIEL JAEGER

What I know... How can I tell you? You can't see it, or feel it...
You live in a universe with little hard limits... You know nothing...
You can't feel the sunset against the wall outside... or the people moving...
Lines of energy... the ocean of movement... the great waves...
It's all nothing to you.

Extra-sensory perception is a unique gift of nature—or is it an affliction? To Hilda, Michael Bristowe's power to perceive forces beyond the limits of the five basic senses offers the promise of some brighter future for humanity, and yet for the bearer himself—dizzied by the threat of sensory bombardment and social exile—the picture is not so clear.

First published in 1927, Muriel Jaeger's second pioneering foray into science fiction is a sensitive and thought-provoking portrait of the struggle for human connection and relationships tested and transformed under the pressures of supernatural influence.

BRITISH LIBRARY
SCIENCE FICTION CLASSICS

SHORT STORY ANTHOLOGIES
EDITED BY MIKE ASHLEY

Nature's Warnings
Classic Stories of Eco-Science Fiction

Lost Mars
The Golden Age of the Red Planet

Moonrise
The Golden Age of Lunar Adventures

Menace of the Machine
The Rise of AI in Classic Science Fiction

The End of the World
and Other Catastrophes

Menace of the Monster
Classic Tales of Creatures from Beyond

Beyond Time
Classic Tales of Time Unwound

Born of the Sun
Adventures in Our Solar System

Spaceworlds
Stories of Life in the Void

Future Crimes
*Mysteries and Detection through
Time and Space*

o————o

CLASSIC SCIENCE FICTION NOVELS AND NOVELLAS

By John Brunner

The Society of Time

By William F. Temple

Shoot at the Moon
Four-Sided Triangle

By Ian Macpherson

Wild Harbour

By Charles Eric Maine

The Tide Went Out
The Darkest of Nights

By Muriel Jaeger

The Question Mark
The Man with Six Senses

o————o

We welcome any suggestions, corrections or feedback you may have, and will aim
to respond to all items addressed to the following:

The Editor (Science Fiction Classics)
British Library Publishing
The British Library
96 Euston Road
London, NW1 2DB

We also welcome enquiries through our Twitter account,
@BL_Publishing